I0748287

Marie's Merry Gentleman

THE BOOKSHOP BELLES
BOOK TWO

CATHERINE BILSON

EBONY OATEN

Copyright © 2025 by Catherine Bilson & Ebony Oaten

Published by Shenanigans Press

PO Box 323, Morayfield, QLD 4506

All rights reserved.

This novel is a work of fiction created entirely from the authors' imaginations and deep love of history. The story, all names, characters, and incidents portrayed in this production are fictitious. No identification with actual persons (living or deceased), places, buildings, and products is intended or should be inferred.

No part of this book may be reproduced in any form or by any electronic or mechanical means, including information storage and retrieval systems, without written permission from the author, except for the use of brief quotations in a book review.

Content Advisory

- Emotional abuse from relatives
- Unfaithful partner
- Death of parents
- Rampant unfairness and sexism because women were considered second-class citizens
- Cats breeding uncontrollably as desexing pets had not been invented

We also advise people not to take any of the herbal remedies mentioned in these books. While some might work, they are not always reliable and indeed the quantities and efficacies would vary from person to person. Please do not constitute anything in these books as medical advice.

Prologue

Baxter's Fine Books, Hatfield, England
August, 1814

"Cumbria. What an absolutely ridiculous idea!"

Marie Baxter, the second eldest and definitely the most sensitive of the four Baxter daughters of Baxter's Bookshop in Hatfield, Hertfordshire, looked at the correspondence in her hand and sighed with frustration.

The composer of the correspondence may well be an Earl, but there was simply no way she was about to travel all the way to Cumbria and deliver two books. No matter how valuable they were. She lifted her pen and wrote a note of response, the nib digging into the paper with her frustration.

> *"I have neither the time, nor the inclination to subject myself to the interior of a mail coach with all and sundry for the best part of a fortnight to deliver two books. There are people I trust in Hatfield who could*

easily do this task, whilst I remain at the bookshop and keep an eye out for more of the titles on your list.
Yours etc, M. Baxter."

Why would this man not entrust a messenger to carry the books? His entitlement knew no bounds! She sanded the letter, then folded it and headed straight to the Red Lion next door to get it on the next postal carriage taking the Great North Road. The late afternoon had turned cool and she wrapped her shawl around her shoulders and ears to keep warm.

The door bell tinkled as she re-entered the shop. Crafty the cat did not bolt for the door as she expected. Now that she thought about it, she hadn't seen the rotund black cat for a little while now. She'd either escaped when nobody was paying attention, or she'd found somewhere to make a nest for her soon-to-be-born kittens.

September 1814

The next letter from the earl was no better.

"I trust nobody to deliver these titles other than your good self. Third parties are worse than useless, they are careless. The books may arrive, but in what condition? Only someone with your breadth of knowledge and experience would understand not merely their monetary value, but their symbolic and deeply intrinsic value to the

world of literature. That is why you and you alone must deliver the books to me. You will be compensated accordingly for your time and trouble. They would be here already and you would be well on your return journey if you'd done as I originally requested."

Marie rolled her eyes. They weren't requests, they were demands, and they were growing more demanding.

"We would have successfully concluded our business by now. No more delays. Bring me my books.

Renwick."

She showed the letter to her sister Louise, who was stretching out her back after stirring a fresh vat of stinky glue. The cooler autumn wind howled through the windows and nipped at their necks, but open windows were the only way to draw the stink out.

Crafty's little kittens scarpered through the bookshop like fluffy black voids. When two of them rolled about and played together, it was impossible to see where one kitten began and another ended.

"They are so adorable," Louise said, laughing as one of the kittens pounced on a trailing boot lace.

"That they are, and we shall need to find homes for them very soon."

"Why can't we just keep one of them, to give Crafty company?"

"Because if we kept a boy, he'd grow up and spray his scent on the books. And if we kept a girl, she'd probably be just as bad as her mother. Then we'd no doubt have two batches of kittens to find homes for at some point," Marie said practically. Someone had to be practical.

"Then I shall enjoy them while they are small and adorable," Louise said, scooping up a passing kitten and smushing its soft little body against her face. "You'd better write back to the Earl of Demanding and tell him where to shove his demands."

"I need to be nicer than that! He sends another letter every time we put an advertisement in *The Times*, requesting we add more books to the order. It's almost a hundred pounds' worth by now."

Louise whistled between her teeth in an unladylike manner. "Perhaps you should go. Estelle definitely would have."

That truthful observation caused Marie a pang. She had faithfully promised their eldest sister that they were perfectly capable of running the bookshop in Estelle's absence.

The four Baxter sisters had already been running the bookshop in their father's absence. Then Estelle had married her dear Mr Yates and was currently in Ireland visiting his mother.

Louise was right: Estelle would have long since set off for Cumbria, viewing the trip as an adventure. Marie, however, considered it a nightmare. She had never been further away from Hatfield than London, and on that trip had despised both the journey and the city. The noise of the city drilled into her head, giving her the worst megrims. The very last thing she wanted to do was spend a week or more each way in a crowded, stuffy coach being jolted through every rut from here to very nearly Scotland!

Marie came up with an excellent rebuttal: "Estelle would have taken the books, come back, and then been immediately confronted with an order for more books," she pointed out.

Louise nodded. "Fair point. Well, you'll have to find some way to convince him, Marie. A hundred pounds is not to be sneezed at!" She kissed the kitten one more time, making it squeak in protest, before setting it down and making her way back upstairs again.

Marie penned her reply and was as polite as possible, which included the final paragraph;

> "We are short staffed at the moment and I cannot leave the responsibility of the bookshop. Please reconsider your preferred delivery method.
> Yours, M Baxter."

October 1814

> "Where are you, and where are my books?
> I need them here by Christmas!"

This last missive from The Earl of Demanding really irked Marie. They were coping well enough without their father and Estelle, but their workload had increased of late. They were lucky to have some extra help with young Ruth Millings and their cousin Brutus Baxter assisting in the store. Brutus also didn't mind the glue stink and seemed genuinely excited to be learning the craft of repairing and binding books, proving a competent and enthusiastic apprentice to Louise. They were able to increase the number of titles they could repair and bind in any given week, which was a welcome boost to the bookstore's income.

To their delight, two crates of books had arrived in quick succession, and the titles had proved incredibly popular. Selling them was easy, and helped them build funds towards paying off their father's enormous bank loan.

Even more delightful than the books was finding a short note from Papa, which was an incredible relief. It was undated, however, which proved an irritation. Louise cleverly spotted the clue about the date in Papa's hastily scribbled note.

Am in Tours again. Heavy autumn rains roads north miserable at best.

"Aha! The last note said he'd arrived in Tours," Lousie said. "That one did have a date on it. So this one says he's in Tours *again*, therefore, this note was written after the previous one." It almost had to be, since that note had arrived almost three months previously, but it was good to have confirmation.

"You're a genius!" Bernadette said.

"I have my moments." Louise grinned at solving the puzzle.

Marie chuckled and said, "He's obviously having far too much fun." It was a relief that Louise had worked it out so quickly. They were a good team.

But if Marie left Hatfield to travel, the previous work of four sisters would land on only two sets of shoulders while she was away. She was the eldest sister left at home

She couldn't go. She absolutely couldn't.

Not even with two additional books the Earl had requested, bringing his total order to a hundred and ten pounds.

It was entirely out of the question.

CHAPTER 1
Alston Calling

Early November, 1814

"If you are unwilling to deliver me the books I require, I shall cancel the entire order forthwith and seek them from a provider who is punctual and reliable."

This most recent letter from 'The Earl of Demanding' - Louise's nickname for him had stuck - was absolutely the last straw for Marie. If only it hadn't arrived at the same time as their account from the insurance company.

It wasn't that Marie had forgotten that particular creditor. She kept excellent ledgers and knew when each bill was due. Alas, she hadn't counted on the bill being a good deal more than that of the previous year. Why was everything getting so expensive? She scowled at the two letters, lying side by side in front of her on the shop counter.

Things were busy in the lead up to Christmas, as customers stocked up on books to read through the winter and as gifts for the holidays. Then they would grow lean until about mid-February. If the Earl of Demanding could wait, Marie would be able to travel without worrying so much for her sisters.

By February, the roads, of course, would most likely be worse, so there was that consideration.

Louise and Bernadette were busy unpacking a fresh crate of books that had arrived from their father in France just that morning, stacking them in neat piles while Marie worked on the accounts and correspondence.

Taking another look at the calendar, Marie calculated that if she left for Cumbria soon, she'd be on the road for about two weeks, could deliver the books and get her payment, then be back well in time for the last flurry of book trade before Christmastide.

Bernadette asked, "Is there a letter from Papa here?"

"Not that I can find," Louise said. "Marie, do we have enough money for us to get by until February?"

"If we're careful, but we shall have to be *very* careful. And hope for a lot of book sales."

Bernadette shook her head as she checked another French book for letters or notes from their father that might fall out from between the pages. "Maybe you should go to Cumbria then. The Earl of Demanding's order is more than enough to cover all the bills."

Marie huffed crossly, even though Bernadette was

saying exactly what she was already thinking. And already mostly planning in her head. "I know."

She had been on the verge of writing to the Earl of Demanding and suggesting he send his own trusted servants to come and collect the books. He was probably so demanding his staff had all fled in terror, so maybe he didn't have any. Why else would he write, "I trust only your good self,"? She had visions of the earl to have the appearance of an ogre sleeping on a pile of books, like a dragon might lie on a mountain of treasure.

"And the longer his books sit here, the longer they won't be paid for," Bernadette added.

Marie answered waspishly, "I'm well aware of that." She pinched the bridge of her nose.

Louise gave her shoulder a rub and said, "You're doing an Estelle, thinking we can't manage without you. Brutus and Ruth are doing much more than you think. And Rosie comes in to help Mrs Poole."

Rosie was an extra housemaid Felix Yates had generously supplied for them, to help Mrs Poole so that Mrs Poole had time to be at the committee meetings with Miss Yates, and she was a great help to them all, a hardworking, friendly girl.

Bernadette and Louise kept on at Marie until she sighed noisily. "Fine, you win. I'll leave next week."

"Or you could leave tomorrow," Bernadette said. "The sooner you go, the sooner you'll be back."

Marie hated when her sisters made good sense.

"No," she said stubbornly. "Have you even looked at the route I'd have to take?"

Both Louise and Bernadette had to admit they had

not, so Marie pulled out the road-book and coaching timetable she'd thumbed through far too many times of late.

"Look, this is where Alston is. About ten miles from Carlisle, hard by the Scottish border."

"That… is a very long way," Louise said, peering over her shoulder.

"The mail coach goes straight to Carlisle, of course, changing horses regularly, but I will need to stop and rest myself. Which means some overnight stays, and I want to send letters ahead to reputable inns to ensure I have rooms for those nights."

Bernadette nodded reluctantly, obviously seeing the sense in that. "Peterborough, Lincoln, York…"

It was a vast distance, and would no-doubt be uncomfortable. Marie's neck and back began to ache at the thought of it. "All the way to Carlisle, where I'll have to hire a hack-chaise or something to take me the rest of the way. And I shall need to write ahead to arrange that, too."

Even though she didn't want to, Marie had suspected this was coming. She'd planned it all out. Just in case. Planning things helped her feel calm, and if the worst came to pass, well then she would know exactly what to do.

At least the Earl of Demanding had promised to pay all her expenses, so she would stay in quality hotels and inns and present him with a list of accounts on her arrival - and request as much reimbursement again for the return journey.

Marie knitted to pass the time in the cramped mail coach, each jolting yard bruising what felt like every bone in her body. Days of long travel were wearisome and frustrating. Her destination was still a day away, but she was at least thankful she'd made good time so far. The roads had been reasonably clear and the horses had made good time without being reckless. She was not going to say anything about how lucky they'd been though, because she didn't want to tempt bad fortune.

Nevertheless, Marie was beginning to feel as if this journey would soon be over. She'd deliver these books, get the money and be home by Christmas.

Cumbria was such a long way, though, and as much as she'd planned out this trip, her nerves were on edge for things to go wrong. She'd never been this far away from home and everything looked so different. The stones people made their houses from were a different colour. The hedges along the boundaries weren't the same plants she was used to. And the further north they travelled, the colder it became. She thought she'd packed enough warm clothes, but if it got colder she might have to wear them all at the same time.

The Earl of Demanding had better appreciate her efforts.

Knitting calmed Marie. Having something to claim her concentration helped block out the smell of bodies crushed into the carriage. The inane chatter coming from those same bodies still managed to break through, though.

"What are you knitting here, dear? Oh! That rhymes," the woman beside her asked, with a silly giggle.

Why did people persist in asking her questions? Especially strangers who she would most likely never see again? It was fine with Hatfield folks, she knew them and they seemed happy with a polite nod and a, "How are you this fine day?" To which she knew the reply; "In fine fettle, and your good self?" That always made them smile, nod and move on.

But these strangers? They weren't following the correct script.

What did it matter about her knitting, anyway? The pattern was in her head and they would be unlikely to see the finished product.

"A scarf," she said, not looking up from her needles. It wasn't a scarf really, but that was a handy response. It was *almost* a scarf, but one for her ears. Alas, she hadn't really come up with a name for her design other than ear mufflers, as they muffled the sounds of the world around her. It was a circular knitted band of her own devising, with thicker, wider sections to go over her ears and muffle the sound. It was too hot to wear them in summer, obviously, but now the cold weather was here, onwards she knitted. Knitting gave her something to help pass the time on this uncomfortable journey, even if she did drop stitches regularly and have to pick them up again.

Much to her dismay, she had discovered around the end of the very first hour of the first day of the journey, that trying to read in the coach made her feel quite sick. Fortunately she had put some wool and needles in her travelling bag. When they came to their first stop after a few hours, she tried casting on.

"You already have a scarf," the woman said.

Marie blinked hard and fought the urge to grunt at her fellow passenger. She paused and searched through her mind for a suitable response, missing her sisters so much at this moment. Estelle would know what to say, and Bernadette would match them and then turn the topic to herbs and gardening. Louise would probably bluntly tell the woman to mind her own business, but Marie couldn't bring herself to do that.

Marie settled on, "It's much colder here than I expected."

"Looks rather narrow," the woman said. "Is it for a babe?"

Marie breathed slowly and had to blink. She should add an extra shilling to the fee to the Earl of Demanding, for her pain and suffering. Or an extra pound. He could obviously afford it.

Answering the woman only encouraged her fellow passenger to ask more questions, which was not the desired effect Marie wanted. The sooner she could hand over these books, the sooner she could return home to Hatfield and the cosy counter with her ledgers and abacus.

Being in the bookshop so much, she'd forgotten how much regular people irritated and confused her. And there were so many of them!

The coach jolted on another rut and she dropped a stitch. Blast!

The woman beside her decided to start a conversation with another lady in the coach. This was a magnificent relief to Marie, but only for a little while as the inanity of their conversation made her ears itchy.

"Prattle prattle, chat?"

"Oh, yes, chat chat prattle."

"La! Chat, prattle. Prattle!"

At least they weren't expecting a response from her any more, and the interior of the coach was dry and quite warm from the many bodies in here. The howling cold and rain surrounding them removed any thoughts of taking an outside seat.

The weather was becoming foul. The passengers riding on the outside would be frozen to the bone, the poor things.

The town of Carlisle came into view at long last. Her bottom and her back ached from sitting on the uncomfortable wooden seat with her feet propped up on the precious box of books in the footwell. Several passengers had complained about the box taking up too much room, but there was no possible way Marie was letting such valuable cargo out of her sight, and certainly not risking it getting wet in the bad weather. Or falling off the coach! By the time they'd packed the Earl's full order, there was almost a hundred and fifty pounds' worth of books in the box. All of them carefully packed in with lambswool and an oilcloth cover Louise had actually stitched on in order to ensure it would be waterproof.

"The Coach and Horses, Carlisle!" the driver shouted from above, pulling the horses to a halt in a great clatter of iron-shod hooves on cobblestones.

"An original name, indeed," Marie muttered as she clambered stiffly off the seat. "Thank you, I'll carry that myself," she said as a man reached to pick up her box. "My bag... oh."

The bags were being thrown down at that moment, and Marie sighed, looking with a jaundiced eye at the puddle her portmanteau had just been tossed into.

"That one," she said, nodding to it. Then she gave the porter and extra coin to help carefully carry the trunk of books into the inn.

The wind slammed the door shut behind her as she spoke to the landlord. "I have a room reserved. Miss Baxter."

At least her meticulous preparations meant she was shown upstairs quickly to a comfortable, if small, private room. A little while later, a maid brought a tray with a bowl of stew and some crusty bread. There was also a pat of butter and a mug of pressed cider. Exhausted after so many long days of travel, Marie ate her dinner and toppled into the narrow bed, thinking gratefully that at least she would reach her destination on the morrow... even if she would have to turn right around and start back home again.

Her dreams were full of a beastly man who lived in a cold dark cave packed only with books.

Her plan figuratively fell to pieces the following morning, when she inquired about the hack-chaise she had ordered to take her to Alston.

The innkeeper laughed at her. "Ain't no hack-chaise getting up that road, ma'am!" His accent was so thick she could barely understand him. She did manage to hear the words "up road" and frowned in puzzlement. "I don't understand. It's a little less than ten miles, according to the map."

"Aye, but a fair bit of it straight oop!" He tilted his forearm to indicate a steep slope, before pointing out the front door of the inn at the Pennines looming in the near distance. "Oop there!"

"Oh." Marie had not considered the elevation. Several times on the journey north the mail's six horses had been supplemented by two more. They were heavy plodders to help drag the coach up steep inclines. It hadn't seemed that steep because she had focused on her knitting. But now she looked at the hills around her, a single horse drawing a hack-chaise wouldn't be able to take such slopes.

"A bigger coach, then?" she asked hesitantly, wondering if there would even be one available.

"Wheer is it yer goin'?"

"Alston. Alston Castle, to be exact."

The innkeeper pulled at his lip in thought. "And ye're wanting to take that there box wid ye?"

"I *have* to take this box with me," Marie corrected. "And I have to go today." That last part might not be precisely true, but delaying would mean her carefully planned schedule for the return journey would be ruined. If she wanted any chance of getting home by Christmas, she really needed to leave for Alston now.

"Can ye ride? I can get ye a lady's mount with a sidesaddle, and a donkey to carry yer box." The innkeeper shrugged. "Best I can do, today."

He'd said the magic word, "Today" and she was grateful. "Then that's what we shall have to do." Marie lifted her chin. "Have the animals brought around as soon as you can, please. Daylight's wasting."

It hadn't taken her long to realise that the winter days were getting even shorter the further north she travelled, even though Midwinter was still a little more than three weeks away. It was nine o'clock in the morning and the sun was barely up, not that she could even see it at all through the thick grey cloud that hung so low in the sky. Still, she should be able to make five miles an hour on horseback, which meant a twenty-mile round trip should be concluded in four hours or thereabouts.

Six hours later, she still hadn't reached Alston. Marie ran out of curse words as she struggled to drag her extremely recalcitrant pack donkey up the steepest hill she'd ever travelled in her life. In this mountainous country, she had wildly overestimated her possible speed. To make things worse, the weather had turned nasty and bitterly cold. Sleet whipped at her face, stinging her cheeks with icy needles and chilling her to the bone.

"That must be Alston," she groaned as the spire of a church finally came into view after another hour. "Come *on*, you horrible beast!"

The sleet fell sideways on her glasses, which she regularly had to wipe in order to see where she was going. It left blurred streaks in her vision. Finally she saw some people, but they delivered her startled looks as they moved about quickly between shops. Alston had a single narrow street and the dark clouds were even lower, making everything feel unwelcoming and ominous. Too tired and annoyed to manage her manners, she stopped the next man she saw.

"Where is Alston Castle?" she asked bluntly.

His accent was even thicker than the Carlisle innkeeper's had been, but she managed to decipher that she still had two miles to go. He pointed farther up the street and then held two fingers aloft.

Marie thought she might scream. Two more miles? It may as well be ten.

There was an inn. It didn't look much of a place, however. It was a single storey, dilapidated wooden building with a sign swinging outside proclaiming *The Sally*, painted with a gaudily coloured image of a rather buxom wench. After one horrified glance, Marie abandoned any thoughts of seeking refuge in such a suspicious-looking place and forged onwards.

The sleet landed heavier, stinging her ears and neck. Marie cast a worried look at the box of books strapped on the donkey's back, hoping desperately that Louise's waterproofing would hold. It didn't bear thinking about what the Earl of Demanding might say if she arrived with water-damaged goods.

"Stupid man!" she shouted at the silent hills. "Stupid, demanding, entitled man!" The donkey balked yet again, so she turned her fury onto him. "And you, you stubborn son of a, a, a, SWINE!"

Darkness was falling but the sleet was at least turning into snow. It wasn't quite as wet when it hit her face; an infinitesimal improvement. An irregular shape ahead of her interrupted the jagged outline of the Pennines against the grim grey sky.

"That... can't be it." Marie stared and gulped. "It's a ruin!"

The pile of crumbling stones made a hideous first impression. Not far from the dark ogre caves of her confusing dream the night before.

But here it was. Alston Castle, and it was clearly and obviously a ruin. Gaping blackness in glassless windows, a huge archway crumbling and broken, massive stones fallen all around.

A substantial poplar tree grew within it, where a staircase should be.

For an awful, horrifying moment Marie thought she must have somehow mistaken the direction. That there was another Alston Castle in Cumbria, and she was going to have to retreat to the village and spend the night in that worrying-looking inn. There was no possible way she could get back to Carlisle tonight.

But no. Her horse had kept walking, dragging the donkey that was tied to the saddle along with it. Onward the horse walked, taking them through a dilapidated arch into an open grass bailey. There in front of them was the *real* Alston Castle.

Her body sagged with relief at the sight of it. A relatively *new* Alston Castle, and even against the blackening sky, it was magnificent. A vast edifice of crenellated grey stone, windows shining golden-bright with warm welcoming light within.

"Thank goodness for that!" Marie said gratefully, and urged her horse and the donkey forward. Finally she pulled up outside the huge timbered front doors. Climbing down stiffly, she approached the doors and swung the massive iron knocker.

The butler who opened it a couple of minutes later

looked startled to see anyone, much less a bedraggled woman in a riding habit holding the reins of a horse and a donkey.

"Are you lost, madam?" the butler asked. He was an older gentleman with a rather magnificent curly white moustache and twinkling blue eyes filled with mirth; Marie thought he looked kindly but also had the capacity for mischief, even if his tone was a bit stiff.

"Is this Alston Castle?"

"Why, yes, madam."

"Then I am exactly where I am supposed to be." Marie drew herself up as tall as she could manage. "I am Miss Marie Baxter, and I am delivering books from Baxter's Fine Books of Hatfield, as ordered by the Earl of Deman... ah, the Earl of Renwick."

She pronounced it ren-wick, and the butler frowned slightly.

"The Earl of *Rennick*," he corrected her pronunciation.

"Of course, like Berwick and Alnwick," she murmured to herself. "I do beg your pardon. I have only dealt with his lordship via correspondence."

"Whoever is here, Mr Martin?" a deep voice demanded from further inside the castle.

"A lady from Baxter's Fine Books, my lord," the butler turned his head.

"A *lady*?" The second voice said. The door was pulled open wider, and a tall, dark-haired man with a strong jaw, wearing a very fine dark navy coat, stared down at her.

"The Earl of Renwick," the butler said, rather unnecessarily. "Miss Baxter, my lord."

Marie was rather too busy gaping at the earl, who

looked nothing like she had imagined. Well, she had thought that he might be dark and foreboding, but she had certainly not thought him to be only a little older than she - she doubted he was above thirty years of age! She had for some reason assumed him to be more like twice that. Mostly on account of how grumpy and demanding he was, like an entitled old man.

I should have checked Burke's Peerage before I came, she thought.

"Why on earth are you here, and not Mr Baxter?" the earl demanded, scowling at her.

The snow continued to swirl around them as she stood there with her pack donkey and horse, no longer able to feel her feet. "My father is in France, my lord. You and I have been corresponding for months now." She frowned back at him.

"You're M. Baxter!" The light of understanding dawned in his expression, even if he looked no less displeased.

"Marie Baxter. Indeed. Do you think we might get these books inside? I believe the package to be water-proof, but I'm not quite certain." She gestured at the donkey, and the earl gasped aloud.

"My heavens! Get them inside at once!"

"And the lady too, my lord?" the butler asked.

"Yes, of course, far too late for her to turn around now, it's going dark." Heedless of the thickly falling snow, the earl briskly strode to the donkey and began untying the ropes securing the crate to the saddle. "If these are wet, I'm not paying for them!" he called back.

Marie let the butler take her riding horse's reins from

her numb fingers. "We shall see about that," she muttered under her breath, but she honestly thought she might be too exhausted to even muster an argument right now. Her legs were shaking and by this point she couldn't feel her fingers or her nose.

"Inside, miss," the butler said, his tone much more kindly than that of his master. "You must be chilled to the bone."

"Yes." She took a step towards the door, annoyed to find that she couldn't feel her knees, either. She wobbled. "Oh, dear," she said, quite irritated with herself. "This is no time to come over all faint."

"Miss Baxter!" The butler's voice seemed to come from quite far away as the world began to spin around her.

CHAPTER 2
Definitely Not Fainting

"Don't you dare faint!" Sebastian had just managed to get the box of books off the donkey - which had tried to bite him, the rotten little creature - when he saw Miss Baxter begin to totter. She sort of collapsed against the door and he shoved the books inside on the floor and grabbed at her, catching both her arms.

Why, she's only a bit of a thing, he realised. She was quite short, and there wasn't much of her as he hauled her inside and put her on the settle in the hall.

She blinked up at him from hazel-green eyes fringed by long damp lashes behind rain-speckled glasses. With a note of indignation in her voice, a voice he'd immediately noticed had the accents of a well-educated, gently bred lady, she said, "I never faint!"

She'd given a fair impression of fainting, he thought, as his attention was torn between his books and the young lady. All this time he'd believed he'd been communicating with a tradesman. His letters had grown increasingly terse with his fear they might not arrive at all. He'd kept ordering more in the hope that the size of the delivery would make it worth Mr Baxter's while.

Yet all along, he'd been berating a young lady while her father was in France. That would explain one of her letters claiming they were low on staff.

He gently patted her hand and said, "You're out of the weather now, but you cannot go out in it again this day. It will be dark soon and the road back to Carlisle will be far too dangerous."

"I do not need to go as far as Carlisle." The young lady sat herself up a little and turned her feet back and forth at the ankles, no doubt to see if she could feel her toes. He would wager she could not. "I can stay at the inn I passed in Alston."

"That is no place for a lady," Sebastian said in imme-diate rejection; he wouldn't send any woman to The Sally, never mind a pretty, well-bred young lady! The moment the words were out, he knew the only answer was for her to stay here. Well, they had plenty of rooms. Mrs Ellwood and young Morag would assist. In fact, if he summoned them, they'd take her under their care and he could get to his books. He'd waited long enough to get them!

Mr Martin, his butler, reappeared with the two women required, and also a footman who then went outside to take the horse and donkey around to the stables.

"You read my mind," Sebastian said with relief.

Mrs Ellwood immediately began to cluck over Miss Baxter like a mother hen. She patted the girl's hand and exclaimed, "Morag, she's cold as ice!"

Morag nodded and said something agreeable in tone, but utterly undecipherable - the maid was from the Scottish Highlands and spoke English with an accent so thick even Sebastian, who had grown up here close to the Scots border, struggled to decipher.

Mrs Elwood said, "Let's get you into some warm dry clothes, Miss."

"Call me Marie," the lady replied. "Please don't fuss. I will be all right. I have dry clothes in my portmanteau."

Confident that she'd be well taken care of, Sebastian left Miss Baxter to the women and set upon his parcel of books. The wrapping was tight and very well put together. Mr Martin appeared beside him with a small knife to cut through the leather straps that would not loosen thanks to the freezing conditions. He could, of course, wait until they dried but that would mean waiting for his books.

He'd waited far too long already.

With a flick, the leather snapped loose and he attempted to unfasten the oilcloth wrapping, only to realise it was actually stitched together. He reached for the knife again. It was only one layer, but when he rolled it back he found there was yet another layer underneath. Once he got the box open he found that each book itself was individually wrapped with rolled strips of lambswool tucked in between them, to prevent them rubbing against each other and moving inside the box.

He grinned like a child, impressed at how cleverly and carefully they had packaged this. Maybe he really could have trusted them to ship him the books after all!

He removed the last layer of protection and gasped at his new, much-longed-for prize, the first of the three-volume folio of *Antiquities of Athens* by Stuart and Revett.

He raised the book in his hands, as if holding a holy relic. The leather binding was cold to touch, no doubt from the weather. It was completely dry. He walked over to the candelabra and opened the cover to look at the frontispiece.

Stunning. His breath caught in his throat in wonder, as he carefully turned each page.

"Perfection," he whispered, before reverently carrying the book into his library and laying it on the desk. If the other two volumes were in as good a condition as the first, the twenty pounds he'd agreed to pay for them was an absolute bargain.

"Shall I bring the rest of the books in for you, my lord?" Mr Martin inquired from the doorway.

"No, don't touch them! I shall bring them myself." Sebastian smiled an apology at the butler, who knew his quirks well and nodded in grave acceptance.

"As you wish, sir." Mr Martin paused, cleared his throat and said delicately, "As the young lady will be staying the night, shall I set a place for her to dine with you?"

That would mean he'd have to make conversation, and spend less time with his new treasures.

"She might like a tray in her room," he suggested.

He was feeling rather clever at that, but Mr Martin gave him a gently reproving look. Sebastian sighed. He supposed making the effort to socialise was the least he should do for Miss Baxter, after the long, wet and perishingly cold journey she'd just made. "Yes, very well then. Set two places for dinner."

"Very good, my lord." Mr Martin bowed and with-drew, leaving Sebastian in peace.

He reached for his pile of goods and reverently unwrapped each title. His heart soared as he looked at each one. They were cold bricks of leather and paper that came to life in his hands as he opened each cover to look inside.

The work and skills to write them, then bind them so beautifully. They were works of art and they were here with him now.

He didn't think he'd ever been so happy in his life.

The clock struck five, startling Sebastian out of his absorption with his new treasures. He reluctantly closed the book he'd been perusing and rose to his feet, supposing he should go and wash his hands. Dinner would be served shortly.

Miss Baxter was coming down the stairs with the housekeeper as Sebastian stepped out into the hallway, and he paused to look at her. She'd seemed a bedraggled waif when she arrived, but dry and in a clean dress, she was actually passably pretty, dark brown hair curling around an oval face, those hazel eyes huge behind her glasses.

"Good evening, Miss Baxter," he said politely. "I trust Mrs Ellwood has taken adequate care of you?"

"Indeed, my lord." She reached the bottom of the stairs and made him a neat little curtsy. "Your staff have been everything gracious. And I do appreciate your kind offer of hospitality for the night," she added, as an apparent afterthought.

It was pitch black outside and the snow had increased to almost blizzard conditions. Wind howled around the castle's turrets. Sebastian shuddered to think of anyone having to be out in such weather, much less a young lady like Miss Baxter. "It was the least I could do, considering how far you have come," he said honestly. "Please, allow me to escort you in to dinner." He offered his arm.

She looked at it as though surprised, then looked back at his face, her expression slightly quizzical. "Thank you," she said finally, then put her hand on his arm and allowed him to lead her into the dining room.

"You mentioned your father is in France?"

"Yes, on a book buying expedition now that Napoleon is safely in exile."

"I almost envy him," he said. "Let me know the moment he returns, he has an excellent eye for quality."

She hesitated just as they walked through the doorway, a quiet "Oh," escaping her lips.

Sebastian tried to see the dining room through her eyes; a vast polished oak table, big enough to seat twenty, with several multi-branched silver candelabras atop it, the lit candles chasing away the dark. A roaring fire in the grate provided heat and a comforting glow. Silver and glassware glinted from the two place settings at one end of the table.

Sebastian escorted Miss Baxter to her seat, took his own, and tried to make small talk as a footman brought in the soup.

He had never been good at it, however, and was

several years out of practice. "Your father is Mr M Baxter?"

"Yes," she said, in between mouthfuls of soup.

"And you are Miss M Baxter."

"Correct."

"You signed your correspondence M Baxter."

She nodded and added nothing further.

He tried a few more topics and she mostly answered in monosyllables. Sebastian found his questions seemed to be getting ever more inane due to her lack of responses.

It was at some point after the pheasant in cherry sauce had been served that Miss Baxter set down her fork, turned to him and said;

"You don't have to entertain me, my lord. It's perfectly fine if you do not wish to talk. I don't mind silence."

Startled, Sebastian paused with his own fork half-way to his mouth and stared at her. She gave him an odd little smile.

"Did you not expect me to say that? I'm sorry if I startled you. I always seem to discomfit people when I say honest things like that."

"You didn't discomfit me," Sebastian managed. "It is... rather a pleasure to find someone who shares my inclination not to fill silence with idle chatter."

She smiled at that, a true, genuine smile rather than the socially polite efforts she had offered thus far, and he smiled back at her before lifting his glass of wine and raising it in a silent toast.

It was a pleasant meal, in the end, both of them enjoying their food without feeling the need to chatter, and Sebastian found that contrary to his expectation, he hadn't minded having his solitude broken at all.

"Would you be interested in seeing my library, Miss Baxter?" he asked as the footman cleared the last dishes away.

She responded with a shining smile of gratitude, and he found himself automatically smiling in return.

"Select whichever book takes your fancy to read this evening," he said as they entered the library.

She made a soft "Oh!" of wonder as she took in the library.

He puffed with pride, because this was his favourite room in the castle. It had been smaller, many years ago, but he'd extended it outward and created an arch where a wall had previously been.

He had his new delivery of books to entertain him, and sat by a desk to absorb the beauty of them. For her part, she took her time perusing the shelves until she selected an atlas of the new world. She took it and sat near the fire in a comfortable wingback chair.

In companionable calm, they spent the next hour or so reading their selected titles. On occasion he looked up to make sure that she was comfortable and had whatever she needed. Mr Martin quietly placed a glass of sherry on the side table beside her. She nodded her thanks but did not look up. Then Martin brought a glass with slightly more liquor in it over to him for a nightcap.

Not needing to talk was so comfortable. No, not comfortable, enjoyable.

He'd be happy to invite her over and not talk any time she liked.

The following morning, the snow lay deep and heavy around the castle and Sebastian knew Miss Baxter would not be going anywhere. He pointed this out when she came down to breakfast, and she looked at him with horror all over her pretty face.

"I need to return to my sisters!" she protested.

"Write them a letter, I'll frank it for you. It will reach them in better condition than you would if you went out in this."

"But I must get home. They need me."

Sebastian firmly disagreed. "You're not from here, you're not used to the conditions." She didn't even have a suitable coat; the thin thing she'd arrived in last night would have done little to protect her against the icy Pennine winter winds. She wouldn't even make it as far as Alston village in this weather without doing herself a mischief, never mind all the way to Carlisle. He simply would not have that on his conscience. He would forbid the grooms from saddling her horse, much less tying the donkey to her saddle, and that would be that. Folding his arms across his chest, he shook his head sternly. He couldn't believe she was in such a rush to leave. He'd given her payment for the magnificent books, and extra for the return journey. He'd parcelled it into smaller amounts so that nobody would see the entire sum in one glance and make her a target for opportunistic thieves.

Mr Martin said, "The lady does seem determined to injure herself."

"It's only snow," she said, sounding confident. "It's

almost finished falling. It's not the wet sleet I arrived in, and I have extra scarves." She bid them farewell and turned to head out the door.

Sebastian shook his head in silent dread, but she seemed determined to hurt herself.

Dutifully, Mr Martin opened the large front door for her. Coldness filled the entry hall as she walked down to the front steps.

"It is cold, but it's so much clearer than last night." She turned and looked back to Mr Martin and himself. "I shall make it back to Carlisle and send another letter on ahead of me." Then she turned and took the next step.

With a sudden yelp, she flailed and fell straight down. "Owww!" she yelled in pain, clutching at her left ankle.

And there it was. "I told you so," Sebastian said as he made his way carefully down the steps to their injured guest. "Probably black ice under the snow that you can't see."

"I'll be fine," she said as she sucked her breath through her teeth.

"You may have broken your ankle!" Sebastian disagreed as he scooped her up in his arms to bring her back inside and away from the snow and ice.

"It's not that bad," she protested.

He looked at her face and recognised the set of her jaw. "You're doing a passable job of hiding it, but you must be in agony. You have at least given it a bad sprain."

"No I haven't." Her lower lip jutted out mulishly.

He wanted to laugh at how ridiculous she was being. "Saying that does not make it true," Sebastian pointed out, carrying her slowly back up the steps. He didn't want to slip on the ice and fall himself, or they'd both be in a pickle.

Once inside, Martin shut the doors to keep the ice and snow out. Sebastian deposited Miss Baxter on the same settle as he'd placed her on the night before.

Trying to sound kind, Sebastian said, "At least now you'll have to stay until the weather improves. I just hope it's not broken."

Tears spilled down her cheeks, causing his heart to wrench unexpectedly at the sight of her misery.

"I suppose we might need to send for the local doctor," she conceded with an unhappy sniffle.

Oh dear, she really had no concept of how things worked around here. "We would, if there was one," he said, shrugging regretfully. "I like Alston because it's so remote, but the remoteness means we must do without. However, I have a great many medical books I can consult. Let me fetch one from the library."

Marie could not believe she'd been so foolish. Black ice? She'd heard about it but had never experienced it. She'd been so keen to begin her return she hadn't given it a thought. Now it became painfully clear. The sleet from last night would have made the steps wet. The first layers of snow to fall on top of that moisture would have frozen hard. Then more layers of soft snow above would make it all but invisible.

If only she'd kept walking forward instead of turning back to boast about how safe she was! What a fool she'd been. Now she could be stuck here for goodness knows how long!

"The light is better in the upstairs guest room Miss Baxter occupied last night," Mr Martin suggested as the earl returned from the library with a thick book in his hand.

The earl reached down to lift her up, but Marie put her palm up to stop him. "I'm sure I'll be fine," she said.

It wasn't right to have an earl carrying her about like a porter at an inn carried luggage. Cautiously, she sat up and turned her body so she could stand, being careful to balance one hand against the wall and place her weight on her uninjured right foot.

Pain throbbed in her left foot as the blood flowed south. The second she tried to put her weight on it, agony speared through her leg and she sat down immediately.

She might have even sworn involuntarily under her breath.

The earl passed his medical book over to his butler. She recognised the title as one from their family shop.

"Is that Fyfe's *Systems of Anatomy*?"

"It is indeed. I purchased it from your father a few years ago. An excellent reference, I've found."

She couldn't fault his taste in books, at least.

With a gentle huff, the earl once more collected her into his arms and carried her up the stairs.

Heat branded her from where his arms made contact, even through his thick coat and her riding habit, and somehow the heat made it all the way up to her face, flushing her cheeks pink. If her sisters could see her now, she'd never live it down.

CHAPTER 3
Trapped at Alston

M arie tried very hard not to shriek in pain as the earl's warm fingers probed at her ankle. It hurt, rather a lot. She tried very hard to pretend he wasn't an actual earl with his hands on her limb. *Just pretend he's Dr Rasley*, she tried to tell herself. To absolutely no avail, because there was an actual earl with his hands on her limb! A young, rather dashing earl instead of the town elder from Hatfield.

"I need to remove your boot," he said, glancing up at her from where he crouched at the foot of the bed. "Is that all right?"

Dear heavens, this was far too intimate for such a short association. Alas, she didn't suppose she had much choice, so she nodded. Fortunately, the housekeeper Mrs Ellwood bustled in at that moment with cries of horror, so at least they were appropriately chaperoned.

Marie bit down hard on the inside of her cheek as the earl very carefully unlaced and removed her boot. Hard enough that she tasted blood, and had to make herself unclench her teeth.

"It's swelling already. Mrs Ellwood, would you have Morag go out and gather some clean snow? We need to ice Miss Baxter's ankle."

Marie propped herself up on her elbows and scowled down at her ankle, extremely annoyed to see that the earl was correct. Her ankle was distinctly thicker than it should be, and already turning a distressing shade of purplish blue.

It ached so fiercely. She'd never in her life experienced anything like this sort of pain or injury, was entirely unaccustomed to being so helpless. It was a dreadful feeling.

"A sprain, I'm quite sure," the earl said authoritatively. "Let me consult my book for the correct treatment, but I believe icing it to be the first recommendation, so let us begin with that."

He left for a few moments, presumably to consult his book, and Mrs Ellwood came over to remove Marie's other boot and swathe a blanket over her legs, tutting away the whole while.

"Whatever were you doing, Miss, going outside in such weather? Why, your skirt's all wet too, we must change your gown once the master's done what he needs to. Ah, here's Morag!"

The maid was lugging in a pail full of snow; she set it down at the end of the bed and produced some linen strips.

Marie's breath hissed between her teeth as they wrapped a strip of linen around her ankle and then packed snow tightly around it. Just moving her foot enough to wrap it sent bolts of pain up her leg. Numbness was soon spreading from the cold snow, however, and she rolled her head back against the pillows and stared at the ceiling.

"What a very stupid thing to do," she chastised herself quietly.

"Arah, nae worrit, miss, we've all tekken a twa hipper skitie afore. Scunners!"

Marie looked at Morag, who was smiling cheerfully at her, and then at Mrs Ellwood, confusion creasing her brow. Mrs Ellwood hid a smile behind her hand.

"Go and brew some fresh tea for Miss Baxter please Morag, and bring up something for her breakfast. Toast and jam, perhaps."

"Aye, mam!" Morag covered the bucket and rushed out.

"Whatever did she say?" Marie begged.

"She said you shouldn't worry as everyone's had a nasty fall on slippery ice. Roughly. She's Scottish and even when she speaks English, the dialect is a little confusing if you're not used to it." Mrs Ellwood took a seat beside the window and seemed disposed to chat. "Where exactly is it that you've come from, Miss Baxter?"

"Hatfield, in Hertfordshire. It's around twenty-five miles north of London."

"A mort long way from here!" Mrs Ellwood gasped, hand to her throat. "And you came all that way, *alone*?"

"I had to deliver the earl's books. His lordship was quite insistent on it."

"That one and his books!" Mrs Ellwood gave a delicate little sniff. "Scarcely cares about anything else. Won't trust any of his staff to fetch them either! Well, I'm right sorry he's dragged you all the way here only for you to suffer an injury. We'll take good care of you until you're well enough to go home, I promise."

Marie thought bleakly that it wasn't herself she was worried about, not really; it was her sisters, and the bookshop. She'd come all this way expecting to take a large amount of money home with her. She had the money safely tucked away in her bags, but she needed to get it to Hatfield. At this rate, she might not make it home for another month, or even more!

"I need to write to my sisters," she said.

"Of course, miss. I'll get you some writing materials." Mrs Ellwood bustled off again, passing by the earl as he entered the room.

Book in hand, Renwick stood at the end of the bed, frowning down at the pages and not even looking at Marie. "It says here that if it's a sprain, it should be tightly wrapped and kept elevated," he murmured, running his finger down the page. "And yes, iced if possible, but not continuously nor directly against the skin, lest you get frostbite."

"May I look?" Marie asked as he set the open book down on the bed and frowned over her ankle. He glanced up at her, then shrugged and handed over the book. She read down the page, looking at the diagram of bandaging as he began to unroll a long strip of linen.

"Under the sole of the foot, then cross over the top,

then firmly about the ankle," she directed, and the earl looked up at her with an amused glint in his eye. He followed her instructions, though, eventually tying the bandage off with a neat knot. Marie tried to wiggle her ankle and found that she could not.

"Treated to your satisfaction, Miss Baxter?" the earl asked.

"Nothing about this situation is to my satisfaction," she said. Her words were harsh to her own ears, and she wished she could be more polite. Pain had a way of making her irritable.

"Understandable, and I am sorry for it." He came around beside the bed. "Your pillows are slipping; allow me?"

She nodded, pushing herself up on her arms. The earl leaned over her to shove the pillows back in.

"Father!" a youthful voice shouted, high with glee. "Father, there's a *donkey* in the stables; did you buy him? Can we pet him?"

Startled, Marie looked over towards the door, noticing almost absently that the earl stood up straight very quickly, a flush darkening his face. For an instant she thought she was seeing double, but no; there were two boys at the door, near-identical at first glance, though as they came into the room she saw there were differences. One was an inch or so taller, his hair a lighter shade of brown, his eyes blue where his brother's were brown.

It was the shorter of the two boys who had spoken, his dark eyes turned curiously on Marie now. "Who's she?"

"That is rude, Richard," the earl chided, though his

tone was not unkind. "When you meet a lady, that's not how you ask to be introduced. You have to ask someone already acquainted with her for the honour of an intro-duction."

Marie guessed the two boys to be about eleven or so, around her cousin Brutus' age or a little older. They could not be more obviously the earl's sons, though now she wondered at her initial assessment of his age at around thirty; he seemed too young to be their father. Unless he'd married young himself, which she supposed was quite likely. Especially if he'd been the only heir in line to the title; the aristocracy often arranged marriages when their heirs were still children, she knew.

"I beg your pardon, Father," Richard said penitently. "Will you introduce us to your lady friend?"

"Indeed I shall, since you have remembered your manners. Miss Marie Baxter, please allow me to present my sons. Richard William and," his voice changed a little, becoming oddly strained, "George Francis."

The boys made very creditable bows, looking at her curiously, and Marie smiled. "How do you do?"

"Very well, thank you." George edged forward, eyeing her foot. "Did you hurt yourself?"

Badly, she thought, blaming herself for being so foolish in the first place. "I'm afraid so, I slipped on the front steps and have turned my ankle."

"Sprained," the earl corrected.

She shot him an annoyed look. "Possibly sprained," she conceded reluctantly.

"Gosh, how jolly awful! But why have you come to visit?" Richard asked.

They were curious boys, if somewhat socially inept - but considering their father's awkwardness, what else was to be expected? Marie rather liked them both immediately.

"I came to deliver some books your father ordered," she confided.

"Books!" Two pairs of eyes lit up, and she smiled.

"Of course you are raising two more book connoisseurs," she said to the earl, who smiled rather reluctantly in return. "I shall take note of potential future customers for the shop."

"You have a *bookshop*?" they chorused in near-unison.

Oh, she liked them even more now!

"Boys, you mustn't bother Miss Baxter," the earl began, but Marie shook her head at him.

"I beg your pardon, my lord, but with my present injury, I have literally nothing else to do. I should be delighted to tell your sons anything they should like to know about my family's bookshop."

"They do have lessons to attend. Where is your tutor?" the earl asked.

Richard and George both looked a little evasive, mumbling something about the stables. Marie hid a smile. Typical boys, they would far rather be doing anything but conjugating their Latin verbs, unless she missed her guess.

Footsteps outside heralded the arrival of the boys' tutor, who was duly presented to Marie as Mr Charles, a young man of around her own age.

"He's going to be a vicar," George confided, sitting

down in the window-seat, "but he's quite nice anyway. Not preachy."

"An excellent quality in a vicar," Marie agreed, thinking glumly of the Reverend Millings, back home in Hatfield. "I am regularly afflicted with an extremely preachy vicar. We call him Old Brimstone!"

The boys both giggled, Mr Charles tried to look disapproving and failed, and even the earl cracked a small smile.

"Would you like to join us for nuncheon, Miss Baxter?" George asked eagerly, as Mr Charles attempted to herd his charges back to their lessons. "We always have nuncheon with Father, would you join us?"

"Is this an attempt to get out of your French lesson?" the earl asked severely. "Because it won't work. We always converse in French at nuncheon," he advised Marie.

French? How wonderful! "Oh, I should be delighted to join you then, my lord. I speak excellent French," she replied cheerfully.

The earl gave her a slightly doubtful look as he left the room in the boys' chattering wake, and Marie smirked to herself. The earl was in for a surprise, and she found that she was rather looking forward to nuncheon.

As the boys, their tutor and their father departed the room, Mrs Ellwood came back in with tea on a tray and a black bottle Marie recognised.

"Laudanum?" she questioned.

"It's up to you, dear," the housekeeper said kindly. "His lordship told me to bring it up. Thought it might help you rest for a while."

Marie thought about it. Her ankle was throbbing quite agonisingly, and the pain was beginning to give her a megrim. While she usually only developed megrims from extended periods of noise, when they came they could be quite incapacitating. She had found in the past that judicious use of small amounts of laudanum could help.

"One drop," she said, "in the tea, please. And even if I ask, please don't give me any more until tomorrow."

"Very wise, miss," Mrs Ellwood nodded gravely, and carefully tapped one drop into the teacup. "Now, just leave the cup there beside the bed when you're finished, and try and get some rest."

Marie's eyelids were drifting by the time she finished the tea, so she set the cup aside, snuggled down in the comfortable bed and drifted off into a blessedly pain-free sleep.

She woke to find Mrs Ellwood gently packing snow around her foot again, but the housekeeper hushed her and told her to get some more rest.

"I don't want to miss nuncheon," Marie mumbled.

"Never fear, you won't." Mrs Ellwood chuckled. "Those boys won't let you."

Marie smiled as sleep pulled her under again.

She woke a second time to a tap on the door, heralding the arrival of the earl and his sons, the two boys asking eagerly how she was feeling and was she ready to come to nuncheon.

"Indeed I am, I'm quite famished!" Marie smiled at them, and unwarily tried to get up. The moment she moved to swing her legs off the bed, she wished she hadn't. Bolts of pain raced up her left leg and she sucked in her breath, trying not to shriek in agony lest she frighten the boys. Very slowly and cautiously, she eased her legs back to where they had been.

Young George looked perceptively at her, his eyes full of concern, before turning to the earl. "Father, could we have nuncheon in here with Miss Baxter instead?"

All eyes turned her way and she felt guilty for holding them back.

The earl nodded and said, "If Miss Baxter cannot come to nuncheon, then I suppose nuncheon can come to Miss Baxter." Then he added in French, "I shall not, ah, compare you to a mountain, nor... Mohammed."

Marie smiled broadly and corrected his grammar, also in French.

His eyes rounded in surprise.

Marie beamed with confidence, despite her aching foot, pride surging through her with her skills in her mother's language.

Mrs Ellwood and Morag bustled in with trays of tea, and plates of sandwiches sliced into peaks, making them appear like the surrounding Pennine mountains. Two footmen soon followed with a selection of side tables and chairs.

Mr Charles took a seat and directed his attention to the boys. His next remark, in French, directly translated as, "This is a select lovely of food bites."

The earl looked to Marie to correct him, because he'd heard the poor delivery as well.

Marie gladly provided the more correct, "Oui, c'est un délicieux repas léger." *Yes, it's a delicious light meal.*

The earl's smile filled her with warmth and confidence.

Throughout their meal, Marie gladly spoke her mother's language freely, gently correcting the boys through some truly tangled sentences. When she'd hurt her ankle, she had berated herself for being stupid and making herself useless to anyone. Now she could be of use after all; she had skills the boys very much required.

Still speaking in French, she asked Mr Charles about how the boys were faring at Eton. Through stilted words and mangled verbs, he managed to convey they were doing very well in Latin and Greek.

Which was a credit to them, but French clearly came a distant third, which Marie deplored. How many occasions were the boys likely to have a need to speak Latin and Greek in their lives? French was far more likely to be useful, as was mathematics.

Cricket was something else at which they apparently excelled, although it wasn't a specific subject like the languages, the boys explained. It was something everyone enjoyed playing in the lead-up to the King's Birthday every June.

They did their best to explain how the school halves worked, and when they were due back, slipping into English when they struggled.

Mr Charles wasn't that much help, as he valiantly tried to explain in tortured speech, "More boys at Eton stay at Christmastide and special boys these are."

"Voulez-vous dire que la plupart des élèves restent à l'école pendant la période de Noël au lieu de rentrer chez eux?" *Do you mean that most students stay at school over Christmas instead of going home?*

"Oui," he replied, with a relieved, heavy sigh. He appeared to have a sore head from thinking so hard. No wonder the children were not doing well in that language when their tutor was not so well-versed himself.

"We shall speak in French as much as you like," she told the boys in that beautiful language, "To help improve your skills in the time that I'm here."

Mr Charles curled his lips down with a sad expression and managed, "Dans ce cas, il n'est pas normal d'être heureux que vous vous soyez fait du mal. Mon français est vraiment déficient." *In this case, it's not right to be happy that you've hurt yourself. My French is so lacking.*

True, but kind of him to say nevertheless. She didn't remark on his poor French, just accepted a slice of cake from the plate George was offering to her, and thanked him.

The tea was hot and welcome as Marie sipped and smiled. Her ankle hurt like blazes now that the laudanum had worn off. But the distraction of the lovely food, the sweet boys, the struggling tutor and the surprisingly charming earl all worked a spell on her and she found she could go several minutes at a time without thinking about her pain. They talked long into the afternoon and Mr Martin arrived with the boys' French readers, so that they could study what was expected of them.

Marie read out a range of verbs, the boys repeated them back. Mr Charles joined in as well, the tutor temporarily becoming the student.

"Je marche, Je marchais, Je vais marcher," she read out

to them. All three replied, trying hard to mimic her accent. *I walk, I walked, I will walk.*

She added something relevant to them. "Je vais marcher jusqu'à Alston et remettre une lettre." *I'll walk to Alston and deliver a letter.*

As much fun as this was, she really did need to get a message to her sisters. It would be most convenient if someone could walk to Alston and post a letter for her.

CHAPTER 4

Painful Truths

M arie woke in the morning with pain throbbing in her ankle. She must have turned it in the night, despite sleeping with her foot above the covers. When she cautiously pressed her fingers down her leg, her ankle felt puffy and hot under the bandage.

Mrs Ellwood helped her out of bed and dressed her. She felt as useless as a babe, being unable to do the most basic things for herself. Even more than that, a night's rest had done nothing at all to repair her joint. It really had to be sprained, or worse. She sent up a prayer begging for it to only be a sprain.

"It's all right, dear," Mrs Ellwood said. "I know you're a lass that is used to getting things done in her own way. You're not used to relying on others, are you?"

"That I am not," she admitted, enjoying the house-keeper's sing-song lilting northern accent. Morag, however, completely defeated her and all she could do was smile and nod when the maid tried to make conversation. It gave her a deeper insight into how Mr Charles must feel as he struggled to speak French.

Her foot hurt so much, as Mrs Ellwood helped her hobble across the room to where a comfortable chaise longue near the window provided exactly the right kind of comfort for someone who needed to keep their leg elevated and steady.

Silly, silly girl, she scolded herself. Why had she been so determined to ignore the earl's warnings?

At least she was dressed and reasonably presentable, as the throbbing in her ankle continued to pulse and ache with every beat of her heart. Thankfully though, her head remained clear, and she declined firmly when Mrs Ellwood held up the bottle of laudanum, a silent question on her face.

"No, thank you. I don't need it."

Morag prattled on, but she had such a sweet expression as she talked, Marie didn't have the heart to send her away. "Maybe if you sing," she suggested, "It will distract me so much better. Do you have any songs you like to share?"

The girl beamed and launched into a haunting tune that sailed around the upper registers like a bird on a wing, before fluttering down and heralding misfortune. Marie had no idea what the song was about, but the melody was enchanting and dramatic. Morag had an incredible voice. Eyes turning misty, Marie wondered what the words meant. Clearly they meant a great deal to young Morag, judging by the yearning expression on her face.

"It's so beautiful," Marie said when the song ended, "I'd love to know what the song means."

Morag smiled sweetly and said, "Tha e ciallachadh bàs dha na Sasannaich a ghoid mo ghaol."

Mr Martin appeared at the door just at that moment and said to Morag, "You'll not be wishing ill of our guest."

Marie had no idea what had just transpired but the young maid ducked her head in a sign of guilt.

Then Mr Martin looked to Marie and said, "His Lordship has asked after his patient."

Marie sighed balefully and said, "I am impatient to leave, but my ankle has not healed."

"May I examine it?" the earl said, as he strolled into the room.

As Morag was still in here for propriety's sake, and Mr Martin (who carried the medical text) stood by with the doors wide open, she could hardly refuse.

And anyway, how would she get out of this room, let alone the castle in her current state? It was all so frustrating.

The earl knelt by her foot and gently touched her big toe.

"Hsssst!" Marie hissed with discomfort.

He palpated the sides of her foot and ankle, each tiny movement punishing her muscles. Marie gripped her skirts so tightly her knuckles turned white, with the effort not to shriek.

With her pained responses, the earl eased his touch so that he was barely feeling the joint. "It is as I thought. Sprained, and badly at that, but it is not broken."

"You can tell just by touching the area?"

"The swelling is down a little, which is a good sign."

Marie tried not to whine, but she couldn't help it. "Yet it feels worse than yesterday."

"I'll carry you downstairs. No point staying up here where you can't do anything. You may as well come and keep me company in my library, and the boys can join us for nuncheon later."

With one smooth lift, he had her up off the chaise and pressed closely against his body. The pain wasn't as acute as when she'd first injured it, but by heavens it throbbed something awful.

Feeling utterly miserable, she buried her head into the earl's shoulder and began to cry.

"Have I made it worse?" He sounded stricken.

"No," she sniffled, "Merely capitulating to self-pity."

He chuckled with what sounded like glee.

Marie accused, "You're enjoying yourself, aren't you?"

He laughed out loud at that and her whole body reverberated as he held her so closely.

"Merely capitulating to *self-congratulation*. I knew it was sprained, not broken, and I am right."

"Hmph," Marie said.

As he carried her easily down the stairs, seeming to take no apparent notice of her weight in his arms, Marie reluctantly added, "You *were* right, my lord, and I am grateful for your medical knowledge. I might have done permanent damage if I had tried to continue yesterday."

"You might indeed." He carried her into the library, set her on a comfortable armchair near the fire, and brought over a footstool, lifting her foot very gently to prop upon it. Standing over her, she had to crane her neck to look up at him.

"And thank you for your hospitality. Your staff have been extremely attentive," she thought to add.

"I'm glad they are looking after you properly, but it has been made clear to me that I am to do my share." He nodded, rather gravely. "Which means that it falls to me to entertain your mind. What can I get you to read?" He gestured around him, at the vast, beautiful library.

"I daresay there are worse places to be trapped for a few days," Marie said happily.

The earl turned back to her, eyes widening slightly. "Miss Baxter... from everything I have read, it will be rather more than a few days, I'm afraid. Sprains can take from three to six weeks for a patient to regain a modicum of usefulness in the affected limb, and three to six months for full recovery. Certainly, I cannot possibly let you attempt the journey home until at least three weeks have passed, and by then it will be just a few days to Christmas. Please, allow me to extend the invitation for you to spend the holidays with us, and return home in the New Year? Mr Charles will be taking the twins back to Eton in time for term commencement. You can travel far more comfortably in their company, in my coach, than you possibly could going by post."

This was quite the longest speech she had heard him make thus far, and Marie took a few moments to think through the offer.

"I do not suppose I have much choice," she said with a sigh. "Even attempting to move my foot is very painful, and I'm quite sure I can't put any weight on it."

"It could be worse," the earl said, and she thought he was trying to be kindly. "I broke my leg when I was fourteen, falling off my horse. I was laid up for eight weeks, quite miserable."

So he did understand how she felt.

She nodded. "It could be worse." She could easily have broken her ankle, falling on that ice. "Well, I shall accept your very kind invitation to join you for the holidays, my lord, and repay your kindness by teaching your sons French!" It was the least she could do in return.

"I must ask how you learned such excellent French?" the earl said. "Mine is school-learned, and then practised only by reading in the language rather than conversing in it, but yours sounds almost native."

A smile broke free. "My mother was French," Marie admitted. "From the Loire region. My father is English, and my sisters and I were born here in England. I have never been to France, but Mama raised us to speak in both."

"I see!" The earl hummed for a moment. "Your father is there now, as you've mentioned, hunting for more books."

"He had correspondence from France urging him to travel. Several chateaux were being raided and soldiers were destroying valuable books."

The earl's face fell. "That's criminal!"

Marie agreed with his assessment, as it was also her father's view. "Naturally, he was in great haste to get there and rescue what he could."

"I hope his journey is successful," the earl said. "Would you care to read in French? I have several volumes I'm not sure have ever even been touched. Let me fetch them over for you and you can peruse them at your leisure."

One of the books he brought over was a stunning calf-bound *Ménagerie du Musée National d'Histoire Naturelle*. Marie selected it with delight, carefully turning the pages to admire the gilt edges and beautiful plates depicting exotic creatures from far-flung regions of the globe. She quite lost herself in the book, and the earl watched for a few minutes with approval for her delicate handling of the valuable item. He then selected a book for himself and settled down in another armchair.

They read in happy, companionable silence until a knock at the door heralded Mr Martin coming in, asking politely if they would be happy for the young masters to join them for nuncheon.

"Of course," the earl said. "That large table over there should be quite sufficient for the tea-trays with enough food to satisfy everyone. I'll bring a plate over to you, Miss Baxter, if you wish?"

"Certainly, thank you," Marie agreed, discovering she was quite hungry.

The boys erupted into the room just ahead of Mrs Ellwood carrying the tea-tray, Mr Charles trailing along behind looking a little harried. Marie supposed it must be quite difficult managing two high-energy young boys all day, especially as the weather made it quite unfit for them to run around outside at the moment.

Deliberately, she addressed her remarks in French primarily to the earl and the two boys, leaving Mr Charles to sit and eat his meal in peace.

When the meal and French lesson concluded, she diffidently asked the earl for some paper in order to write to her family and let them know she would be delayed. She had asked Mrs Ellwood for something similar the day before, but she'd left the items up in her room.

Expecting small note-sized paper, she was very impressed when the earl bought her several large sheets of expensive, quality paper, ink, a quill, a blotter and even a small writing board that she could balance horizontally across the arms of her chair.

What incredible bliss! He also mentioned that he would frank the letter for her, so she need not worry about her sisters having to pay postage when they arrived. She could include as many pages as she wanted.

The boys were reluctant to leave, and ate their last sandwiches with the tiniest, slowest bites. Marie finished her letter to Louise and Bernadette and then took another sheet and made a quick sketch of young Richard as he took mouse-sized bites. Then she captured George in a few more strokes and played with getting the shape of his hair pattern just so. The earl had said they were twins, not merely brothers, but the more time she spent in their company, the more differences she could easily see in them. She no longer needed to see them together to know who was whom.

"You have captured them both remarkably," the earl said, the moment he realised what she was doing.

"Sit still and I'll make a study of you next," Marie said without thinking. Had she just delivered orders to an earl? Who did she think she was? "I'm sorry, I quite forgot myself!" she exclaimed, flushing slightly.

"Let me see!" George got up from his seat and came over to look at the page. He gasped and said, "Gosh, that's jolly good! Dickie, look at this!"

Richard was by her other shoulder in a moment and said, "She really got your nose right!"

George shot back, "And your sooky bottom lip!"

"Boys, I'm a little out of practice, I shall do better on the next one," Marie said. "You'll need to forgive me."

"It's jolly good, all the same," Richard said. "You could be our artist in residence!"

Marie began sketching the earl, adding him into the image as if sitting beside his sons, a fond smile on his face as he watched them.

"Make sure you get his flappy ears!" George said with a laugh.

"He has very nice ears," Marie corrected, before realising what she'd said and flushing to the roots of her hair. "As do both of you!" she added hastily. "Ears are unique, once you start really looking, you begin to notice no two people are identical. But obviously the Renwick traits breed true." That was no better! Oh! She needed to stop talking!

The earl stood up and abruptly walked out of the room, surprising her. The sketch was almost complete, though, and she finished it off quickly.

"I shall enclose them in my letter to show my sisters what lovely people I am staying with. A pity the weather isn't good enough for me to go outside to sketch the castle…"

"Well, there is a painting of it on that wall," George said, pointing. "Couldn't you copy that?"

Marie turned to look. "So there is! Very well. I would like my sisters to see what Alston Castle is like… none of us have ever had the opportunity to stay in a castle before." Flipping the sketch of the earl and his sons over, she drew the castle in sure, quick strokes, glancing up at the painting regularly to check she had the proportions approximately correct.

The twins watched over her shoulder the whole time, raptly attentive.

"Before you leave," Richard asked in a small voice, "would you make a drawing like that for us? Then we could look at it when we're at school."

"Of course I will," Marie said immediately, realising that they must be at least a little homesick when they were away at Eton. Perhaps that was why the earl had brought them all the way home for Christmas; they were, after all, still very young.

Or maybe he just missed their company, she thought as she folded up her letter and the drawings. Just as she was already missing her sisters. With the boys away at school, she thought that Alston Castle was probably a very lonely place for its master.

On returning to the library, Sebastian found the boys still there, bothering Marie. "Out," he said, not unkindly.

"Yes, Father," they chorused obediently, and trailed Mr Charles out, though Sebastian did catch both of them sneaking glances back at Marie. He caught Mr Charles sneaking a look too, and firmed his lips. That young man was in no position to be admiring Miss Baxter. Even if she did look very pretty with a smile on her lips and her hazel eyes shining as she bid the boys a good afternoon.

"Is that your letter to your sisters? I shall take it to Alston personally in the morning." He held out his hand for the letter. "And though Alston is small, I assure you that our postal service is quite good even in poor weather. A rider goes down to Carlisle three times a week. Your sisters should receive your letter in ten days or so. I shall have your hired horse and donkey returned to Carlisle in the next few days too, so you need not worry about them."

"I appreciate you taking the letter to Alston, my lord. I'm reassured to think it might even reach them before they originally expected me back. It will ease their concerns when I do not arrive with the payment for your books."

His jaw dropped for a moment and he could have kicked himself hard enough to make an injury. "Oh dear, it was quite a good amount."

"Well, now that you raise the topic," she said with a shy smile.

"That was badly done of me. And you're in no state to return any time soon. Plus, we cannot send that much blunt unaccompanied by post. It would never arrive." He thought for a moment about how he could possibly fix this. *Who could he send to Hatfield at such short notice? In this weather?* "Wait, I have it!" He clicked his fingers as a plan came together. "I shall write to my man of business in London. The letter could get to him in about a week. I shall explain all, and ask him to arrange for the necessary funds to be sent securely to Baxter's Fine Books."

"That does sound like the safest option," she said, with only a slight wince of discomfort as she adjusted her sitting position. "I shall fetch the amounts from my bags …oh." She visibly winced as she tried to get up.

"Would you like me to carry you to your room?"

"Yes, if you would not mind."

"It doesn't need to be done right away. I should write to my man of business first, that is far more urgent. I recall the cost of the books came to one hundred and forty-seven pounds. What were the expenses and accommodations you incurred bringing them here?"

"That was six pounds, eight shillings, ten pence and ha'penny," she recited.

"You are magnificent with numbers," he said with a half-grin, a little amused by her pedantry.

He was rewarded with a deep blush. "Thank you for the compliment. I am in charge of the accounts at the bookshop."

He was silenced into shock for a moment. He thought he was being flippant, and possibly a little rude, in noting her exactness. She'd taken it as praise.

"Why don't I round it up to seven pounds then?"

She shook her head, immediately protesting. "I could not, that is far too much."

He slowly shook his head and chortled. What a funny creature she was! "How about six pounds ten?"

He could tell she was pressing her lips together to prevent laughter.

"Please, Lord Renwick. It was six pounds, eight

shillings, ten pence and ha'penny. And not a farthing more!"

"I shall add that to the amount my man will forward to the bookshop."

"Please also subtract the amount you paid for my return accommodations," she said with a stern insistence. "You did offer to have me conveyed back home when Mr Charles takes George and Richard to Eton," she said slowly.

"Yes, that still stands."

"Presumably you will have accommodation arranged ahead, therefore subtract it. When I next am in my room, I shall repay you."

It was clear she would not let him pay a penny more than he owed her.

"One hundred and fifty-three pounds, eight shillings, ten pence and ha'penny," he said, writing the figure out. "I will instruct my man to expedite the payment, so your sisters should receive it soon after your letter arrives. Do you wish to add a postscript?"

"Yes, best that I do." She took her letter back and wrote a brief line on the back of it under the seal.

He showed her his letter to his man of business, so she could give final approval to the total sum. She nodded her satisfaction when she read it and handed it back.

Sebastian was just finishing and sealing both letters when Marie hit him with a question that made him shoot up straight in his chair.

"Mr Charles is a nice young man. How does he come to be the boys' tutor?"

"Er... he is the son of a tenant farmer," Sebastian

said a bit stiffly, unused to being asked to explain himself, and a little uncomfortable that Marie was showing interest in Mr Charles. "His father is a good man, but not well educated; it was apparent from an early age, however, that the son was very clever. He did well at school and when I inherited the earldom I was able to sponsor him to a better school, and then to Cambridge. He will complete his seminary studies next year."

"Ah, so he is well known to the family and under your patronage!" Marie nodded understandingly. "Do you have livings in your gift, to be able to establish him?"

"Yes and no... while there are several livings under the earldom's control, all the incumbents are hale and hearty, and a good many years from retirement. While I will lend Mr Charles my support, I am afraid he will have to earn his living as a travelling curate for a while at least. It will be some years before he is able to support a wife," Sebastian couldn't help but finish.

Marie gave him a puzzled look. "Well, he is quite young to think of marrying, I am sure he will be content to wait until he is established," she said, apparently unconcerned.

Sebastian could have kicked himself. While it had been obvious from the covert glance he'd observed earlier that Mr Charles was quite taken with Marie, it appeared *she* was only asking about the young tutor out of politeness! What if his silly remark about marriage planted the idea in her head of looking at Mr Charles romantically?

He didn't particularly want to examine why that thought bothered him so much, so instead he placed both letters on his desk to take to Alston in the morning, and smiled tightly.

"If I might trouble you," Marie said hesitantly then, not quite meeting his eyes, "I should like to retire to my room for a little while, before dinner."

He figured she would want to return all his money, down to the very last ha'penny. Then he noticed the time, and realised with horror that she probably required a little privacy. Mr Martin had kept them well supplied with drinks and light snacks all day, and Marie couldn't exactly get up and visit the water closet.

"Of course," he said hastily. "Allow me. I shall send Morag to attend to you, and we shall see you at dinner."

"Thank you, my lord."

He was getting to like the way she felt in his arms and the way she rested her head against his shoulder, Sebastian realised as he carried her up the stairs.

It was definitely time to make alternative arrangements.

CHAPTER 5
Home Comforts

S ebastian stretched and welcomed the new day with a hearty yawn. First light peeked over the mountains. He loved this time of year when he could catch the whole sunrise at a reasonable hour. His first thoughts were for Miss Baxter, and whether her pain levels were manageable. They might even watch the sunrise together from the upstairs parlour that faced south.

His valet, Mr Sharpe, commented, "You're in an excellent frame of mind this morning."

"Indeed I am," he agreed far too readily.

"Can we credit this to the presence of Miss Baxter?"

He snapped, "You're out of line." Then immediately regretted being so terse. But also, how dare the valet assume such a thing? "It's the books Miss Baxter delivered, nothing more."

"Apologies, my lord," Sharpe said as he adjusted Sebastian's cravat. "The books are indeed a boon, and an excellent addition to the library."

He shouldn't have been so harsh. Reacting so defensively was a sure sign the valet had got too close to the truth. A moment ago, he'd planned to carry Miss Baxter down to the library... but now he wondered how much his staff had seen?

He was being chivalrous, nothing more. The poor lass was injured and unable to walk. Ergo, she must be carried.

So why was he the one doing the carrying? He wasn't the one who'd hurt her; so his actions were not the result of duty or guilt. In fact, he'd urged her to remain in the house because of the risk of injury.

Cold realisation washed though his body as he adjusted his sleeves.

He *liked* carrying her around. The thought of anyone else performing that duty stuck in his craw.

He really should stop. They were virtual strangers, even if they'd been corresponding for months. Except he'd thought he was addressing Matthew Baxter the father, not the daughter Marie.

Marie was now stuck here, possibly still in a great deal of pain and missing her family. And she was trapped in one room at a time unless someone carried her to the next.

She must be utterly miserable.

He rang the bell for Mr Martin. "Have my horse ready in an hour, I shall be taking letters to Alston."

"Very good," the butler said, and headed off to alert the stables.

Sharpe retrieved a thick scarf and a greatcoat for him. Grey clouds covered the sky, they were unlikely to see much of the sun today. But it wasn't raining just yet.

"Should you take the carriage instead, sir?"

"I'll be faster on Caesar. If I go in the carriage, someone else will have to drive it through the gloom. I should be back within the hour."

He saw Mrs Ellwood in the hall as she left Miss Baxter's rooms.

"Mrs Ellwood, how goes our guest this morning?"

Mrs Ellwood bobbed a curtsey and said, "A little glum, but nothing a visit to the library won't fix."

Sebastian beamed at how much Estelle appreciated his library. He was about to offer to carry her down there before he left, then stopped himself. He had to prioritise the letters. Then he'd see to Miss Baxter's comfort.

"I have an idea," he said to the housekeeper. "Would you please convert the unused parlour on the ground floor into a bedroom for Miss Baxter?"

"Certainly," she said with another bob of her head. "And ah…" she lowered her voice as her expression softened, "Miss Baxter requires some more clothing. She has some things with her, but they are completely inadequate for an Alston winter."

Sebastian indicated they should not stand around chatting, as he did need to get down to the stables. He tilted his head toward the stairs so they could keep walking together and carry on the discussion. It would give Miss Baxter some privacy, too. He didn't feel comfortable discussing women's clothing so close to the door where the lady whose clothes were in question might overhear them on the other side of it.

"I did note the thinness of her coat when she arrived," he said.

"I have warm things she might use, of course, but a lady of Miss Baxter's station does require more than servants' clothes."

"I concur," he said, taking the steps. Then it hit him what his housekeeper was hinting at, "She needs a *lady's* clothing, doesn't she?"

"Thank you, my lord, that she does." Mrs Ellwood stood looking at him, patiently waiting for him to catch up to her thoughts. She knew what had to be done, of course, and so did he, but...

He hung on to the bannister while he absorbed the impact of what the housekeeper was saying and accepted the necessary action. He couldn't go on pretending events of the past had never taken place, no matter how much he tried to lock things away. He took a steadying breath and then continued his descent. "Very well. No use if all those dresses remain mouldering in a trunk. Do as you see fit. I suppose Miss Baxter is of a similar size to the former countess."

How he managed to get those words out and remain upright astounded him. He had hoped to live the rest of his life without ever having to think of that woman ever again. It was bad enough that the boys were a constant reminder.

"Thank you, my lord. I shall find something suitable, and warm. Some of the plainer gowns will do nicely. And I am sure there are some warmer coats -"

"Yes, very good," he said in clipped tones.

"I recall a rabbit-fur lined cloak," Mrs Ellwood said with a hopeful tone.

Sebastian stopped and faced the overly-helpful housekeeper. "Is this your way of telling me you've already gone through the trunks?"

She bobbed a curtsey and said, "I am terribly sorry, but the poor lass did need something warmer."

She was right, of course. Mrs Ellwood was a wise woman and he knew it. She had merely required his permission to do the right thing, which she had clearly already done. He nodded abruptly and hurried away from the pitying expression on her face.

He couldn't get out to the stables fast enough. The cold winter air on his face would do him the world of good. As much as he yearned to gallop, it would be fool-hardiness itself to encourage Caesar to go any faster than walking pace. The snow on the ground might look pretty, but there was no way of judging the obstacles or rabbit holes beneath it.

Black ice was also a certainty. Blasted stupid black ice was why Miss Baxter was still in his home, and why, indirectly, he was now in a foul mood. Not because of her exactly, but because of the feelings she'd stirred up that he'd long since buried.

The horse let out a complaining huff, and pawed the ground.

"It's all right, Caesar, I'm not cross with you," he told the stallion with a pat on the neck. He must have been holding the reins too tightly.

Caesar snorted and tossed his head in understanding. Plumes of steam erupted from his soft brown nose, and Sebastian huffed out his own breath.

He had to relax. "The outing will do us both good," he told the horse, but he still found himself turning to look back to the castle before he rode under the ruined arch. He looked up at the window to Miss Baxter's room. Was she sitting there?

The curtains were still drawn, however.

The icy wind would cool his inflamed nerves. This journey to Alston would do him the world of good.

When he returned home, his limbs were so stiff from the cold he almost had to be prised off Caesar's back. That Miss Baxter had survived her much longer ride in even worse conditions raised her higher in his esteem. A determined, stubborn woman, he thought, who would accomplish whatever task she set herself to no matter what unexpected obstacles might present themselves. How frustrated she must be at being trapped now by her injury!

Instead of heading directly inside, he corralled a couple of grooms in the stables and directed them to affix wheels to a chair so that Miss Baxter would be able to move from room to room without needing to be carried.

"Can we also somehow brace something to the chair for her left leg, so that it remains level or raised in some way? It's for the lady who has badly sprained her left ankle and this will help enormously."

"We'll do our best," one of the grooms said.

The other nodded and said, "It'll be grand, m'lord, leave it to us. We'll bring it in shortly."

Smiling with the expectation of success, Sebastian headed inside to the comforts of his warm library. He rang the bell and told Mr Martin to let him know when Miss Baxter was in a state to receive visitors. Then he picked up the book he'd been devouring and returned to the page he'd reached last night before he went to bed. Mr Martin silently left a pot of hot coffee at his elbow, and Sebastian murmured his thanks without looking away from the page.

He sat by the fire and thawed out nicely, wiggling his toes as his feet came back to life. At least Miss Baxter had worn decent boots on her journey to Alston. They were firm fitting and had probably prevented even greater injury to her ankle.

He should not be thinking of Miss Baxter's ankles, but that's where his mind took him.

He should not be thinking about Miss Baxter at all.

Within the hour, the grooms proudly delivered him an old dining chair which had been modified with wheels attached to the feet and a short plank attached on each side protruding forward with a cross-brace nailed between them. They'd wrapped a thick pad of leather around the wood for comfort.

"Very good," Sebastian approved, eyeing the chair. "That will help enormously."

Miss Baxter would be able to rest her injured foot on the cross-brace and the other on the floor, then scoot herself about from room to room, as long as she went slowly. "Thank you, lads, a fine job!"

Mrs Ellwood was the next to arrive, telling him that the unused parlour had been cleaned, a fire lit and a bed brought in.

"I took out the rugs that were on the floor, too," Mrs Ellwood said, looking at the wheeled chair with an approving nod. "That's a right clever contraption, my lord."

"Let us hope Miss Baxter approves too. Is she ready to come down?"

"I think so. I didn't tell her we were preparing a room for her downstairs." Mrs Ellwood beamed. "Thought it'd be a nice surprise to cheer her up, like."

The housekeeper didn't miss a thing. Poor Miss Baxter must be miserable. "You think she needs cheering up?"

Mrs Ellwood shrugged. "The lass is hurt and far from home and family. She's putting a brave face on, but I've seen a few tears."

He had, too; she'd cried into his shoulder, wrenching at his heart. He nodded, determining then and there to do everything in his power to give Miss Baxter all the comforts Alston Castle could possibly provide while she resided there. "Treat her like a duchess, Mrs Ellwood," he instructed. "I feel dreadful that this happened to her; it's my fault she came all this way in the first place. I should have trusted them to package and send my books properly."

"Trust don't come easy to you, my lord." The housekeeper looked at him with a penetrating gaze, and then she gave a small smile and nodded. "But I quite understand why. I think Miss Baxter is one as you can trust, though. A real lady, for all her family's in trade."

Was his housekeeper... *matchmaking*? Sebastian gave a stiff little nod, his distrust extending to himself as he couldn't figure out how to respond the right way.

He marched off towards the stairs. The sooner he brought Miss Baxter down and into her movable chair, the better. Once she had her movable chair and was settled in the converted downstairs room, he wouldn't need to carry her about any more, which meant he wouldn't smell the lavender water she obviously rinsed her hair with, or feel the way she trustingly rested her head against his shoulder...

Stop it, Sebastian, he told himself, very firmly. *This way lies heartbreak.*

Marie's face when he showed her the wheeled chair was a picture; he set her carefully down on it and lifted her foot onto the padded cross-brace. Privately, he tried not to think too much that this would be the last time he carried her about, but it was best for his sanity that he keep his hands off her.

"If you hold onto the arms and push on the floor with your good foot, you should be able to scoot around. Slowly. I don't think it will turn corners very well..."

Marie experimented, a grin dawning on her face as she was able to navigate her way across the library.

"My lord, this is simply marvellous. You made this?"

"Well, two of my grooms made it," he demurred. "I just told them what I needed." All the same he couldn't help grinning at how happy he'd made her.

"It is exceedingly clever! All the more so as it must have been put together from bits and pieces you had on hand. I am impressed by your ingenuity, my lord, and indeed by your grooms' craftsmanship."

Sebastian felt the tips of his ears heat. He ducked his head a little bashfully. "The least we could do, Miss Baxter. But I have more to show you. If you'll allow me?"

He put his hands on the back of the chair. "I think it will steer better with someone pushing."

Mr Martin opened the library door for them with a broad smile, and Sebastian pushed Marie across the hallway and down a wide corridor. Opposite the dining-room another door stood open, Mrs Ellwood waiting there for them with a welcoming smile.

Sebastian had to pause and steel himself before pushing Marie into the parlour that had once been the former countess' favourite room. Looking about, though, he noted gratefully that Mrs Ellwood had done a marvel-lous job. Though the walls and drapes were still the pastel pink shade he had come to hate, the monstrously ornate, gilded furniture was gone, probably banished to some far reach of the attics, replaced with a simple chaise upholstered in sage-and-cream striped satin and a bed with matching covers, set discreetly behind a woven wicker screen. A fire crackled merrily in the grate, a tea-tray waited on a side-table beside the chaise, and several lightweight chairs were placed along the walls, out of the way for now but easy enough to drag up to the tea-table.

"His lordship thought this might be more convenient for you," Mrs Ellwood said kindly, as Marie looked about.

Marie didn't say anything for a long moment, and Sebastian began to wonder nervously if there was some-thing about the room that displeased her.

"Is it to your satisfaction?" he asked anxiously.

Marie turned to him, eyes brimming with tears, her hand over her mouth in shock. She pulled it away and confessed, "This is quite the kindest thing anyone has ever done for me. It's too much, my lord! I am already inconveniencing your household quite enough..."

"Nonsense," he said robustly, "you must never think that. We are delighted by your presence here, especially the boys..."

Who erupted into the room at that precise moment, and promptly began shouting with glee as they examined Marie's wheeled chair. She laughed, knuckling away her tears, and graciously gave permission for them to push her about the room, so long as they were careful not to bump into the furniture.

Sebastian stood back near the door and watched, aware after a few moments that the tutor Mr Charles had come up beside him and was watching too.

"Miss Baxter is very good with George and Richard," Mr Charles commented. "It is good for them to have a female figure in their lives, I think."

Sebastian bit down hard on the inside of his lip, not trusting himself to say anything. Fortunately, he didn't have to, as Morag arrived just then carrying the first of several trays of sandwiches and pies for nuncheon. The boys called for him to come and sit with them.

"Pardonnez-moi, qu'avez-vous dit? Je ne comprends pas l'anglais," he said teasingly, making them laugh.

Richard stumbled through the invitation in French, gently corrected by Marie, and then Sebastian accepted graciously and came to the table, bringing one of the chairs with him to sit on. He tried not to resent Mr Charles taking a seat too and eagerly joining in the conversation. He couldn't begrudge the young man taking the opportunity to improve his French.

Somehow, he was going to have to manage the unpleasant curdling feeling in his belly whenever Mr Charles cast one of those admiring smiles at Marie, or whenever Marie laughed at the tutor's efforts to make jokes in French. He had no business feeling jealous of their innocent interactions.

None at all.

CHAPTER 6

Mixed Signals

Marie looked around the parlour-turned bedroom, her heart full. It was truly kind of the house-keeper and staff to have gone to so much effort, though she was well aware that Mrs Ellwood would have done no such thing without explicit orders from her lord and master. Marie still wasn't quite sure what to think about the earl at times, but there was no doubt he could be extremely generous when he wanted to be.

It was so much more convenient to be on the same floor as the other rooms she liked to visit, especially the library. She didn't want to be ungrateful at all, but the room's decor wasn't really to her taste. The walls were a slightly nauseating shade of pink and the curtains a darker pink in heavy silk that must have cost a fortune. The furniture was rather nice, even if it didn't quite match and she was sure it had been brought in from another room. Once the gentlemen had departed after nuncheon, she wheeled herself slowly about the room, pausing to look at the charming writing-desk by the window, well-stocked with paper, ink and quills. Having just written to her sisters, she thought she would not need to write again for a few days. Perhaps she'd make some more sketches to share in the next letter, and she would enjoy telling her sisters what she'd been doing, with the lovely people she'd met.

There was another door on the opposite side of the room to the one she had entered by. Curious, she opened it to find a large room on the other side with all the furniture blanketed in Holland covers.

"That there's the music-room," a voice said behind her.

Caught snooping, Marie jolted guiltily in her chair. "I'm sorry, I didn't mean to be nosy," she began.

Mrs Ellwood laughed, coming to stand beside her. "Miss, if his lordship didn't want you in there, he'd have told me to lock the doors. The twins are allowed in whenever they please, to come and look at that picture." The housekeeper pointed across the room, to a large portrait hanging on the rear wall. It was of an extraordinarily beautiful woman dressed in a pink gown. Golden ringlets cascaded over creamy shoulders, her mouth open in a soft laugh. She looked so vibrantly alive Marie half-thought she might step out of the portrait.

Mrs Ellwood said, "That's their mother."

Marie blinked, looking back at the housekeeper. "George and Richard's mother?"

"Aye, the last countess." Mrs Ellwood's mouth screwed up as though she'd tasted something bad. "We try not to speak of her in this house. But she did leave something behind which may be of use - trunks and armoires full of clothes! Morag and I have brought a few things down you might like to try on."

"I couldn't possibly!" Marie exclaimed in horror.

"But you must!" Mrs Ellwood shook her head. "You've only a couple of dresses with you, and you'll be here for weeks - and his lordship agrees with me, what you have isn't suitable for our cold northern winters. Now come over here with me…"

Mrs Ellwood could be rather forceful when she set herself at something she perceived to be a problem, and Marie found herself wheeled over to the bed, where Morag was piling dresses in what looked to be every conceivable shade of pink.

"The former countess liked pink, then?" Marie asked. That would explain the curtains, and the walls.

"Didn't wear much else." Mrs Ellwood made that face again. "Except after the old earl passed. Wore some darker clothes for a while then, though nothing like what I'd call respectable mourning. Come to think of it… Morag, go up and fetch that nice dark blue wool dress, and the lavender one. They'd both look very nice on Miss Baxter."

"Aye, mum." Morag trotted off again, and Mrs Ellwood held up a lovely pale grey cloak, the hood lined with a soft silvery fur. It was quite beautiful, and Marie couldn't resist reaching out to feel the thickly woven lambswool.

"More your style, Miss Baxter?" Mrs Ellwood asked knowingly.

It was beautiful. "Oh yes, if I could afford something of this quality!"

"Does no good mouldering away here, Miss. You should wear it."

She barely believed her good fortune. "And... his lordship is happy for me to use these things?" Marie asked, a little doubtfully. From the tiny clues of context Mrs Ellwood had let slip, she wondered if the staff hadn't liked the former countess much, but the earl must have loved her, surely? The woman was stunning. Doubtless the earl kept her portrait in the music room where he rarely went because it must break his heart to look at her.

"He said I could give you anything you'd find of use," Mrs Ellwood replied, and Marie didn't remark on the fact that the housekeeper hadn't actually answered the question she'd asked.

Morag returned with three more dresses, in navy, lilac, and a lovely rust-coloured gown Mrs Ellwood exclaimed over, saying she'd not noticed that. "I don't think the countess ever even wore it, decided she didn't like it after it was delivered. It'll look a treat with your colouring, Miss Baxter!"

It was a beautiful dress, skillfully made with fine lace at the collar and the cuffs of the long sleeves. Marie rubbed the thick, warm wool between her fingers before nodding. "It's lovely, Mrs Ellwood." Marie looked over the rest of the outfits and declared, "If you're quite sure it's all right... I think perhaps I'll avoid wearing any of the pink gowns as I wouldn't want to cause anyone any distress. But these three here in colours she didn't wear, I could borrow those."

"Very good, miss. We'll take these pink ones back upstairs when we've helped you dress."

Carefully, the housekeeper and the maid helped Marie into the rust-coloured gown. These warmer clothes were made of thicker cloth than she was used to; they were heavier on her body, and she had to be careful not to lose her balance as she placed her weight on her right foot.

With the fire burning away in the hearth, she felt properly warm for the first time since leaving Hertfordshire. With tender care, Mrs Ellwood pulled an oversized sock over Marie's injured foot to keep her toes warm.

The pale grey cloak sat perfectly on her shoulders, as she tucked it about the chair so that it didn't become caught in the wheels. "Thank you, Mrs Ellwood, thank you Morag, these clothes shall do me very well."

Mrs Ellwood beamed at the compliment. "It's a good thing you've darker hair than the late countess, otherwise his lordship will think he's seen a ghost."

It was an overdone compliment. Bernadette was the beauty in the Baxter family, not she. And compared to the countess's portrait, Marie was but a sparrow. But it was nice to be compared to a woman with such beautiful features all the same.

"He must miss her a great deal," she said.

"That's one way to put it," Mrs Ellwood said cryptically.

Morag said something unintelligible, but the tone sounded rude to Marie's ears.

A silence descended as Marie wheeled herself back toward the music room, guessing at what might be under those Holland covers.

"Is that a pianoforte?" she asked, pointing at a familiar shape.

"It is at that. Do you play?" Mrs Ellwood asked as she and Morag moved toward it.

"I do," Marie said as the women carefully removed the cover and stirred up a little dust.

With some help from Morag to steer her chair, she found herself sitting next to the pianoforte, her hands reaching the keys. She pressed a scale of notes and pulled her hand up in surprise. "It's in tune?"

"Aye," Mrs Ellwood confirmed. "Han't been played f' years, but his lordship gets it tuned ev'ry autumn'n any case."

Her accent sounded thicker and Marie saw her wipe away a tear.

"You must miss her so much as well."

Mrs Ellwood straightened up, pursed her lips and said, "Her companion Miss Ramsgate was a dear lass, but after the countess died, she went back home."

Again, not really answering the specific question Marie had asked. It was as if the housekeeper was doing everything she could not to mention the late countess at all.

Instead of pressing her on the issue, Marie began to play a French folk tune her mother had taught her, about a woman waving her sweetheart goodbye as he set off to make his fortune.

"Her ghost is waiting still, by the window sill, for the beau that never came…"

"Bit maudlin, innit?" Mrs Ellwood said.

"Yes, you're correct, I shall…"

In the corner of her vision, she saw two little heads

pull back from behind some more furniture, also covered in blinds.

She exaggerated her speech so they would hear her. "It appears, Mrs Ellwood, that I have a larger audience than I expected. Two little mice hiding behind the chaise!"

"Mice!" Mrs Ellwood exclaimed, spinning around in horror.

"Not real mice. We heard the pianoforte," young Richard said, poking his head out and grinning at Marie.

"And we wanted to see who was playing," George finished for him.

"Did your mother play often?" she asked, thinking the children might not be so reticent with information.

"Her friend Miss Ramsgate did, but she's not here any more."

"Do either of you play?" she asked.

They shook their heads in unison, emerging from their hiding spot and coming to stand beside the pianoforte.

"I suppose your days are full of other lessons," she said.

"I'd best get back to it," Mrs Ellwood said, excusing herself. She tisked toward Morag for her to leave them alone as well, even though Morag appeared to be enjoying herself. "Come on, lass, we've those other dresses to put away. Let's be about it."

"Thank you again, both of you, for all your help," Marie said as they made their way out. Then she turned to the boys and asked, "Do you sing?"

They curled up their noses and shrugged their shoulders.

"I'm sure you're both very good. Do you know The Twelve Days of Christmas?"

"I like that one, it's fun!" George said, his face brightening a little. "Birds everywhere!"

Marie began to play the opening notes and they sang together with vigour, not caring if they hit the wrong key in their singing. As they reached some of the later days, the twins became muddled with the order of swimming swans, leaping lords and ladies dancing and fell into fits of laughter. Marie kept playing and laughing at the same time. The boys drew in a huge breath ahead of crying out, "Five goooooooold rings!"

By the time they reached the end of the song they were red in the face and out of breath, their faces split with happy smiles.

It took them a while to get their breaths back, but soon they were sitting down and begging her to play another song.

"I'm not positioned quite correctly to get to all the notes I want to reach. Could you help me adjust the chair?"

Her wheeled chair was not as close to the pianoforte as the regular playing stool would be. George carefully rolled the chair back and forth a little until she had a much better position.

"Do you know this one?" she asked, playing another hymn that her mother had taught her. This one was in Latin, so the boys would most likely pick it up.

"*Adeste Fideles laeti triumphantes, Venite,*
venite in Bethlehem. Natum videte, Regem Angelorum;

Venite adoremus, venite adoremus, venite adoremus Dominum!"

The boys joined in heartily.

"We sing that at school," Richard said.

"Excellent!" She tried another that she was sure they would enjoy, even if they didn't know the words. "I saw three ships come sailing in," she started. It was a lively tune and the boys clapped along. They soon picked up the repeated lines and joined in the song.

When that song was done, they all cheered each other.

"I'm so glad you're staying for Christmas," George said.

"Could we learn singing instead of French?" Richard asked.

Marie laughed at their lack of enthusiasm for that language, but she was beginning to feel personally invested in improving their fluency. Understanding and speaking French would get them further in life than Latin, she was sure of it. "How about I teach you a French song?"

"Yes please!" they chorused.

Marie moved to place her hands on the keys but suddenly stopped. "I've just had an idea. How about we put on a concert for your father for Christmas?"

The boys' eyes rounded with surprise and delight, and they immediately began to speak over the top of each other about how much fun that would be.

Mr Charles came in just then, obviously alerted to his charges' location by hearing the singing, and George and Richard immediately begged their tutor to allow them to rehearse for a Christmas concert.

To Marie's delight, Mr Charles seemed quite enthused about the idea.

"It can be a surprise for Father!" George said happily.

Marie met Mr Charles' eyes, and saw her own amusement reflected there. Keeping a surprise of this sort of volume wasn't going to be possible, even in a place the size of Alston Castle.

"The earl does like to go out riding most mornings," Mr Charles said thoughtfully, playing along with the ruse. "Perhaps when we see him go out on his horse, we can come here and rehearse, if Miss Baxter is willing to play for us."

"And if Morag can be permitted a small time off from her duties, she could join us," Marie suggested. "She has the most beautiful singing voice, and perhaps she knows some Christmas songs in Gaelic. I'll ask Mrs Ellwood."

When the housekeeper popped her head around the door a few minutes later to find them singing "God Rest Ye, Merry Gentlemen", Marie asked if Morag could be spared to join the rehearsal.

"Aye, I suppose," Mrs Ellwood said, though she did pause for a moment first, looking at Mr Charles. "I'll send her down."

Marie noticed the glance and wondered if there was something she shouldn't ask about. After all, she was merely a guest and did not want to pry.

A few minutes later Mrs Ellwood and Morag arrived at their impromptu salon.

Morag nodded to Marie, then smiled at Mr Charles and moved to stand beside him at the pianoforte. Mrs

Ellwood quickly placed herself bodily between the two people and ushered Morag around to the other side. "Your voice is higher, you should be on the other side," the housekeeper said.

"Aye an oot o' the way!" Morag muttered under her breath as she took up position on the other side. She smiled warmly at Mr Charles, who made a slight gulp and hastily turned his gaze away, fixing it firmly on Marie.

Marie might not literally understand what the young maid was saying, but she was getting a fair idea from the looks passing around the room.

She cleared her throat and asked, "Morag, do you have a carol we might all sing?"

Morag's voice was clear and sweet.

"Shid ald akwentans bee firgot, an nivir brocht ti mynd? Shid ald akwentans bee firgot,

an ald lang syn?"

Marie quickly picked up the tune as she'd heard it before over the past few years. She knew the chorus and had the rest of them joining in with a mix of Gaelic and English.

"Fir ald lang syn, ma jo, fir ald lang syn, wil tak a cup o kyndnes yet, fir ald lang syn."

Morag was in her element, directing her song to Mr Charles. The tutor appeared transfixed and yet also trapped. The sooner this song finished, the better for the poor young man. But lo, Morag had another verse in her:

"An sheerly yil bee yur pynt-staup! an sheerly al bee myn! An will tak a cup o kyndnes yet, fir ald lang syn."

Marie stopped playing and applauded, "Bravo, how beautiful!" George and Richard did the same. Soon she began to play a sweet little French rhyme she hoped everyone would know.

"*Frère Jacques, Frère Jacques, Dormez-vous? Dormez-vous? Sonnez les matines! Sonnez les matines! Din, din, don. Din, din, don.*"

This led perfectly to singing rounds, with Marie and Morag starting off, Mrs Ellwood and Mr Charles singing the middle and the boys bringing it all home.

When it came to the end, there were smiles all around at how well they sang together. Morag said something to Mr Charles, but he either couldn't understand her or pretended not to. He then turned to Marie and said, "I'm terribly sorry to spoil the fun, but I must take the boys back to the classroom for the remainder of their lessons."

Richard and George made some low mutters of displeasure, but Marie assured them they could come back for more singing tomorrow, as soon as their father rode out.

Mrs Ellwood moved quickly to intercept Morag as she made a beeline for the tutor. Marie could hear her, but the teacher and the boys were already walking away by this point.

"Pull yer eyes back into your head, lass. You're reaching much farther than your sleeves will let you with that young man!"

The particular expression was unfamiliar to Marie, but the tone of the housekeeper was not. Marie might need glasses to read, but she could clearly see how Morag was besotted with the young tutor. He was handsome, so it was not unexpected that he could turn heads, but his future was in the church and he would need a suitably dutiful and possibly more placid life companion than this wild, uneducated Scottish lass.

All the same, Marie felt sorry for the young maid. She must be lonely on this mountain surrounded by no suitable suitors of her own age.

Morag made herself busy with re-stocking the fire, then curtseyed and took the cold tea tray away to the kitchens for a refill, her pretty face sullen the whole while.

"It's all right, Mrs Ellwood," Marie said as the maid departed, keeping her voice low. "She may be young and a little silly, but I'm sure she meant no harm."

"That matters not. What matters is that Mr Charles is a respectable young man who doesn't need distractions coming between him and a life of service in the Church, especially from a heathen!" Mrs Ellwood tutted and shook her head. "There's plenty of men will be keen to court a pretty lass like that one, once spring comes and folks are stirring from their hearths again. She needs to stop making eyes at those who aren't for her. Especially his lordship!" The housekeeper swept out on that final word, leaving Marie suddenly wondering if that last line had been aimed in her direction. Did Mrs Ellwood think Marie had been making eyes at the earl? She hoped not. Marie wasn't silly; she was well aware that the earl was far, far out of reach for the likes of her.

With a sigh, Marie gently closed the lid of the pianoforte and pushed the toes of her good foot against the floor, pushing her chair back so she could begin the laborious process of steering herself back to her room. She was tired, the slightest beginnings of a headache making themselves felt after the noisiness of the last hour. Perhaps she would lie down for a little while before joining the earl in his library.

CHAPTER 7

Good Memories and Bad

S ebastian was in the middle of rearranging a shelf in his library to correctly incorporate some of the new acquisitions Miss Baxter had delivered for him when the first notes from the pianoforte startled him so badly that he dropped several of the books he was holding.

"Blast it!" He stooped and carefully picked up the books, checking each of them for damage. His frown deepened as the music continued, scales resolving into a tune, and then a sweet alto voice raised in song... in French.

A small smile twisted Sebastian's mouth, in spite of the emotions roiling through him at hearing the pianoforte being played. Miss Baxter - Marie, as he was beginning to think of her all too often in the privacy of his thoughts - must have discovered the music room. His feet took him in that direction without consciously choosing to do so, but just as he arrived at the door in the parlour which led into the music room, two younger voices raised up in song.

By the time the twelve days of Christmas had been sung through, in a great muddle and a tremendous amount of laughter, Sebastian was holding in his own chortles. Marie really was quite wonderful with the boys, he thought.

And then he heard another voice. Mr Charles had joined the group, and soon all four were singing together rather beautifully.

While the sound of the pianoforte had at first brought uncomfortable memories of his late wife to mind, they were quickly banished. Marie's voice was nothing like Francesca's, he thought; Francesca had been well-trained by London masters and sang in an operatic style, showing off her soprano voice, whereas Marie's was a lower alto, sweet but obviously unschooled.

Altogether, he enjoyed today's singing far more. Perhaps especially because Francesca would never have deigned to sing something as simple as children's songs or Christmas carols. And never in a hundred years would it have occurred to her to invite a maid to join the choir!

Unable to resist, Sebastian eased the door open the smallest amount, just a crack wide enough for him to peer through. And there was Marie, her face alight with joy as she played and sang, hazel eyes bright behind her glasses.

He'd thought she'd be wearing pink, but the rust-coloured gown she wore was surely not one of Francesca's. It looked lovely on Marie, bringing up the deep reddish tones in her brown hair, the colour lending a warmth to her pale cheeks. With the lace collar at her throat and the grey fur-lined cloak about her shoulders, she looked every inch a fine lady.

He could just see Mr Charles, standing on the other side of the pianoforte, hands behind his back as he raised his voice in the carol. The young tutor had a very nice baritone and was keeping his eyes on Marie, a slight flush on his cheeks as he watched her and sang.

Sebastian tried not to grit his teeth. Was he actually going to have to tell Mr Charles to keep his distance? He kept watching, growing more and more annoyed as the young tutor never took his eyes off Marie.

I'm spying on them. He realised it as Marie moved, her eyes flicking briefly in his direction, and Sebastian suddenly froze. He should not be spying on them; it was quite ridiculous, he told himself sternly.

He should go in and join them, but he couldn't move. Indeed, it was a good thing he hadn't gone in, he thought a moment later, as he heard Richard and George excitedly talking about "a surprise Christmas concert for Father!" A wry smile crossed his lips. Bless them, they wanted so badly to please him, to make him proud of them. They were good boys, and he was trying, he really was. It was easier with Richard. If only he didn't see Francesca every time he looked into George's blue eyes!

I need to do better. Stepping back and closing the music room door very quietly, Sebastian looked about thoughtfully. Though tastefully decorated, the parlour was quite a dim and dull room; it could definitely do with some brightening up. Making his way back out into the hall, he found Mr Martin standing listening to the music drifting out of the music room with a smile on his face.

"Quite puts one in the Christmas spirit, doesn't it, my

lord?" Mr Martin said cheerfully as Sebastian approached.

"It does, rather," Sebastian agreed. "And to that end, I think the castle could do with a little brightening up for the holidays." He pointed to the stairs. "When my mother was alive, I remember that she used to tie swags of red and green ribbon up the spindles and banisters. Do you think we might still have any about somewhere?"

Mr Martin's smile broadened. "I do believe I know the exact trunk in which that ribbon is stored, my lord. Lady Renwick, God rest her soul, did love Christmas. It's been many a year since Alston saw such cheer as she used to bring."

"I think it's time to revive a few of her traditions, don't you?" Sebastian wasn't even sure he remembered all of them - his mother had died when he was only ten - but Mr Martin and Mrs Ellwood had been at Alston since before he was born. They'd remember what he'd forgotten.

"I think that's a simply marvellous idea, my lord."

"Very well." Suddenly invigorated, Sebastian nodded. "Would you fetch my coat, Martin? I'm going to head out to the stables and fetch a couple of the grooms. We'll see if we can find a hefty Yule log, and cut some holly and ivy for wreaths."

"I shall return with Lady Renwick's decorations, my lord." Martin looked enthusiastic as well.

"And when I come back, I'll talk to Mrs Ellwood and the cook about some Christmas dishes!" Sebastian was sure they might have had some celebratory dishes planned, at least, but he wanted those he remembered from his childhood; roast goose and plum pudding, mince pies and iced gingerbread, hot cider... he grinned to himself as he shrugged into his coat and tramped out into the snow. He'd enjoyed the hot cider as a boy, and probably the twins would like it, but perhaps he might graduate to mulled wine now he was an adult.

He laughed as the snow crunched under his boots, suddenly very much looking forward to Christmas, for the first time in a very long time.

Outside it was perishing cold. The wind howled and for a moment he almost lost his nerve. Snow on the pine boughs slid off in the wind, exposing the deep green needles. They would look festive inside, and bring a welcome scent with them.

The grooms were there, and he congratulated them again on the tremendous success of the wheeled chair they'd made for Miss Baxter. "It surpassed my expectations, and I thank you once again for your speed and ingenuity," he said.

The men beamed at his compliment and replied with eagerness that if there was anything else he needed, he only had to ask.

Which he did. "I require decorative pine branches, any holly and ivy we might find, and a Yule log."

They both looked at him with furrowed brows, and then one of them said rather hesitantly, "Yer'll not be thinkin' of bringing the greenery inside yet, will yer m'lord?"

"Well, I was thinking we'd need to dry it out for a day or two first, perhaps," Sebastian said, but the men were shaking their heads vigorously.

"No, my lord, it's terrible bad luck to bring greenery inside 'afore Christmas Eve!"

He hadn't known that, but he wouldn't for the world upset any superstitions his people might hold. "Very well, let us hold off on cutting the greenery for a few days yet. But we'll still need to find a Yule log and get it under cover to dry out, or it'll never burn for twelve days and nights."

They agreed to that, and consulted quickly with each other on where they might find a good log, before setting out towards the edge of the woods. There weren't a great many trees this high in the Pennines, but there was a small wood in a narrow valley just below the castle, and Sebastian hoped they'd find a decent specimen there.

When they realised he was following rather than returning to the castle, the grooms became confused. "Yer Lordship needn't bother, it's well in hand," one said.

He grinned at their caution. "Call it temporary madness, but I'd rather like to be involved."

They looked at each other with raised brows and then shrugged and one of them said, "Let's get to it then."

The axe Sebastian carried was hefty and sharp. He felt rather workmanlike as the three of them strode through the snow, searching for just the right log.

They came across a fine fallen tree at last, mostly buried in snow. It would be perfect and was large enough to burn from Christmas Eve to Twelfth Night, once it had dried out a bit.

There was no way they'd be able to get it into the house in its current state. It wouldn't even fit through the front doors. Sebastian considered the tree, noting which branches would need to be chopped off - most of them - and stamped a bit of snow away to give himself somewhere stable to stand while he cut. The grooms gave him worried looks, that he might injure himself in the process of wielding the axe and they'd be blamed for it.

One of the grooms said, "I'm more than happy to cut the log, yer lordship."

"All right, you can get it started," he said, handing over the axe.

The men took turns in giving several whacks to cleave the branches from the trunk and then set to chopping a great length out. After a few whacks each, they removed their own coats as they began to perspire.

When one tired, the other took his place, puffing and huffing, cheeks turning red with effort.

"May I...?" He wanted to contribute something to the work.

"It should come clear with not too many more," the groom said, stepping back from the endeavour. "Careful, mind. Bring it down but don't swing too hard or ye'll cut your awn leg awff."

If the axe took such chunks out of hardwood, he imagined it would make short work of his limb. He followed their instructions and brought the axe down firmly, as close to their previous marks as he could manage. It made a slight indent, and he had to wriggle the axe out from its cut. A second whack, and he needed to take his coat off as well. His shoulders couldn't move properly under the extra weight, and he was roasting hot already from the effort.

"Aye, cut your own wood and it warms ye twice!" one

of the grooms said, laughing. They weren't laughing at him, though, nodding approval of his efforts.

Sebastian shrugged off his coat and tossed it onto a branch, then dried his perspiring hands on his trouser legs. With an almighty effort, he lifted the axe and brought it down hard, again and again, until the notch deepened. The wood creaked and cracked. The grooms rocked their weight on the end of it and the huge log fell away from the trunk.

The three of them cheered with their success. The grooms had smaller hand axes with them, which they used to quickly remove the remaining side branches.

He was relieved it hadn't taken any more whacks to separate the log. He'd put so much into that last swing he would wake up very sore tomorrow.

He couldn't believe he was standing out in the snow with only a shirt and trews on, and still felt hot.

The heat continued in his arms and legs as the three of them tied ropes around the log and dragged it in stages, all the way up to the stables. It was only once they got there and Sebastian saw Caesar looking over the stall door at him that he laughed out loud.

"We're fools, lads! Why didn't we harness a horse to do all that pulling for us?"

Both grooms laughed and shrugged their shoulders. "'Tis done now, my lord!"

"Done indeed." They rolled the log into an empty stall, where it could dry out before they took it inside to light on Christmas Eve. Sebastian smiled with deep satisfaction, dusting off his grimy hands.

"A very good afternoon's work, you two. Tonight you

deserve to wet your throats, I'll let Mr Martin know you're to have an extra pint of ale each."

They thanked him with broad smiles, and Sebastian left them in good spirits, striding back across the stable yard.

Just as he got to the castle doors, he remembered he'd left his winter coat back on a tree branch and ran back through the snow to retrieve it. Darkness was falling, and the snow was beginning to fall again with it as he dashed back inside. Snowflakes caught in his hair.

"Have yourself a good time, my lord?" Mr Martin asked dryly, accepting the coat when Sebastian held it out.

"Do you know, I did, rather." He pulled off his gloves and looked down at his hands. "Although I believe I might be developing a blister. Chopping wood is jolly hard work."

"Perhaps a bath before dinner, sir?" Mr Martin suggested discreetly.

Sebastian caught a glimpse of himself in the large hall mirror hanging on the wall behind the oak settle he'd set Marie on that first day, and began to laugh. He was filthy, as grubby as either of his sons might be after they'd had a wrestle on the floor of the stables! "I think so indeed, Martin. Mr Sharpe will not be pleased with the state of my boots, either!"

His valet indeed threw up his hands in horror when Sebastian went upstairs, but soon rallied and had a hot bath ready for him to soak in while Sharpe fetched clean clothes.

There were pine needles in his hair, Sebastian discovered, and he scrubbed vigorously. What a mess he must look! He was naturally quite fastidious, preferring to be clean and tidy in his dress, even if some did think his taste in clothes quite dull, tending as he did toward more muted colours and less flamboyant styles.

"Not that black coat," Sebastian said, watching Sharpe lay out his clothes on the bed. "Maybe… maybe the green one." The green would look nice with Marie's rust-coloured dress, he mused silently.

"I don't think you've worn that green coat since we returned from London, my lord." Sharpe's surprise was evident.

"Have I grown fat since then? Do you think it won't fit?" Sebastian teased gently.

Sharpe snorted a laugh, but he looked even more surprised. The valet had a wit as sharp as his name, and exercised it frequently at Sebastian's expense, though he was careful to remain respectful. He wasn't used to Sebastian being the one to make the jokes.

"I'll get the green coat, my lord," Sharpe said, and fetched it from the dressing-room while Sebastian finished his bath.

Soon he was making his way downstairs, trying to suppress that treacherous leap of excitement in his stomach at the thought he would soon be spending time with Marie again. Mrs Ellwood greeted him at the foot of the stairs and he paused to discuss Christmas dishes with her. The housekeeper looked delighted at the thought of engaging in Christmas festivities and promised to consult with the cook on the morrow, so that they would have plenty of time to send down to Carlisle for anything special the cook might require.

"Thank you, Mrs Ellwood. Oh, and Martin! I forgot to mention it earlier, but I promised the two grooms an extra pint of ale each tonight, for their hard work with the Yule log. Would you see to it, please?"

"Of course, my lord," Mr Martin said cheerfully.

Sebastian entered the parlour, surprised to see it already looking a little more festive - extra candles were lit and the whole room seemed brighter. Marie was sitting in her wheeled chair by the fire, a glass of sherry on the table beside her, a book in her lap.

"Good evening, my lord," she said, looking up with a bright smile.

"And a good evening to you too, Miss Baxter. I hope I find you well?"

"Oh, very much so."

"And your ankle?"

She grimaced a little. "I find if I try not to think about it, it hurts a little less."

"Mrs Ellwood does have some laudanum…"

Marie held up a hand to forestall him. "I accepted a drop on the first day, but I prefer not to use laudanum often. I find it can make me quite unwell. Rest is all I require, my lord, and your staff have been exceptionally helpful and attentive."

"I am glad to hear it."

"Dinner is ready, my lord, Miss Baxter," Mr Martin said from the doorway.

"Thank you, Martin. May I push you in, Miss Baxter?"

She smiled and thanked him, admitting that the chair,

while excellent in every way, could be just a little hard to steer unassisted.

"I shall not tell my grooms that. I praised them to the skies for making it," Sebastian confided.

"Indeed, do not hint of the slightest flaw! I would be mortified if they thought I was critical of their skills."

That was very kind of her, Sebastian thought. Just as it had been kind of her to invite Morag to join their little choir practice earlier. Marie didn't seem to care about what station people occupied in life, she treated everyone with exactly the same respect. Which he very much appreciated. He'd mostly broken his staff of the habits of excessive formality his father had demanded of them. Being bowed and scraped to could get very wearisome over the years, Sebastian had found. In his own home, he preferred to be more casual.

Sebastian pushed Marie up to her place at the table, where the regular dining chair had been removed, and took his own seat beside her.

Although they began their meal in comfortable silence, as the fish was brought out it occurred to Sebastian that there was something he wanted to mention.

"I heard you playing the pianoforte earlier," he said.

He hadn't expected her to drop her fork, her face turning pale as she stammered out an apology.

CHAPTER 8

Good Moods and Bad

Guilt swirled through Marie and she didn't know where to look. She'd really thought Renwick was out of the house at the time, or surely he'd have heard the noise and come to see what they were doing.

She picked up her dropped fork, her mouth dry. "You heard me playing?"

He nodded, his face stern. "And singing, with the boys."

Her heart sank. The playing must have reminded him of his late wife, and stirred up so many difficult emotions. "I was teaching them some French as well, I promise you it wasn't all frivolity. And it is nearly Christmas and the songs were most suitable for them, I assure you. I am sorry the noise carried so far. Please allow me to keep playing, though, it's a beautiful instrument and the boys are so looking forward to putting on a..." she suddenly stopped herself. While she'd thought they wouldn't be able to keep the secret for long, she hadn't planned to reveal it so soon herself!

One of his eyebrows rose and she could have kicked herself for letting the boys' secret out.

"I already know about the concert," he said, the corner of his lip curling up in the smallest hint of pleasure.

"Oh!" Her racing heart slowed a little. *He's not angry.* "Oh dear… it's meant to be a surprise and I've ruined it."

His face softened with a full smile that sent a jolt of warmth into her system. "You can relax. The music was delightful, by the way. And no, you didn't ruin it. I overheard the boys talking about performing. Nevertheless, I shall play along and be surprised and delighted when they announce their secret plan."

Marie pressed her lips together to stop a laugh escaping. How kind of him, to humour the boys in such a way!

He gave her a mocking frown and said, "I am rather looking forward to it, so don't you give anything away."

"Oh, I shan't," she said, and this time a laugh did escape. It was one of relief, that she was not in trouble and had not caused problems with her enthusiasm on the pianoforte. Renwick could be stern but she was also learning he could be rather adorable. To think she'd called him the Earl of Demanding for so many months as they'd exchanged letters, yet just a few days in his company and she was witnessing a completely different man. Not an ogre hoarding his vast book treasure, but a determined man who cared deeply for his family and even his staff.

A little later on in their meal, Marie said, "The pianoforte is a lovely instrument, and I'm glad you've kept it in tune."

His face fell a little and she instantly thought she'd said the wrong thing.

"It is a good instrument. My late wife enjoyed it, though it was always her companions who actually played while she sang."

The phrase, "You must miss her," was on Marie's lips. But she didn't say it. Of course, he must miss his late wife. Grief had no time limits. If the portrait was even a little true to life, the former countess was an extraordinary beauty and the boys had clearly adored her too. The staff were no doubt still mourning her loss as well, as she'd noticed they wanted to keep changing the subject when Marie asked about her. Although, now she gave it some thought, Mrs Ellwood hadn't seemed so keen... perhaps just a clash between a long-serving housekeeper, who had been here since before Renwick's birth, and a very young new mistress?

She shouldn't add to Renwick's burden, so she changed the subject to something far more pleasant.

"Would you tell me about your Christmas traditions?" she requested. "The household seems enthused about the season, all of a sudden!"

He put his knife and fork down and thought for a moment, his stern expression giving way to a smile. "My mother was fond of wrapping the bannister in great swags of ribbon to brighten the hall, and Mr Martin says he knows where that ribbon might be stored. We have many spruce and holly trees we can harvest for greenery so we shall bring that in on Christmas Eve and make a great mess of it for the boys, of course. Then there's the Yule log."

Marie felt heat on her face at the mention of the Yule log. She'd seen him in action earlier that day. The image of Lord

Renwick chopping wood, his shirt stuck to his perspiring frame, was seared into her memory. She should not have been looking. But the noise of the men outside had her pushing her chair towards the window in the music room. She had thought it might be staff cutting firewood, and not in her wildest dreams did she think she'd see the lord of the manor performing manual labour. Yet there he'd been, ruffled and red-faced, his perspiring hair sticking to his neck as his strong arms thwacked into the dead wood. Then the three of them had toiled valiantly with the enormous log to drag it into the stables. They'd put on a marvelous show. She was sure nobody had seen her looking.

The display had transfixed her to the spot. Even if she hadn't been in her awkward wheeled chair and had retained full use of her limbs she doubted she would have been able to turn away from the incredible sight of him.

"I was out with the grooms chopping it," Renwick held his palms up with a look of pride, "I think I even gave myself a blister!"

Marie burned internally at the memory of watching his athletic prowess.

He continued, "You know, I don't think we've had a Yule log since my mother passed. It's drying in the stables, and we'll bring it in on Christmas Eve."

Would they be chopping anything else? Marie might need to check out the window more often to see him perspiring like Hercules performing one of his feats.

He was looking at her, his gaze searing into her soul.

Heat stole over her face and she felt so guilty for ogling him she simply had to confess, "I'm sorry, I watched you carry the log to the stables and I shouldn't have been spying but I couldn't help it."

He grinned, "You watched me?"

Marie covered her burning face, "I should not have. It was improper of me to stare like that."

"You *stared*?"

If she wasn't in this chair, if she hadn't sprained her ankle, she'd flee the room and hide from the deep embarrassment flooding her system. But she was stuck here at the table and had no way to flee.

He made a low chuckle and said, "As long as I put on a good show and didn't disgrace myself."

She could not speak, could not look at him. Drawing a slow breath, she had to remain at the table and keep breathing through her mild humiliation.

They had often sat together in silence before, but at this moment she needed to talk about something. "Did you know Yule logs are also a French tradition? Mama said they would take logs from fruit bearing trees like almond or olive, but oaks are very good too."

He creased his brows for a moment in thought until he said, "Of course, the acorns would be the fruit of the oak tree. Unlikely to be an almond or an olive up here though, I'm sure it's far too cold to grow those kinds of trees this far north. I think this one was an ash."

Relief spread through Marie that they'd been able to change the topic from her ogling this man as he swung his axe. "It snows in Hatfield, of course, but I've never experienced anything as cold as this."

"In that case, may this be your most memorable

Christmas," he said, holding his glass of wine aloft to salute her.

She returned the salute with her glass, knowing it already was. When else would she ever get a chance to spend Christmas with a real live earl, in a real castle? She was going to enjoy it to the full, sore ankle or not!

As the days passed, Marie found herself settling into a comfortable routine at Alston Castle. Morag would bring her breakfast in her room and help her dress, and then Mrs Ellwood would usually stop by for a cup of tea and a chat. Marie was beginning to think of the kindly house-keeper as a dear friend; they would talk about anything and everything, Mrs Ellwood sharing lots of details about life at the castle and even asking for Marie's advice on some points. She asked too if Marie had any favourite dishes, and promised to have Cook make them.

"You're far too kind, Mrs Ellwood. You needn't put Cook to the trouble."

Mrs Ellwood disagreed. "The menu could always use a little more variety. That soup sounds delicious."

They discussed Christmas traditions too, and Marie thought of a few French dishes her Mama used to make. Some of them would be too difficult to obtain this far from London, like lobster and oysters, but others might be done. Marie described her mother's recipe as best she could remember. Butter and flour to form the roux, then the chopped leeks, a few ladles of stock from the pot, then the potatoes. Toward the end, stir in cream.

Mrs Ellwood wrote the recipe down precisely, asking for clarification on quantities and cooking times, and then asked if Marie had any other recipes she might suggest.

"There's gratin Dauphinoise," she said. "That was always one of my favourites, if you have garlic. Potatoes sliced thinly and cooked with cream and garlic, seasoned with pepper and nutmeg."

"Sounds quite delicious, that will go well as a side to the roast goose!" Mrs Ellwood beamed and made a note in the journal she carried everywhere with her. "All the special things we requested from Carlisle came up on the cart yesterday. I know there was garlic in there, and we have pepper and nutmeg already, of course."

"We could have flan Parisien too. That's a custard tart, basically..." Marie wrote the recipe down and handed it to the housekeeper as well.

"Wonderful, Miss Baxter, I shall take these to Cook. Well, I'd best be about it." The housekeeper rose, gathering up the tea tray. "You have a pleasant day, now!"

"I shall, and you also." Marie smiled warmly as Mrs Ellwood left.

She pulled the writing desk closer to her body and wrote to her sisters again, apologising for not being home and missing them so very much. Once she'd finished her letter, she folded it and got up from the chaise, moving carefully over to her wheeled chair. After almost three weeks, she could now put a little weight on her foot, very cautiously. It was getting easier to transfer herself about from her wheeled chair to the chaise or the bed, but she did not want to press her recovery and put too much weight on her bad ankle.

Settling herself in the wheeled chair and putting her left leg on the rest, she was about to head in the direction of the music-room when movement outside the window caught her eye, and she paused to look.

The snow was thick on the ground still; there had been no thaw and it had snowed on several occasions since she arrived. Sebastian had mentioned that the drifts were as tall as a man in places, but he still ventured out of doors every morning, saying that he enjoyed the exercise.

She swallowed with anticipation as she wondered if he were about to chop more wood and begin to perspire.

To her shock, she found she was actually salivating in anticipation.

When had she become so debauched?

Was it the time she'd watched him riding his big bay horse, Caesar, into Alston? Or the other time he'd ridden Caesar across the moorland area and down to the edge of the woods. She'd craned her neck to follow his progress but lost sight of him.

It wasn't Caesar that Sebastian was leading across the snowy landscape now, however, but a heavy draught horse, dragging a... was that a sleigh? Intrigued, Marie pushed herself closer to the window and peered out. She'd seen drawings of sleighs before, but had never seen a real one! Whatever was he doing?

There were two grooms accompanying Sebastian, and as she watched, they stopped by a pair of holly trees and began to cut branches.

Of course, Marie realised. Tomorrow was Christmas Eve, when the house would be decorated with greenery!

They must be cutting it today so it would have time to dry a little, before bringing it into the house.

Leaving the holly, the three men took the horse and sleigh and made their way to the edge of the woods, where they began cutting fir and spruce branches and piling them high on the seat. Marie watched, fascinated, and more than half-hoping Sebastian might grow over-warm and take his coat off again. The memory of his strong shoulders surging beneath his thin shirt had disturbed her dreams on several occasions in the last weeks.

"Miss Baxter!" a knock at the door startled her, and Marie winced, hastily dragging her gaze from the view outside.

Whatever was she doing? Ogling the earl?

"Miss Baxter?"

"Yes, Mr Martin, please do come in," she said, recognising the butler's voice.

He entered, offered a respectful bow, and held out a silver tray. "A letter arrived for you, miss. His lordship asked me to bring it to you once you and Mrs Ellwood had finished your conversation."

"Oh!" she reached eagerly for the letter, overjoyed to recognise Louise's beautiful script on the outside. "Oh, it's from my sisters! How wonderful." She had hers to send back, but would most likely add more to it in reply to their letter.

"The letter you've been waiting for, hm." Mr Martin gave her a benevolent smile before discreetly withdrawing, and Marie returned to the window, cracking the seal on the letter hastily. She'd begun to fear that her own letter to them had somehow gone astray, it had taken so long for a response to come. As she read it, that fear was quickly alleviated, because Louise and Bernadette had obviously received her missive.

Don't worry about a thing, Marie, everything is well in hand at the bookshop. Another crate of books from Father arrived - he must be doing very well in Tours! - we enclose a list just in case the Earl of Demanding would be interested in some of the volumes.

Marie choked back a little laugh. It had been quite some time since she'd thought of Renwick as the Earl of Demanding, but of course her sisters didn't know him the way she had come to. She would add an explanation about that in her reply!

The writing changed then from Louise's to Bernadette's, commiserating about Marie's ankle and suggesting some herbal remedies she might try, if she had access to them, but otherwise rest and elevation were the best cures.

I hope they are taking good care of you at Alston, Bernadette concluded. *From your sketch it looks a very grand place, and those two boys quite charming... and the Earl of Demanding far more handsome than I think any of us imagined!*

Marie smiled, her gaze drifting back towards the window. The sleigh was piled high with greenery now, and Sebastian had tossed the axe in on top before going to the horse's head and turning the animal back towards the stables. She watched him striding through the snow, quite transfixed, until a sound from the music-room made her jump.

"Miss Baxter, are you there?" a youthful voice asked, and George poked his head around the door. "Father is outside and we're ready for practice!"

"I'll be right along. I'm just reading a letter from my sisters!" She held it up. "I'm almost finished, though."

There were only a few more lines to the letter, in Louise's hand.

We received the funds from Lord Renwick's solicitor, so we are quite flush. Do not worry about us, and enjoy your Christmas, dearest! All love,
Louise and Bernadette.

With a happy smile, Marie folded the letter and the attached list of books, and put them in her pocket. She couldn't show anyone the letter - she would pass away from mortification if anyone at Alston ever found out she and her sisters had nicknamed Renwick the Earl of Demanding - but she could certainly tell him about it, and show him the separate list.

"Ready for practice?" She wheeled herself towards the music-room. "We only have two days left to get this absolutely perfect!"

She and the boys sang and played songs in English and French, and their voices harmonised so well. Morag joined them but Mr Charles had stayed away today, much to the maid's obvious annoyance. After each song, they would listen out for the sound of the Earl's return, then proceed with the next song. Marie also felt her playing had improved with the repetition of practise, although her voice simply could not compete with Morag's hauntingly beautiful voice. She truly had the sound of a fallen angel, the notes were clear and high, but somehow there was a deep sadness within. Marie sincerely hoped Morag would one day find a suitable husband, who would enjoy her singing and bring happiness to her life.

CHAPTER 9

Christmas Eve at Alston Castle

On Christmas Eve, the castle bustled with activity. Mrs Ellwood and Morag wore gauntlets to protect their hands and forearms as they travelled from room to room with baskets of spiky green holly and prickly spruce branches. Soon every mantle in the castle had a pretty arrangement of green holly and red berries, along with sprigs of green pine needles and brown cones. Every portrait had ivy trailing along the tops of its frame, and the curtain rails had the plant wound along the rods and dangling beside the portraits of long-passed Renwick ancestors.

The scent of pine and spruce filled the castle, making Sebastian nostalgic for Christmases in his youth. He stood in the hallway, watching as Mr Martin worked his way up the stairwell banisters with much help from the twins, tying swags and bows of red and green ribbons. The bows were rather more lopsided than the ones his mother had made, but Sebastian didn't care; his heart was full as Alston Castle came to life as it had not in many years.

"Those ribbons make the hall look so bright and love-ly!" Marie said from by his side, and he looked down and smiled broadly at her.

"They do, don't they? Perhaps it's time to think about redecorating for the rest of the year as well. It is rather gloomy in here most of the time."

"Oh, but it has so much character! Well." She paused and looked around, then up. "Do you know, if you painted the ceiling white, that might help."

It would never have occurred to Sebastian to paint the ceiling. He tilted his head and looked straight up, seeing the dark oak timbers that made up the base floor of the castle's second storey.

"Do you know, I think you're right," he said thought-fully. "It might be tricky - we'd have to build some sort of scaffold in here for the workers to get up that high - but it could be done. What a clever idea, Miss Baxter! I shall see to it, in the springtime."

She beamed at him, her eyes sparkling behind her glasses. "I wish I could see it when it's done, my lord. It will be a pleasant surprise for the boys when they come home for the summer." She turned away again, looking back at the twins giggling as they became tangled in a great length of ribbon, unaware of the emotions her words had just stirred up in Sebastian.

She won't see it. She won't be here. The thought was an unexpected wrench, and Sebastian realised how incred-ibly comfortable he had become in Marie's company in the last weeks.

They had fallen into a comfortable routine, happy to talk or remain in peaceful mutual silence as the mood took them, reading quietly or getting into an animated discussion over their books. She always had some thoughtful remark to make, some insight which made him look at the world in a new way.

Alston Castle will be the poorer without her presence. I will miss her very much when she goes home.

The feeling that churned in his stomach at the thought discomfited him so badly he had to turn away, striding up the stairs to go and rescue Richard and George from the muddle they'd made of the ribbons before poor Mr Martin despaired of them.

When he came back down again, Marie had been joined by Mr Charles, who was as usual looking at her with great admiration.

Sebastian's gut clenched with an ugly feeling he refused to acknowledge. Perhaps it was time he had a quiet word with the tutor, Sebastian reflected; it did the poor man no good to break his heart over a woman he couldn't possibly marry.

Not that Sebastian had any power to prevent the match! He would not be so petty as to withdraw his financial support from Mr Charles before his ordination: and he certainly had no authority over Marie, but he would not for the world see Marie marry a man who could not support a wife in reasonable comfort. A woman like her deserved the very best.

Morag came out into the hall just as Sebastian reached the foot of the stairs, and Sebastian stopped short at the look on the redheaded maid's face. It was pure jealousy, directed at... Marie? And then Morag looked at Mr Charles, making a bee-line towards him, and the light dawned.

What a tangled web, Sebastian thought wryly, *of people pining for those they can't have.* Morag for Mr Charles and Mr Charles for Marie. He refused to include himself in that situation. He marked himself out of that equation with his very next breath. Obviously he would never marry again.

Before he could contemplate the situation any further, Mrs Ellwood marched into the hall, caught the maid by the arm, neatly turned her about and marched her off again. The housekeeper was muttering under her breath and firmly shaking her head.

Well, at least his redoutable housekeeper was aware of the Morag situation, and obviously had the problem well in hand. Mr Charles would be gone soon enough, returning to Cambridge to complete his own studies and be ordained this summer, after which his visits to Alston would be few and far between. It meant Sebastian would need to find a new tutor for the boys, though. His heart sank a little at the thought. Mr Charles had been so good for them. Perhaps the soon-to-be curate might be able to recommend an acquaintance from Cambridge who would be interested in the position? Someone young, with plenty of energy.

He should speak to the tutor now, while he still had the chance.

"Would you have a moment, Mr Charles?" Sebastian said. "In my study? If you'll excuse us, Miss Baxter."

"Why, of course, my lord." She smiled up at both of them from her chair, and the men bowed politely to her.

As soon as Sebastian had closed the study door, Mr Charles asked, "How may I assist you, my lord?"

Sebastian took a seat behind his desk and invited the tutor to take a chair. "I want to commend you for your attentiveness to the boys," Sebastian said. "They are still boisterous, but they are no longer as heedless and thought-less as they were when you first commenced your tutelage. They have matured and thrived under your direction."

Mr Charles beamed happily, obviously pleased at his praise. "They are good boys, and clever. A credit to you, my lord. I have no doubt they will do very well in life."

"Sadly, they will not have you for the next holidays, as you will be going on to bigger and better things yourself, as you well deserve. I was wondering if you could think of anyone you might recommend for your replacement?"

"Oh." Mr Charles tapped his finger against his lips in thought. "I might, at that. Please, allow me to make some enquiries among my fellow students when I return to Cambridge, and I will write to you with a list of potential candidates."

"Very good." Sebastian hesitated, but he thought it best to approach the next topic head-on. "I am not sure whether you are aware that the maid Morag might fancy herself a little in love with you?"

"Oh." Mr Charles looked exceedingly embarrassed. His cheeks pinked and he cleared his throat. "I hope you do not think I have given her any encouragement in the slightest, my lord!"

He wanted to laugh at how uncomfortable the young man was, but he spared the tutor any further embarrassment. "I did not think it for a moment. Mrs Ellwood has the matter well in hand, but I do caution you against leaving your door unlocked at night."

Sebastian felt a tinge of colour come to his own cheeks even as Mr Charles blushed furiously and nodded in agreement.

Both of them ended up laughing at how awkward the situation was.

"Was there anything else, my lord?" Mr Charles asked once he had recovered himself.

Sebastian tapped his fingers lightly on the desk. "There is one other small matter. Miss Baxter..." he paused, trying to think of how to phrase his words without sounding accusing. Drat it all, this was a tricky tangle. He tried approaching the topic from a different angle. "Unfortunately, as I have no currently available living to bestow upon you, you will need to make your way as a curate for a while, and that lifestyle will not enable you to support a wife."

He was almost pleased with how diplomatically he had put it, but he dare not smile.

"Indeed not, my lord, I should not think of it," Mr Charles agreed promptly.

Sebastian sighed with relief.

Then the expression on Mr Charles' face changed as he obviously put two and two together from Sebastian having accidentally let Marie's name slip at the start of his sentence. "Wait, you don't think I... and Miss Baxter... oh no, goodness no my lord!" He blushed furiously again. "Miss Baxter is everything admirable of course. Even if I were ten years older with a living of my own..." he was stumbling over his words, obviously in a frantic rush to get them out and convince Sebastian of his sincerity. "I know my place, my lord! Miss Baxter is far beyond my reach."

He wanted to sigh with relief, but he held it in. "I am glad to hear it confirmed, that you are as sensible a man as I have always believed you to be," Sebastian said, a feeling of intense happiness coming over him. He stood up and offered the tutor his hand.

"And I thank you, my lord, for your faith and generosity in me. I shall always be in your debt," Mr Charles said fervently, shaking his hand.

"You have amply repaid it already with what you have done for the twins," Sebastian disagreed.

Thank goodness that artless, floundering conversation was concluded.

They returned to the hall together to find Marie at the foot of the stairs with the boys sitting in front of her chair, listening raptly as she spoke to them in her perfect French.

"Admirable as she is," Mr Charles said, a little diffidently, "it strikes me that Miss Baxter might well be wasted as mistress of a parsonage somewhere."

"Oh?" Sebastian found himself bristling a little on Marie's behalf. He didn't like the direction this was taking.

"Indeed." The tutor cast him a knowing look.

Something ominous flipped in his stomach.

Mr Charles then added, "I do believe she would be much better suited to be mistress of a far greater estate. Somewhere like Alston Castle, perhaps?"

Sebastian's ears grew very hot, and there was a faint ringing in them. He mumbled something, he knew not what, and hurried hastily forward, desperate to disengage from Mr Charles and the conversation which had taken a most uncomfortable direction.

"Boys, come along! The ribbons may be done in here, but I want to hang ivy from the beams in the parlour, and I shall need your help!" he exclaimed.

He had no idea where he'd managed to rescue that line of thought from, but he was grateful that the boys jumped up, eager to help. Sebastian followed them into the parlour, careful not to look at their tutor who stood watching him, with a knowing look on his face.

That was so utterly uncalled for, but he shook his head and decided the young man had merely been having fun, perhaps caught up in seasonal cheer. He shouldn't have reacted so badly, as it must have been a jest.

Redirecting his energies into putting up decorations with the boys helped Sebastian overcome his acute embarrassment at the tutor suspecting the direction of his feelings to Miss Baxter.

"Dear boy," he said to George, "I'm going to lift you up, so you can hang the branch from the rafter above me."

"Yes, Pa," George said, holding a branch in one hand and a knot of sap in the other. "Ready!"

Sebastian lifted him up by his middle, but there was still far too much distance the boy's hands and the beams.

This was not going to work. "Hold steady," he said, bringing the boy down and into his chest. "Keep your torso firm, I'll lift you by your thighs."

With a little grunting and adjusting, Sebastian lifted him closer to the ceiling and the boy reached the rafter and stuck the greenery to it.

There were grunts of achievement and effort, and Sebastian brought him gently back to the floor.

"My turn next," Richard said.

His heart was puffing from the exertion but he was ready to go again. "All right, Richard, ready?"

Richard nodded and held his arms upwards.

This time Sebastian bent his knees to grab the lad, again from the thighs to give him more height, then hoisted him skywards.

"Nearly, nearly, nearly. Got it!" Richard cried.

The three of them cheered with success.

Sebastian brought him back down again and ruffled his hair. "Good job, Richard."

Mr Martin came in and said with droll delivery, "We have a ladder, my lord. Shall I…"

Had the man waited for him to almost injure his back before making the suggestion?

"Bring it in, yes, please do," Sebastian agreed with a laugh at his own expense. The boys were getting too big for this, already as tall as his shoulder, they were almost young men now. He really couldn't lift them repeatedly without doing himself an injury. He already had an injured Miss Baxter, he didn't want to add to his staff's woes by hurting himself.

His eldest came over with another bough and said, "Ready to go again. Lift me up, Pa."

"Steady, lad," Sebastian put a hand on the boy's shoulder. "I don't need to do myself a mischief, and wiser heads have prevailed. Mr Martin is fetching a ladder for us."

Mr Martin came in with a ladder which they could lean against the wall. Mr Martin held one side steady, Sebastian held the other side and held his hand out for the boy.

"Righto junior, up you get."

As he watched the boy ascending the steps, his vision caught on the sight of Miss Baxter wheeling her chair to the doorway. He acknowledged her presence with a nod, but then turned back to keep an eye on the child at the top of the ladder to make sure he didn't fall.

"Easy!" the boy said as he stuck his prize to the cornice. "Can I come down now?"

"Yes, mind your footing," Sebastian said.

With Mr Martin's help and the boys' enthusiasm, they soon had the room bursting with greenery stuck on every imaginable surface. Was any of it level or co-ordinated? Not a chance. A troll could have sneezed in the room with more care, but it did look festive and that was the plan.

More than that, the pine scents really brought the seasonal joy indoors.

"Well done lads," he said, giving Richard another tousle of his hair. "Now, off for more lessons and I'll see you at nuncheon."

"Bye, Pa," they said as they left the room, "See you soon, Miss Baxter."

She'd been there the whole time, watching them decorate. He couldn't help but smile at her and the rosy glow on her cheeks.

Mr Martin picked up the ladder and bid them both farwell.

Miss Baxter hid a small giggle behind her hands. "They have done a … remarkable job," she said.

"That's one way to describe it," Sebastian laughed at his own expense. "I'm hoping they fall down on their own accord at some point as the sap dries. Otherwise someone will have to climb up and get them down,

"You didn't hurt yourself lifting the boys so high?"

He rubbed his lower back and said, "I hope not, but I might need a hot compress tomorrow." Then he stopped. "I have nothing to complain about. How is your ankle?"

"Mending at speed," she said. She used her good foot to wheel herself into the room.

Sebastian closed the distance between them. "Allow me," he said, grasping the back of the chair to push her along.

"Thank you," she nodded. "I am so grateful for this chair. The boys have taken turns to gently push me around. They've offered to give me a tour of the castle as soon as I can walk a little, which I am greatly looking forward to."

"Have they now?"

He moved her to the centre of the room where she could get a better view of the misshapen and haphazard decorations.

He smiled down upon her, but instead of returning his smile, she worried at her bottom lip.

"I wanted to ask something, but I fear it might not be my place," she said.

He took a nearby seat so they could be at eye level for the conversation. He was in a festive mood. "Ask away."

"It's about Richard … and George."

He tried hard not to wince at the name, and blinked instead.

"There it is," she said.

"There what is?" he asked, suddenly wondering where this conversation was going. He had thought she might ask if she could become their French tutor, to which he would have readily agreed. Instead she was trying to pry open an old wound.

"You treat them very differently, Richard and George."

He breathed in, feeling defensive. "Do I?"

"I've seen and heard you, and I do not want to come across as an unappreciative guest. You have done so much for me, and my sisters already have your substantial payment. Oh, I nearly forgot," she produced a small purse and placed it on the table. "I meant to return this so much sooner, but I've been so entertained I keep forgetting. It's the money for the books and my travel, which I no longer need."

He tried to keep track of the conversation. She'd begun by talking about the boys, but diverted to the money. "To be honest, I'd completely forgotten about it, so I appreciate your honesty."

"Back to what I wanted to ask you about."

He gulped, not sure he liked where this was going.

"I've noticed… you have no hesitation calling Richard by his name, but when it comes to George it's 'dear boy' or something else. It's as if there's some barrier…"

His pulse hammered in his head. She couldn't

possibly know. She couldn't have guessed. If she'd seen a difference in the way he spoke to the boys, well, he'd deny it until the end of time.

It stuck in his throat to outright claim she was wrong, but he couldn't lie to her. He had to think of something.

"He's the heir, even if only by ten minutes or so, he is the heir and will always be treated that way. It's not Richard's fault he's second. I'm trying, in my own poor attempt, to make him feel better at being second."

Her face was so sympathetic. Did she believe him?

"Who's the heir?" Marie pointedly asked him.

His guts churned at having to say his name. "George," he gritted out. There, he'd said it.

Marie nodded, but there was scepticism in her expression.

Sebastian rose from his seat, wanting to be anywhere other than here, under Marie's penetrating gaze. "I must see that Cook has all the ingredients for tomorrow," he said and stalked out of the room as fast as he could.

Marie did not raise the subject again at nuncheon, nor that afternoon when they read together, and by dinnertime he had concluded with relief that she did not intend to. He relaxed, eating his dinner with enjoyment, and afterwards took hold of the back of Marie's chair to push her into the library. Something caught his eye hanging above the door, and he paused, surprised. Who had put that there?

"What's the matter, my lord? Is one of the chair wheels stuck... did my cloak catch in the wheel?" Marie twisted to look up at him.

"No... it's not that." He looked up again, at the sprig

of greenery with white berries stuck above the library door.

"Oh, that's mistletoe," Marie said, promptly identifying it. Then her eyes went very wide, her soft lips parted in an 'O' of surprise.

How could he not honour the tradition of the season, especially when she looked so beautiful? Placing his hands on the arms of the chair, Sebastian leaned down and kissed her, right on that sweet mouth.

CHAPTER 10

Sebastian Gets The Guilts

Marie's lips were soft and warm under his, yielding, her breath sweet from the lemon syrup pudding they'd just finished for dessert. The touch sent jolts of long-neglected sensations through him waking him from a decade-long emotional slumber. She was the answer to the prayers he didn't know he'd made. Sebastian lost himself in the sensation as she returned the kiss just as fervently, until he felt her sharply indrawn breath of shock.

Then he leaped back as if she'd just slapped his face, horrified at himself.

What was he *doing*? He'd just kissed a lady who was a guest under his roof, an innocent at that, and most shameful of all, one who couldn't even run away from his advances! He ran a shaking hand through his hair.

"I most sincerely beg your pardon, Miss Baxter! I was overcome with…"

"Don't you *dare* apologise," she said, quite severely.

"I… what?" he blinked at her, confused. He'd done

the most reprehensible thing, all for his own entertainment, and treated her very poorly.

"You heard me, my lord." A smile quirked those beguiling lips upwards at the corners. "Don't you dare apologise. I have never been kissed before, and that was… quite nice." She smiled serenely at him and pushed her toes on the floor to propel herself past him into the library, leaving Sebastian standing with his mouth flapping open like a stunned carp.

He thought she would slap him.

He thought she *should* slap him!

"Quite… nice?" he croaked finally, turning to find her taking up her usual spot beside the fire.

"Indeed." Marie looked up from the book she had just opened. "Rather an enjoyable first experience, thank you." She nodded, apparently quite calm and composed, a vast contrast to how Sebastian was feeling at that moment, his heart hammering, his knees unsteady.

He debated going outside and throwing himself bodily into the snow, to quench the raging heat her innocent remark had suddenly engendered in his body. Somehow, he made himself walk over to take his own seat.

"Nevertheless," he said, regaining a little of his composure. "If you decline me the right to apologise, so be it, but it should not have happened. It was deucedly inappropriate of me and it will not happen again."

Was it *disappointment* he saw on her face as she glanced up at him and nodded quickly before looking down at the book again? She was going to be the death of him, she really was.

"Are you not reading this evening, my lord?" Marie asked a few minutes later, and Sebastian jumped.

He had spent the last five minutes just sitting there, staring at her. 'Pon rep, he was sunk. He closed his eyes in embarrassment. Not only his manners, but his very wits deserted him in her presence, it seemed!

How was she so calm and even tempered when a veritable tempest stirred within him?

Collecting the book he had begun reading earlier that day, he tried to settle in to read. For the first time since being forced to read dull-as-ditchwater texts in his schooldays, Sebastian could not make himself focus on the words on the page in front of him. His gaze kept drifting upwards, quite outside of his conscious control, and fixing on Marie's serene visage, perfectly lit by the flickering firelight.

"Oh!" she said, startling him as she looked up, and Sebastian dropped his eyes guiltily, hoping she hadn't caught him staring. "I quite forgot, my lord! I received a letter from my sisters."

"At last!" He knew she had begun to be a little concerned that perhaps her original letter had gone astray. "Are they all well?"

"Yes." She beamed at him, fishing two sheets of folded paper from her pocket. Looking carefully at them, she folded one back up and put it away again, before offering him the other. "They confirmed they received your payment."

"Oh, I could not possibly read your letter." He shook his head in immediate denial and did not take the offered paper.

"That's not the letter, my lord. It's the list of books received in the latest shipment from my father in France." She smirked at him a little. "My sisters are well aware of how much you desire rare and unusual books. They enclosed the list in case you would like to order anything before our next advertisement is sent to The Times."

His blood thrummed with delight. "A right of first refusal! How exceedingly generous." He accepted the paper, still barely able to take his eyes from Marie's face.

"I have already written a reply, but am happy to delay sending it for a day or two if you would like to take the time until then to think on anything you might like. Perhaps you will finally allow us to ship the books to you, now?" she teased him lightly.

He blushed with embarrassment as the very gentle barb struck home. But he deserved it. "Seeing how carefully the ones you brought with you were packed, I believe I will. I know I can trust you," he said, almost shocking himself as the words came out of his mouth.

Marie inclined her head, but didn't say anything, returning her attention to her book with a pleased little smile on her face. Sebastian stewed in his own muddled confusion.

He could trust her, and he did. He was in no doubt of that. But how was it possible, when he'd known her for only a few weeks? He'd trusted others he'd known far longer, and had then had that trust thrown in his face in the worst manner possible.

When it came to Marie Baxter, he'd lost his whole, entire, blasted mind. That was the only conclusion he could reach.

And yet still he sat, staring at her face in the firelight, memorising every feature. The way she nibbled thoughtfully on the edge of her lip as she read, the tilt of her head as she moved from the left-facing page to the right, the swanlike curve of her neck, the shadow at the hollow of her throat.

He tried to give his attention to the list in his hand; couldn't make head nor tail of it. It was no use. He needed to get out of her presence in order to focus, or he'd end up handing it back and telling her to keep all the books for him, no matter that he probably already owned a third of them and didn't want half the rest.

"If you'll excuse me," he murmured, getting to his feet, "I think I shall take this to my study and consult with my reference catalogue."

"Of course. Good evening, my lord." She nodded to him before returning her attention to her book.

It was almost a relief to get out of her presence, and yet the desire to go back and stare at her again was strong. Sebastian pinched himself, hard.

"Snap out of it," he muttered, firmly closing the study door behind him. "You've acted like the veriest donkey all day!"

He'd been acting the fool ever since Marie Baxter had turned up on his doorstep looking like a bedraggled brown wren, he acknowledged wryly to himself. Somehow, he didn't think a stern talking-to was going to improve matters much, but he tried it all the same.

He imagined Mrs Ellwood giving him a set down over his behaviour, but that didn't work. Next he pictured Mr Sharpe's withering disdain, but that didn't work either.

Sitting down at his desk, he unfolded the list she'd given him and attempted again to read down it... but all he could see were a pair of bright hazel eyes, shining with light and laughter behind round glass lenses.

Martin arrived and cleared his throat. "The boys have asked about when they might bring in the Yule Log."

What a cloth-eared dolt, he'd completely forgotten that most important event. And he'd sweated and laboured so hard for it! Sebastian stood up and said, "Thank you, my good man."

The boys were waiting behind the door and ran in, already holding their coats, ready to don them for the cold and dark conditions outside. Mr Charles followed in their wake.

Sebastian then corralled Martin and Sharpe and two footmen to assist, along with the grooms who'd helped cut it down in the first place. With ropes, coordination and a great deal of effort, the eight men and two boys brought the Yule log in from the stables to the front of the house. The doors were wide enough to let them all through. Which had the consequence of letting in plenty of cold wind and snow. Working carefully not to damage the flooring or hit the walls, they dragged the log on an old rug through the entry hall and into the great room, which had the largest fireplace. Mr Martin hurried back to close the front doors, much to everyone's relief.

The fire in the great room was already lit, ready for the enormous log to be put there so it would burn constantly until Twelfth Night. Only the end of the log had any chance of fitting over the fire; the remainder of it rested on the paved hearth and would be pushed a little further into the fire each day. Martin had already arranged a roster of the staff to take it in turns to sit in the great room twenty-four hours a day in case the fire ran too far down the log.

Mrs Ellwood and Morag arrived, pushing Miss Baxter's chair into the room so that she might witness the event. Puffed but delighted from their efforts, everyone cheered as the first flames caught on the bark, dancing and twisting as it began to burn.

Richard looked up to Sebastian and said, "I was reading about a tradition we might include. Everyone lights a candle from the log and makes a wish, and if their candle burns all the way down without going out, they get their wish!"

Sebastian hugged the boy and laughed. "That sounds like a most excellent tradition." He turned to George, noting he had an enormous audience. "And George," he forced himself to say the name without hesitation. "Do you have a tradition we should observe these holidays?" He was so pleased he'd announced the lad's name without a stammer. He could do this.

The boy beamed. "Yes, we... we must eat pudding every night until Twelfth Night, or... or the wishes won't come true either!"

Richard cried out, "You just made that up!"

"Fine!" George said. "I'll eat your pudding if you don't want it. Then you won't get your wish!"

The room filled with laughter and frivolity. Soon, Mrs Ellwood had an array of candles and holders at the ready.

"Why don't you go first, Richard, as it was your suggestion?" Sebastian said.

"Thanks, Pa." The boy solemnly chose a candle and a holder, then stood close to the fire and held the candle's wick near the flame on the Yule log. He withdrew it when the wick began to glow and placed it on the holder. With a palm guarding the flame from movement, he placed it down on the table and closed his eyes.

Everyone in the room followed, including Morag who was only too keen to make a wish, staring blatantly at Mr Charles all the while. The poor man seemed almost ready to hide behind Sebastian for protection.

Then George said, "Miss Baxter, I'll push your chair closer for you, if you like?"

"Thank you," she said, as Richard grabbed a candle for her and said in a loud whisper, "Don't tell anyone your wish or it won't come true!"

The solemn expression on her face showed Sebastian she was taking this tradition, and the boys, seriously. George maneuvered her chair toward the hearth and angled it so Miss Baxter could reach sideways and light her candle. Then she too held her palm in front of the flame so that it would survive the journey to the table as the boys carefully pushed her in that direction.

Sebastian pretended to admire the boys, but his gaze kept straying to Miss Baxter's face.

She was so lovely, it was hard to look away.

Marie wanted to cry with how lovely everything was. This was the most perfect Christmas Eve she could have imagined. More staff arrived to gather for the occasion of witnessing the Yule log on the fire, and to make their own wishes. The log burned steadily, while the candles on the table kept their wishes alight. She had made a rather selfish wish, that she would one day soon return to Alson Castle. In her heart, she knew she'd have to go home soon, but her wish was that it would not be too long before she could come back. There was something so warm about this estate, even though it was surrounded by snow. Mrs Ellwood cared for her as if she were her own child, the boys were so charming and playful, and the earl had kissed her so delightfully only a short while ago.

That kiss, a first for her, had branded her heart. Who knew kisses could have that effect?

Perhaps she should have wished for another kiss? They were out of candles now, so she'd missed her chance. No, she'd made a very wise wish, in wanting to return to Alston. She would never tell anyone what her wish was, either. Richard had warned that if she did so, it wouldn't come true.

And she very much wanted that particular wish to come true.

But another kiss would be an excellent outcome as well.

CHAPTER 11

Christmas Day at Alston Castle

Mother Nature had no respect for the importance of Christmas Day, Marie thought as she carefully moved to her wheeled chair and pushed herself out of her makeshift bedroom. Cold winds howled outside, bringing more snow from a dark sky. Being on the ground floor, she was close to the great room and it didn't take long before she reached the open doorway.

The Yule log still burned magnificently in the hearth, and the candles on the table had melted overnight into a strange layered mass that looked like the surface of a badly made cake. A few had gone out early and could be reused, but the rest had burned all the way down. She looked at the section of table where she'd placed her candle. To her surprise, it had burned all the way down. Perhaps her wish - that she would return here to Alston - would come true. She found she was missing the boys already and would so love to see them again in the near future. They were lovely children, and deserved a bright and happy future with their father. In time, she hoped

Lord Renwick would recover from his heartache and marry again, giving the boys the mother they obviously craved.

A cold shiver ran through her at the thought of him kissing his new bride on their wedding day, some day in the future, and Marie shook her head, wondering at herself.

She couldn't possibly be jealous. That was out of order. For her to be jealous, she'd have to have formed a deep attachment and perhaps have some kind of promise of reciprocation. How could she be jealous of an imaginary person?

That kiss had clearly addled her brain. She'd read many of the Minerva Press books and had vicariously lived out many such romances. But the reality of a magnificent kiss was something else entirely.

The tell-tale noise of two lively children echoed in the hall. George and Richard ran in so they could check their candles. "It melted all the way!" Richard gasped with wonder. "That means..."

"... Don't say it out loud!" George elbowed him.

Marie playfully put her hands over her ears so she wouldn't accidentally hear the secret wish.

Richard clapped his hand over his mouth in an exaggerated effort. When he pulled them away he said, "Phew! That was close."

George pointed to a candle that had burned only part way down before blowing out. "I think that one is mine. Oh well. Looks like I won't get pudding every day after all."

Marie giggled at that. "You might still, if you are ever

so good."

The boys turned to face her, as if they suddenly realised they were not alone, and greeted her. "Good morning, Miss Baxter! Merry Christmas," they sing-songed together.

"Good morning George, good morning Richard. Merry Christmas to you both." She held up her arms, and they both ran over to give her a hug and kiss her cheeks.

"Do you need to go anywhere?" George offered. "We can give you a push."

"Thank you, I should like to visit the library, I am part way through a book."

They took a side each and guided her towards what had become her favourite room in the castle.

George said, "When your foot is better, we can give you a tour of the castle."

"We'll show you our favourite rooms," Richard finished.

"That would be most enjoyable, I shall look forward to it immensely," she said, giving her foot a gentle tilt and feeling only a little resistance. It shouldn't be long now before she could walk a little.

Lord Renwick was already in residence. He looked up and offered his greetings of the season, and asked if they'd had breakfast.

The boys nodded and said they'd had extra honey on their porridge, but were feeling hungry again already.

Lord Renwick grinned. "Ah, the bottomless stomachs of growing boys. Oddly, no medical text I have ever read has been able to explain this curious phenomenon."

"We could play some games until nuncheon," Marie said, then wondered what games she could play that didn't involve having to get up and move around. Hide and go seek was out of the question, even though she dearly would have loved to explore more of this castle. Especially as the boys had offered to be her guide.

"I don't know any," George said.

Marie pressed her lips together in thought. *Buffy Gruffy* might work, or it might result in injury. In any case, there weren't enough of them to disguise their voices and pretend to be someone else. "How about we play *Consequences*?"

"What's that?" Richard asked.

The poor lads, did they truly not know any parlour games? "It's lots of fun," Marie explained. "We need a piece of paper and a pencil."

George ran to the desk and took a sheet.

Marie made herself laugh with an idea and shared her thought, "We can play it in French if you want to make it educational?"

"No thanks," the boys said in unison.

Renwick chuckled, his eyes shining with humour.

"Fair enough, I shall give you a reprieve. All right, here are the rules. I'm going to write the first clue, which is an adjective for a gentleman. I won't say what it is, and then," she wrote down 'A towering brute', "and then I fold it over so nobody else sees it. Now George, you get to write the next part, which is a gentleman's name."

"Right," George wrote something on the paper.

"Now fold it zig zag and hand it to Richard," she said.

Richard had the paper and waited for instruction.

"Richard, you need to write an adjective for a lady."

The tip of his tongue poked out in concentration as he wrote. Then he folded his comment away and said, "I give it to Father?"

"Yes you do. My Lord, you need to write a lady's name."

He chuckled and wrote something, then made a fold. Then the paper and pencil came back to Marie for the next round of prompts. "I now write down where they met," she said, "But I have no idea what anyone else has written." She thought for a moment about writing 'in a castle' but that wasn't imaginative enough. They were in a castle right now. Instead she wrote, 'in a cooking pot' just to be extra silly. Then they went around again. The next parts, if she remembered correctly, were 'what he wore', 'what she wore', and 'what he said to her'. When it was her turn again she said, "And now I must write down what she said to him!" Thinking back on her giggle, she wrote, 'you're standing on my foot' and folded the paper again. 'George, you get the fun part, you get to write, 'what the consequence was', and Richard, you get to have the last laugh by saying, 'what the world said'.

When it was all done, Richard gave the paper to Marie, but she gave it to Lord Renwick instead who read the whole thing out in a deeply serious tone.

"A towering brute, Named Oliver Flint, A fire-headed washerwoman, Flora … oh, I see, *called Flora*. In a cooking pot?"

They giggled.

Marie said, "That's where they met."

"I see, they met in a cooking pot. It must have been enormous. He wore a teacher's robes, she wore a bonnet … made of bacon?"

That set them all off into fits of laughter and it took a while to recover.

Lord Renwick looked unable to continue, so he handed the paper over to Marie, who picked up the concertina-folded paper. "He said to her the sun is out, she said to him you're standing on my foot. The consequence was they had to sleep in the stables and the world said he should be prime minister!"

Both boys were on the floor absolutely howling with laughter, and Renwick's deep chortles made a merry music over it. Delighted with the success of her game, Marie giggled along with them.

"Again!" George gasped, getting to his feet. "Let's have another round!"

They played a second round, which was even more ridiculous as everyone had the hang of the game now and were trying to top each other with silly suggestions.

This brought about another contagious case of giggles that took them even longer to recover from. Marie had to wipe tears away. The boys laughed so hard they stopped making noise altogether. For a moment, they looked as if they were in pain, they were laughing so hard.

They were listening and laughing to Marie reading out the results of the third round when Mr Charles came in to join them, smiling broadly at their laughter.

"Are we playing games? What great fun!"

"Do you know any good parlour games we might play, Mr Charles?" Marie asked.

"Well." He looked at the boys, a grin forming on his face. "Bullet pudding was always rather a favourite when I was growing up."

"Ha!" Renwick chuckled. "I remember that one. Ma wouldn't let us use a bullet, so we used a coin instead. Here, I have half-a-crown in my pocket, that will do. Ring the bell, George, and we'll see if Mrs Ellwood will bring us a plate of flour."

He'd used George's name twice this morning, Marie noticed. And from the beaming smile on George's face, his son appreciated the acknowledgement.

Mrs Ellwood duly produced a mounded dish of flour, and then stood at the back of the room grinning with Mr Martin while everyone took it in turns to use a letter-opener to cut slices off the flour without the coin perched on the top of the mound falling. The mound became thinner and thinner - almost a spire - and Marie breathed a sigh of relief as she managed to carve off a slice without the coin toppling. Surely it couldn't survive another full round!

Renwick was up next, and then George and Richard after that. Both boys were biting their lips, wide-eyed with nerves, and Marie saw Renwick look at them, then glance at her with a small smile on his face, before he took the letter-opener and made a deliberately clumsy slice.

The coin toppled, and Renwick cried "Oh no!" in a very dramatic fashion, before shrugging his shoulders and plunging face-first into the floury pile to retrieve the coin with his teeth.

He did that on purpose, so neither of the boys would have to. The loving kindness of the gesture - an earl willing to suffer such humiliation for his children's sake - melted Marie's heart. The twins might not have a mother, but they were deeply loved, nonetheless.

Renwick emerged laughing and covered in flour, the coin clenched between his teeth, and excused himself to go wash and change, saying he hoped his valet was in a good mood. Mrs Ellwood reclaimed the dish of flour before the boys got into it and made a mess, and Mr Charles suggested a game of spillikins, to which the boys agreed very happily.

Renwick returned a little while later clean and tidy, if with the faintest traces of white still marring his dark hair in front, and brought out a box of beautifully carved ivory dominoes.

It was one of the loveliest Christmas mornings Marie could recall, full of joy and laughter, and then Mr Martin called them in to nuncheon. Renwick had decided they would have the Christmas Day feast at nuncheon, so the boys could join them, and there were a great many exclamations of delight as Renwick pushed Marie into the dining-room, the boys following, and they saw the feast laid out on the long table.

A roasted golden goose was the centrepiece, surrounded by dishes of all sorts; a whole salmon baked in cream and parsley sauce, a pigeon pie, roasted potatoes, mushrooms cooked in butter, green beans and almonds, carrots baked in honey, and more.

"We could not eat all of this in a week!" Marie half-laughed.

Renwick said, "Oh, the staff will feast after we do, and then leftovers will be packed up for the Boxing Day tradition. We deliver it to a couple of the tenant farmers," he explained, wheeling her to her regular place at the table.

There was a large tureen of soup at one end, which Mrs Ellwood said was the potato and leek recipe Marie had provided. Marie felt almost homesick at that gesture.

"But, there's no pudding!" George exclaimed in sudden horror. "It's all savouries."

"There's more to come, of course," Renwick said to the boys.

"There is both plum and treacle pudding, young man," Mrs Ellwood said with a fond ruffle of George's hair as she passed. "As well as a fancy custard tart Miss Baxter gave us the recipe for, and baked apples stuffed with raisins!"

"Hooray!" George and Richard cheered together, taking their seats.

"And what is this?" Mr Charles asked with interest, inspecting a dish close to him.

"I believe that's the potatoes Dauphinoise," Marie said. "A favourite my mother used to make."

"How marvellous!" he replied. "And that reminds me, we should be speaking French, shouldn't we?"

The boys looked a little glum, and Marie looked an appeal at Renwick.

"I think perhaps we might make an exception for Christmas Day," Renwick said with an affectionate smile at his sons. "Since you have been working very hard on your French. Don't you agree, Miss Baxter?"

They had come on in leaps and bounds since she'd been having nuncheon with them, Marie agreed at once, and was rewarded by happy smiles.

"You make French great fun, Miss Baxter. I wish you were one of our teachers at Eton," George said, passing his plate as Renwick began to carve the roast goose.

"Well I am very honoured, George, but I rather suspect Eton wouldn't hire female teachers," Marie said. She entertained a sudden wistful thought of perhaps offering to come and stay with them next summer and tutor them... but all she could really teach them was French and mathematics, and they needed so much more than that. She was being silly. As if the earl would ever hire a female tutor, anyway! Whoever heard of such an idea? It was just as ridiculous as the thought of a female teacher at Eton!

Both boys nodded in agreement, chuckling at the mere idea.

The meal was a joyous affair, if rather over-indulgent. Both boys appeared quite sleepy afterwards and Mr Charles took them away to have some quiet time and probably a short nap himself, Marie thought. She had a little lie down on the chaise in her room herself, but soon enough it was four o'clock, the time they'd agreed on for their concert of carols.

Richard scratched on the door, his face alight with glee. "Everyone's ready, and George has gone to fetch Father! How surprised he'll be!" Richard crowed, pushing Marie's chair into the music room and helping her to get aligned at the pianoforte.

Some extra chairs had been brought in, Marie saw, and all the staff were present, seated and smiling, waiting for the concert to begin. Morag stood by the pianoforte, gazing adoringly at Mr Charles, who was studiously ignoring her as usual.

"Whatever is all this?" Renwick exclaimed from the doorway.

Everyone in the room except for the twins was well aware that Renwick knew all about the concert, but none of them could have guessed as he played his part to perfection, showing surprise and delight as George urged him to a reserved seat beside Mrs Ellwood in the front row.

The concert could be described as nothing less than a roaring success. The boys sang their hearts out, Morag's voice soared like a bird, and Marie thought her face might crack apart from smiling. To everyone's astonishment, there was one real surprise - at the conclusion of the concert, Mr Martin produced a violin and accompanied Marie for the last carol, a rousing rendition of *Hark! The herald angels sing.*

As the boys made bows at Mr Charles' urging when the concert ended, Renwick stood up and clapped so hard Marie thought he might make his hands sore. Then he held out his arms and the two boys ran straight to him for a loving embrace.

Marie had to knuckle away a tear of happiness.

"This has been the best Christmas ever!" George cried happily.

"It really has," Renwick agreed. "And I do believe we have Miss Baxter to thank for that."

"Yes!" Both boys nodded vigorously, and then Richard looked up at his father and said; "Pa, you should marry Miss Baxter. She's terrific!"

Hot flames erupted on Marie's cheeks. "Richard!" she gasped, horrified. "Goodness, you must not say such things! That is highly inappropriate!" She truly did not know where to put herself. In front of all the staff, no less, how utterly dreadful!

Renwick, thank the heavens, looked more amused than offended, ruffling his son's hair.

"Richard, you're embarrassing Miss Baxter. Thank you both so much for my surprise, it is quite the best Christmas gift I have ever received. I am blessed to have such good lads. There's an extra supper for you upstairs, if you have any room"

Both of them ran back to the pianoforte to hug Marie too, Richard whispering a penitent "Sorry!" in her ear.

"You are already forgiven," Marie said fondly, and he rushed off after his brother grinning, shouting to George not to eat all the buns.

"How they can think of eating a thing after that midday feast I can't imagine," Renwick said as the room emptied out, sitting back down in his chair and patting his stomach. "Perhaps a small dish of soup before bed, but certainly no more."

"Not even the soup for me. Perhaps a cup of tea," Marie agreed.

"Thank you for this." He nodded towards the pianoforte. "You have devoted a lot of hours to the boys' amusement and education."

"It was more than worth it to see the joy on their faces," Marie said simply.

"Yes." He seemed to steel himself then, before lifting his head and looking for the first time at the wall on which the portrait of the last Countess hung. "There has been little of that in the last few years, I fear."

"How long ago did the Countess pass?" she asked tentatively.

"Four years ago, almost exactly. A few days before Christmas. News didn't reach me in London until the New Year. The boys had spent Christmas at Eton, as if nothing had changed. Christmas has understandably been a difficult time for them ever since, which is why I didn't want them spending it at Eton ever again." He tore his gaze from the portrait and looked at Marie again. "You have made Christmas a time of joy again in this house, and I can never thank you enough, Miss Baxter."

Embarrassed, she looked down at her hands, still resting on the keys, and almost absently began to play again, a delicate nocturne. "It has been my pleasure, Lord Renwick," she said finally. "Although it is the first Christmas I have ever spent away from my family, sharing it with yours has made happy memories I will carry for a lifetime."

He was silent, listening to her play, and she kept going, playing several pieces from memory until her hands grew weary and finally she finished a piece and closed the pianoforte lid.

"Thank you," he said quietly. "It has been a long time since I enjoyed music for its own sake, but it has been a true pleasure listening to you play." He hesitated for a moment, then said "I am in your debt, Miss Baxter, for everything you have done for my sons. If there is ever anything that is in my power to do for you, you need only name it."

She shook her head with a smile, again saying it had been her pleasure, and he nodded as though that was what he had expected her to say, before getting up, bowing, and taking his leave of her.

Left alone in the music-room, Marie looked out into the darkness outside, a smile on her face.

It truly had been a wonderful Christmas.

CHAPTER 12

Boxing Day gifts

M arie grimaced in anticipation as she placed the slightest pressure on her bad ankle. It held, although it was tender. Nothing at all like the searing pain of the weeks before. Being careful, she would be able to get about a little. Staying close to the interior walls was the best thing, as she could put a hand out and balance her weight.

It wasn't quite the miraculous recovery she'd hoped for, but it was good progress. Enough that she'd be able to join Mrs Ellwood and Morag as they visited the tenant farmers with boxes of gifts for the year.

The carriage was ready and to her surprise, Mr Charles would also be joining them. He assisted Marie into the carriage and Mrs Ellwood pulled her up from the inside and helped her to a seat.

Morag was delighted to see the object of her affection joining them, and Marie wondered if perhaps something had happened between them.

Of course, she remembered a moment later, he was a

son of one of the farmers, and that was why Lord Renwick was sponsoring him.

In the carriage, Mr Charles smiled and politely coped with Morag as she peppered him with questions about what gifts he'd brought for his family. Morag was doing her best to be understandable today. Perhaps she'd been taking some elocution lessons from Mrs Ellwood?

Marie turned to Mrs Ellwood who theatrically rolled her eyes at Morag's display.

It wasn't until they arrived at a farm where the name 'Charles' hung on a shingle near the main gate that she realised why the tutor was accompanying them.

"Here we are," Mr Charles said, as soon as the carriage came to a stop.

It had been slow going because a fresh dumping of snow had fallen over the roads. Mr Charles climbed out first and asked the coachman to take the horses into the barn so they wouldn't become chilled standing in the snow.

Marie carefully eased herself down a step onto her good foot, but she would need to put more weight on her bad one. Mr Charles extended his hands to her and said, "I'll lift you, if you like?"

"Thank you, you're most gallant to offer."

He lifted her by the waist and gently placed her on her feet, where her boots vanished into the snow. She might need some of it to pack around her bad ankle if she did anything silly.

"I'd like a lift," Morag said as she stood on the top step.

Mr Charles gave a hearty laugh and said, "Of course."

He lifted her just the same as he had Marie, and Morag grinned the whole time his hands were on her.

Mrs Ellwood handed them all the parcels, then made to climb down. Mr Charles also offered his services.

"Tosh, I can get down fine on me own." The housekeeper laughed at him, her eyes crinkling at the corners. "No need to be gallant for me, young man!"

Once they were ready, the coachman took the horses into the barn and they entered the farmhouse.

The fire was roaring in the hearth with a Yule log sticking out of it as well. Aromas of burning pine, honey and roasted vegetables filled the air. An older man took the boxes from Mr Charles and beamed, his arms wide for an embrace.

"John, you are a sight for sore eyes!" The two men embraced and Marie realised the older man must be Mr Charles' father.

A woman came bustling in, fresh tears on her face, "My darling John, come here!" She held her son and hugged him, rocking him sideways and nearly throwing him off balance.

A much taller man then walked in, ducking his head as he came through the doorway. He was built like an oak, his legs as thick as tree trunks. "Baby brother!" the giant called out.

"Andrew!" Mr Charles cried. When Mr Charles embraced his brother, there was a marked gap in their heights. Clearly the elder boy had never lacked for food!

Morag gasped, "My word! Lookit ye!"

Had Marie been with the household so long she could truly understand the wild girl?

Mrs Ellwood reached out to correct the young maid, but stopped as the elder son quickly gasped and said, "I shall return the favour, pretty lady!" His eyes were fixed on the Scots girl's fiery red locks.

What had just happened? Marie looked at the maid, whose eyes were virtually turning heart-shaped in front of them. Then she looked up to Mr Charles' brother, who wore an enormous grin in response.

"Morag Campbell, kind sir," the maid said, making a quick curtsey to him.

"Oh dear!" the giant of a man said, "You know what they say, 'Never trust a Campbell'. Not that it's yer fault, like."

"Weil," Morag twirled her skirts, flirting furiously, "If ye think it's a bad name, marry me and i'll change it to yers!"

The parents roared with mirth and laughter. The father said, "She's got yer number, my lad." Then he looked at Morag and said, "Come and sit by the fire and warm yourself, hen. Andrew? Get her a drink. John? Tell me all about how your training is going?"

They spent a wonderful, if confusing, hour at the Charles' farmhouse. When it was time to go, they almost had to drag Morag away from the elder brother.

"Why don't you pick me up later when you're on the way back?" she suggested.

"Morag!" Mrs Ellwood said, sounding utterly outraged, "You'll do as yer told."

As they returned to the carriage, Morag reprimanded Mr Charles. "Whydintya teil me yer brother were so handsome, and like to inherit the farm too! To think ahve bin wasting me time with the likes of ye!"

Marie had to bite the inside of her cheek to not burst into fits of laughter. It was a truly fast turn around in affections from the young maid. Mr Charles was laughing and looking suddenly relaxed. Morag's change in romantic target had quickly resolved a particularly sticky situation of her holding a flame for the tutor who was destined for the church.

The rest of the farm visits were short and merry. With the last one, Marie remained in the carriage so she could rest her ankle. One of the farmer's wives came out to see her and offer her a small apple cake. The kindness of the gesture robbed her of speech. There was a little girl holding on to her mother's skirts. "Can I come in? It looks grand?" the little girl begged, eyes wide with wonder.

"Pet, no…" the mother started.

"Be my guest," Marie said, and nodded to the farmer's wife to climb up as well. It would be warmer in here than standing outside.

"Is this really an earl's carriage?" the girl said, eyes as round as saucers. "Are you a princess?"

"Very far from it," Marie said, "but I do feel very much like a princess in this carriage. It does belong to the Earl of Renwick."

"Are you going to be the new lady in the castle?" the girl then asked.

"Hush child," her mother said. "I do beg yer pardon, my lady, she's at that age when she's full of questions! She didn't mean no offence."

"It's all right, no offence taken, she's allowed to

dream," Marie said, giving in to some fantasies of her own. Riding around in an Earl's carriage was something she could get used to. Not that she should, and not that she'd even let herself believe it was possible. In fact, she really shouldn't let herself dream like that, because before long she would wake up and be back in regular old Hatfield.

"And I'm not a lady." Marie broke her apple cake and offered half to the little girl, whose mouth made an 'O' of surprise.

"Thank you!" the girl said, "Come over again soon and Ma will make more."

The mother chuckled at how much enthusiasm her daughter had. "Come on, little one, they need to get back to the big house before it gets dark."

It snowed so much on the return home, Marie wondered if they might need to find a nearby barn for them for the night, because it would be cruel to keep the horses out in these conditions. The driver too must be buried under a freezing white blanket.

When they did change direction, it was to bring them back to Alston Castle. The horses kicked through the snow and pulled them safely into the stables.

The grooms were quick to give them oats and brush them down, paying attention to carefully get more blood flowing through their lower limbs.

Marie was careful too not to rush back into the castle, knowing a bad step could set her recovery back. To her utmost surprise, Lord Renwick appeared at the stable door with a blanket. He wrapped it around her, then picked her up and carried her back into the castle. He walked her all the way to the library, where George and Richard were sitting by the fireplace, holding an iron shovel full of chestnuts over the coals.

"Have you hurt yourself again?" George asked.

"We were hoping to give you a tour soon," Richard said.

"No, I'm not hurt. Your father decided to be gallant," she said. "But the tour might have to wait another day. I am quite tired, I'm afraid."

"Shouldn't have let you go out in this weather," Renwick said, seemingly chiding himself, as he settled her in an armchair. "Dreadful risk."

"I had a wonderful time," Marie contradicted him firmly. "I haven't been out of doors since I arrived here, I very much enjoyed the fresh air, and meeting Mr Charles' family too."

He looked a little thoughtful at that.

"And young Morag also had a marvellous time," she added. She left the comment there and would tell Renwick more later, when they didn't have an audience.

"I wish we could go out too," George said regretfully as the first chestnuts began to pop. "We haven't even had a chance to build a snowman yet!"

"That must surely be remedied," Renwick said with a laugh. "Let me see what I can do."

The following morning, Mrs Ellwood bustled in to help Marie dress, smiling broadly. "Warmest petticoats today, my dear!"

"Why is that?" Marie asked curiously. Despite the ruined approaches to Alston Castle, the renovated portion was warm and comfortable, with fires lit in every room and few drafts. She couldn't imagine why she would need to dress more warmly even if the weather were to turn worse, and today looked better; the sun had actually come out, shining almost blindingly on the snow-covered landscape.

"His lordship has an outing planned for you and the young masters," Mrs Ellwood said cheerfully, but she refused to share any more details, miming turning a key beside her lips when Marie pressed her.

Mrs Ellwood offered her arm for support, and they made their way slowly to the front door. Her ankle was even better this morning, and as long as she was careful, she would be able to accept the boys' promise of a tour very soon.

Mr Martin smiled and opened the door for her, and Marie cried out in surprise at what awaited her at the bottom of the steps; Lord Renwick there with his two sons, in a horse-drawn sleigh!

"I saw you piling the greenery in this sleigh, on Christmas Eve," Marie said, as Renwick entrusted the reins briefly to George and came up the steps to collect her.

"Quite useful when the snow is this deep - and we don't need to stick to the roads." Renwick lifted her and carried her easily down the steps, then tucked her into the sleigh. It had two bench seats, rear and front. Marie sat in the back with Richard, and George in front with his father, who promptly delighted the boys by cracking the reins and shouting "Ho!" to the horse.

They did not rush off at a great speed despite this, the horse picking a steady pace through the crunching snow. It was a big draught horse, with dense hair around his feet and thick tail and mane to keep him warm. His huge hooves didn't seem to sink so deep into the snow as the carriage horses' slender legs, despite his greater size, and the sleigh was a great deal smoother than a carriage, gliding along with sparkling snow crystals flying up around them from the horse's hooves and the boys' laughter trailing behind. Marie could not stop smiling, even though she had to take her glasses off and put them in her pocket because they promptly misted over with snowflakes.

After twenty minutes or so, Renwick drew the horse to a halt in the lee of a large boulder, and threw a large blanket over the horse's broad back to keep it warm.

"Here is a fine spot for your snowman, boys," he said, gesturing grandly to the space in front of them. "He can look down on the castle from here, like a guardian angel!"

George and Richard cheered, jumping down from the sleigh and running forward. Well bundled up in heavy coats and knitted hats and mittens, they were soon rolling a huge ball of snow for the base of their snowman and arguing good-naturedly about exactly where to place it.

It was an excellent spot, Marie thought. They hadn't come all that far from the castle, Renwick having steered the sleigh in a large shallow semi-circle up the slope, to avoid going too steeply, but they had a marvellous view of Alston Castle below them. From this vantage point, she could see how little of it was actually ruined; it really was only a small section in the front. She wondered how many years Renwick and his ancestors had been rebuilding it for, and indeed when it had originally been constructed.

"Are you warm enough?" Renwick asked Marie. "Half an hour or so and they should be done... there's a blanket under your bench to spread over your legs, if you wish."

"I'm quite warm enough, I thank you!" They were sheltered from the wind, where the sleigh was parked. The sun managed to peek out, and Marie found herself quite warm. She decided to stand up, because the bench seat was a little uncomfortably hard, and Renwick offered his hand to assist her out of the sleigh. She leaned back against the sleigh, enjoying the sun on her face for however long it lasted.

They watched the boys for a little while, Renwick leaning on the side of the sleigh beside her.

"I went through the list," he said, and it took Marie a few moments to recall what list he might be talking about.

"Oh, the list from my sisters?"

"Indeed." He took the folded paper from his greatcoat pocket and handed it to her.

Marie unfolded the list and glanced down it, before beginning to laugh. "My lord, you have ticked verily half this list! Are you sure?"

"Quite sure. And since I have decided to deliver you back to Hatfield in person before taking the boys to Eton, I can collect them myself, without needing to trouble you to post them." He smiled in satisfaction. "I will enjoy browsing the shelves of your bookshop in person at last!"

"Very well." She shook her head, still chuckling. He would be accompanying them back to Hatfield? How marvellous! She wanted to shout with glee, but suppressed the impulse, instead saying sedately, "I will send this back to my sisters and tell them to reserve the volumes for you... and hope none of them have been sold already."

"They had better not!" he looked almost indignant, before shaking his head ruefully. "Goodness me, there I go being demanding. How could your sisters possibly hold all those books, on the off chance that I might want them?"

Marie bit her lip, wondering for a moment whether she should tell him that she and her sisters had nick-named him the Earl of Demanding. *No, best not,* she decided.

"You're not wearing your glasses," he observed, "and yet you read down that list quite well, it seems?"

"I can do some things without them," she admitted, "but it is very uncomfortable. I squint, and if I try to read more than a page or so I will get a dreadful headache. Outside it is better, I can see far away things quite well." She looked up at him. "You, this close - are a little blurry. Still handsome, though."

The moment the words left her mouth, Marie wished them back. Even though Renwick appeared a little blurry without her glasses, she could still make out his expression of startlement.

"You... think I'm handsome?" he said slowly.

Oh she could turn herself inside out right now with how awkward she felt. "Well, you are... tall, and dark, and have very fine cheekbones and a patrician nose and eyelashes so long they are quite wasted on a man."

I'm babbling. Oh no. Shut up, Marie Baxter!

Renwick was smiling, she could see that much. He leaned in towards her and very gently, traced the tip of one gloved finger down the bridge of her nose.

She caught her breath on the gesture.

"Talk about my eyelashes?" he said softly. "Yours are so long they often brush the insides of your glasses."

"How ever have you noticed that?" she said in astonishment.

"Because I look at you far more than I probably should, Miss Baxter."

"Oh." Her breath came short as he leaned closer.

He's going to kiss me again. This time, I'm not going to let him pull away so soon...

"Pa! Come and look!" George's shouts broke the tension, and Renwick turned his head away.

Marie could have quite happily throttled George for his interruption at that moment. She heaved a regretful sigh as Renwick walked away, and she almost thought the glance he gave her back over his shoulder was full of regret as well, for the missed opportunity.

CHAPTER 13

When The Cat's Away

Perhaps standing in the snow while the boys made the snowman had set her ankle the right way at last, because Marie felt steadier than ever by the time they returned to the castle.

George and Richard's faces were alight when she said she could walk a little, and would enjoy taking the tour they had long been promising her.

"We shall still help you up the stairs," Richard bragged, "which a gentleman would do anyway."

Could she adore them any more than she already did? "I would appreciate that very much," she replied.

At the foot of the stairs, she braced one hand on the bannister for balance and gave her other hand to Richard until they reached the landing. Her ankle held, although she barely placed any weight on it.

"My turn," George said, and the boys swapped over so that George could hold her hand until they reached the next floor.

Her ankle held up remarkably. They spent the next

hour solemnly showing her around the rooms. Some areas had not been renovated and the doorknob to those rooms were cold to the touch.

"This one feels haunted," George said.

"It's grandpapa's old room," Richard announced. "He probably breathed his last in here."

"Should we perhaps leave?" Marie suggested, not liking the drop in temperature. The chill wasn't from any ghostly presence, though. A pane of glass in the leadlight window was cracked, letting the elements in. She doubted there had been a fire in the hearth for the best part of a decade.

"Hey look at this," George said, finding a panel of the wall that had a hinge in it. Richard rushed over but they couldn't get it open. Perhaps it was somehow locked from the other side. She wondered if Renwick knew how to open it, and where it led. It was all very Gothic; just like something out of a Minerva Press novel, but Marie was far too sensible to invent horrible stories of skeletons and villains hiding in secret passages.

The furniture was covered in Holland blinds, similar to the music room downstairs. The footprints they made in the dust told Marie that nobody had been in here for years.

"Let's look at your areas, do you have a playroom?" she asked.

Richard crinkled his nose, "Well, we did have a nursery, but we're far too old for that now," he said, as only an eleven-year-old could.

Marie held in a laugh.

They visited more rooms that were used, and had fires

burning merrily in the hearths and worn furniture that had seen better times. Perhaps the staff used these rooms to take a rest between tasks?

Another wing on this floor was completely blocked off. George and Richard showed Marie what it was through a window - an old tower that was in desperate need of repair. It would be quite the task to make it sturdy and liveable again, and definitely not something to be done during the winter.

"This is our classroom," George said, leading Marie into a room that in many ways mimicked the library on the ground floor. Except it was far smaller. There was a broad table in the middle with chairs around it. Sitting by the window with a book in his hand was Mr Charles.

"Hullo!" he called out. Then he saw Marie and he stood up to make a polite bow. "It is good to see you on two feet, Miss Baxter."

"I feel much stronger today. The boys and the earl treated me to a sleigh ride, and I stood about in the snow while they built a snowman. It has done my limb the power of good."

"I thought we had the day off?" George asked. "Why are you here, you're not waiting for us, are you?"

"You do," Mr Charles confirmed. "And no; I am just enjoying my book in a comfortable chair in good light."

The boys both sighed with relief.

Mr Charles made an exaggerated gasp, "I'm not that awful, am I?"

That brought some bashful expressions to the boys' faces and Marie smiled broadly.

"I think they are quite fond of you, really," she said

sotto voce as the boys found a bowl of apples on the table and claimed one each for a snack.

"As I am of them, I assure you." Mr Charles smiled fondly.

"There's more to explore," George said once he'd finished his apple.

"We should play hide and go seek," Richard said.

"All right, I'll count," Mr Charles said, putting his book down.

"In French!" George teased.

"Not fair!" their tutor laughed, "but I think I could manage counting to fifty, after Miss Baxter's excellent tutelage. It should take me about the same time as counting to one hundred in English, I think… so you had better hurry!" He then turned his back, covered his eyes and began counting.

Marie did not run off, but she did follow the boys to another unused room where she could crawl under a table that had a large sheet over it.

The boys scarpered and she was left to her thoughts, which immediately strayed to Lord Renwick. While the boys had built their snowman, she'd been so ready for a kiss from him, but the kiss had not eventuated! She was sure it would be even better than the last one, whenever he did get around to kissing her again. Perhaps she should lure him to stand under the mistletoe.

She heard Mr Charles finding Richard with a loud, "Found you!" and soon after he found George. The boys then helped him find her hiding place, which felt a little like cheating.

"You won," George said, "So you get to count now."

"Shall I count in French?" she asked.

Mr Charles laughed and suggested that would be too easy for her, and she should try Latin.

Marie sat down to count, so she could rest her leg, and she had a good time hunting down her quarry.

They were having so much fun the boys even managed to corral Mrs Ellwood into a short session - with a great deal of pleading and promises to help her with whatever chores she could think of. Richard won the next round, so he counted. Marie found a cosy spot to hide near a window, where she could sit on a chair. There was a privacy screen on the other side of the room, and for a moment she thought about hiding behind that. She didn't need to, as Richard was so slow in his search she wasn't troubled at all, and could admire the view out the window. The view included the hill where they'd taken the sleigh ride, including the enormous snowman they'd built. His tattered brown scarf stood out amongst all the white. Eventually Mrs Ellwood had to bring Richard in to look for her. "There you are!" he cried out in exasperation.

"Thank you for finding me!" It was a relief because this part of the castle had no fires burning and she was starting to shiver.

Perhaps she might knit a scarf if she was to play with the boys again and explore more of the castle.

An idea struck. She'd been wondering about what to get for people for gifts on Twelfth Night, which would be here before she knew it.

"Mrs Elwood, would you know where I might obtain some wool suitable for knitting?"

The woman smiled broadly and told the boys to wash up for nuncheon so they could talk in private. "You're thinking of making something?"

"Yes, I thought I might knit some scarves for the boys. I have some wool in my travel case, but only the one colour, and probably not enough."

"This is Cumbria, wool is the most plentiful thing you can imagine here! I can easily get you as much as you need. I'll leave a basket in your room for you."

True to her word, there was an array of fine soft wool waiting for Marie later that evening when she returned to her room after dinner. Bless Mrs Ellwood, nothing seemed too much trouble for the redoutable housekeeper.

Marie wasted no time casting on and knitting several rows. She didn't even need her glasses once she got into the rhythm of it, and soon she had several inches of scarf descending from her needles. Happy with her progress, and tired after more exercise that day than she had done in weeks, she decided to try and go to sleep.

The castle was quiet as she put down her needles for the night and leaned over to blow out her candle. Suddenly something scurried along the skirting boards that stole her breath. In a flash, it darted under the gap in the door.

She shook her head. If this was back at the bookshop, she'd have to be on the lookout out for the remains of that mouse behind the counter in the morning.

Quickly, she got out of bed and tested her ankle. She had been on her feet for a good part of the day, but had taken every opportunity to rest her ankle when she could.

The limb held, and she pulled on her robe before

making her way to the hall where a basket of correspondence was ready to go to Alston in the morning. She
picked up the letter she'd recently written to her sisters
and took it to the library.

Lord Renwick was sitting in his favourite chair,
reading.

"Sorry to bother you this late, my lord."

"You're not a bother," he said, looking up from his
book. "Anything the matter?"

"I'm adding a few lines on the back of this letter. You
see, ah, how can I put this, you ah… I saw a mouse."

"Oh? I didn't hear you scream."

"Mice don't make me scream, except when I step in
half a mouse. Crafty leaves them behind in the
bookshop."

"Crafty?"

"Our cat, and the most excellent mouser. She had
kittens recently, so if there are any left, we can give you
one to keep the castle mouse-free."

"You don't have to write a post script to that one. You
could write them another fresh letter and I'll be happy to
send it to Alston when you're done."

Marie had spent her life being frugal with paper. The
thought of being able to write another separate letter felt
like luxury.

A light thud in the hallway indicated one more fallen
decoration. They both laughed. Marie carefully walked to
the doorway to find a spray of pine needles on the
boards. She stood for a while leaning on the doorframe,
taking the weight off her bad ankle. A mouse, possibly
the same one from her room, darted across the floor to the

pine needles. It scurried over the greenery and ate at the soft bark holding the needles in place.

"It's the decorations," she said. The moment she spoke, the mouse fled to safety. "That's why the mice came in. We accidentally brought in a ready food supply for them!"

Holly would probably be too tough for them, but the soft bark of the pine stems would be perfect fodder.

Marie knew that if the cats that lived in the Alston stables were only half as good as Crafty, there would be no live mice to be seen inside the castle. Although, if they were like Crafty, they'd also leave eviscerated surprise presents all over the place for unsuspecting feet!

Another thing the mice would love were the mistletoe berries. Perhaps some of the little white fruits had dropped off during the decorating process, leading to more tempting morsels for mice. She could not climb ladders, nor could she reach the higher decorations remaining. Jumping was out of the question.

"Oh dear!" Renwick said, as he looked about at the remaining decorations, complete with mistletoe and holly berries.

Marie nodded. She'd drawn him to the mistletoe quite by accident, but what a happy accident it was.

"I'd best take this down then," he said, reaching up to remove the nearby hanging mistletoe.

Marie remained perfectly still, readying herself for a kiss.

"Did you draw me out here for this?" But his voice had a smile in it and his eyes softened with creases.

"It was a happy coincidence," she said, her heart beating a little faster in anticipation.

Finally, finally his lips descended on hers and she was in heaven.

It shouldn't be possible, but this kiss was even better than their first. His lips pressed on hers so gently and warmly. It was a caress of beautiful intimacy. Her lips parted on a sigh and she pressed into him, deepening the contact. Something delightful flipped behind her ribs at the glorious pressure.

"You are dangerous to my peace of mind, Miss Baxter," he said quietly, a few moments later. "This is unwise."

"I shall not regret it," she answered, eyes still closed and a smile on her lips. She reached up and stole a kiss from him and sparks of delight filled her body at his response.

She heard him laugh quietly. "I shall not regret it either, but it must not become a habit."

Wait, no. It would be a marvellous habit!

His lips brushed her forehead, very gently, and she heard him step back. Opening her eyes, she watched him retreat to the library again.

A little sigh escaped Marie, but she couldn't keep the smile off her face as she returned to her room and climbed back into bed. Renwick was far beyond her reach - she might as well wish for the moon! - but it was really rather lovely to be kissed by him and to kiss him back.

"And to think, I did everything I could to avoid having to come to Cumbria!" she chuckled to herself as she snuggled down into the warm, comfortable bed. "A strange few weeks it's been, but I've made memories enough to last a lifetime."

The following morning, Marie settled herself at her writing-desk to pen another letter to her sisters. A scratch on the door had her calling "Come in!" absently.

"It's only us, Miss Baxter." George and Richard crept in. "May we sit with you?"

"Of course, but where is Mr Charles?"

"He has the sniffles," Richard explained seriously. "He said it's only a cold, but Mrs Ellwood says he has to stay in his room or the whole household will catch it and she won't have that."

Marie grinned as she imagined the diminutive housekeeper shooing Mr Charles back into his room, possibly with a broom in her hand. "Poor Mr Charles! Well, I expect I shall be a poor substitute as a tutor, apart from French…"

"Oh, you don't have to," George said earnestly. "He sent a note and has set us essays to write for History. I have to write about the Wars of the Roses and Richard has to write about… what was it again?"

"Henry the Sixth and his eight wives," Richard said.

"I think you mean Henry the Eighth and his six wives," Marie corrected, amused. "You'd better have another read of that chapter in your history book, Richard. Well, pull some chairs up to the table over there and get started, then. I have my letter to write, so shan't be talking to you until nuncheon and our French lesson!"

Both boys agreed happily and were soon settled at the table, Richard's head buried in his book checking his facts, George's tongue poking out as he began laboriously writing his essay. They were so good, Marie thought, and really very quiet and studious.

She soon finished her letter, as it was really only a note to her sisters to keep one of Crafty's kittens if they had not all found homes yet. She decided to include some more detailed sketches of the two boys. Taking some fresh sheets of paper, she made a careful sketch of each of them, and then drew Renwick from memory, sitting in his reading chair in the library, head bent over his book.

The morning quite flew by, and soon Mrs Ellwood was coming in with the tea tray and some food; hot pies, fresh bread, sliced ham and cheese, and some apples.

"His lordship won't be joining you. Called out to assist at one of the tenant farms - the amount of snow we've had, a barn roof has caved in."

"Oh, nobody is hurt, I hope?" Marie asked.

"No, but some sheep got the fright of their lives, I'll wager." Mrs Ellwood smiled fondly at the boys, already both with their mouths full of pie. "Thank you for minding them, Miss Baxter. If they're troubling you, I could…"

"They are not troubling me at all, they are very good company. How is Mr Charles?"

"He'll be right in a day or two," Mrs Ellwood said wisely. "I'll keep my eye on him. He'll be glad to know you've the boys in hand."

"Please tell him not to worry about a thing, I shall see that they keep up with their studies."

Mrs Ellwood nodded respectfully and left them, and Marie switched into French. The boys really were improving by leaps and bounds, their vocabulary excellent and their grammar such that they could now hold simple conversations without having to pause much to think.

"Let's play a game, that we are strangers meeting for the first time," she proposed. "So you can practice the sort of conversations you might have if you were meeting a French person."

The boys nodded gamely, and Marie began, saying her name and asking theirs.

"D'où venez-vous?" Richard asked, correctly using the formal form one would use when asking a stranger where they came from.

Marie gave him an approving nod before saying "Je vis en Hatfield, en Hertfordshire."

"Oh!" Both boys looked surprised, and then George slowly explained, with only one or two grammatical errors, that they had travelled through Hatfield on their way home from Eton.

"We slept for the night in the inn, the Red Lion," Richard added.

"But that is right next door to the bookshop! You were right next door!" Marie cried out in French, and then had to repeat herself more slowly so that they understood.

Maybe I will see them again, she thought with a sudden burst of happiness, if Hatfield chanced to be a regular stop on their journey to and from Eton.

Then she frowned as she thought back to the maps she'd studied to get to Alston. "Isn't Eton near Windsor?"

The route from there to Cumbria would not likely pass through Hatfield. She scrunched up her forehead, trying to envision a larger map of southern England. No, surely they would have gone through Oxford, and thence to Birmingham.

"Yes, but one of the masters accompanied us to Cambridge where we met up with Mr Charles," George explained.

Now the route made sense, and she nodded in understanding, before frowning again in puzzlement. "Your father must have known the route you would take. I wonder why he did not have you collect the books to bring home with you?"

"I'm glad he didn't," Richard said. "Because then you would never have come to Alston!"

Marie gave him a fond smile. "Well, I would not have missed this trip for the world, truth be told. Meeting you has been wonderful, and if you ever pass through Hatfield again, you must be sure to visit our bookshop!"

The boys enthusiastically agreed, and begged her to tell them more about the bookshop, and for stories of Crafty's mischief. Marie obliged them, all the while still puzzling over why Renwick hadn't trusted his own sons to collect his books. They'd travelled in his own carriage, there would have been plenty of room! She couldn't fathom it at all.

CHAPTER 14

Revelations

M r Charles remained unwell until New Year's Day, and Marie obligingly looked after the twins until the tutor was able to resume his duties. At least she was able to walk about more now, and rather enjoyed exploring more of the castle with them. George and Richard proudly showed off more rooms in their home, explaining that their great-grandfather had begun the renovations some eighty years earlier and each generation since had completed another section of the castle.

"I'm going to do the North Tower, when it's my turn," George said proudly. "I like it up there, it's the tallest tower, but there aren't any windows right now and the steps are a bit wobbly. I don't think it would be safe for you to go up there, Miss Baxter. Maybe you can come and visit in the summer and I'll show you!"

She smiled, thinking that unlikely. It would indeed be lovely to come for the summer. It was sweet of George to suggest it. "I don't think anyone should be going up a tower without any windows in this icy weather," she cautioned gently. "Even if they had two good ankles. It would be very slippery."

They both looked a little sheepish, before admitting they had tried a few days earlier but Richard slipped on the third step and had dragged George down with him as he fell.

"Only a few bruises!" Richard reassured Marie as she looked aghast. "But you're right, and we promise we won't try again. Please don't tell Father, we weren't hurt at all!"

Marie was sure their father would be furious. They could have been seriously hurt. "Promise me no more climbing," Marie said.

"Not until summertime," George put in quickly.

"And not without an adult," Marie said firmly. "Your tutor or your father, or even one of the grooms. Just in case you fall again. Promise me."

They promised, and she hoped they'd remember when summer came.

"You can accompany us in summer," Geroge said cheekily. "You will be married to Pa by then!"

Marie's cheeks burned red at the suggestion.

"Why are you blushing?" Richard said. "Pa really likes you, we can tell."

"Please boys, you're very sweet, but it's not like that."

She didn't want to get their hopes up. Who was she kidding, she didn't want to get her own hopes up.

"Oh yes, I know, this is an *adult* thing, isn't it?" George added. "Whenever we tell someone something obvious, they blush like mad and say it's an adult thing and we wouldn't understand."

"Yeah, like when we told Mr Charles that Morag really liked him," Richard said.

"He went so red and said we must be mistaken, but we could tell."

"Well, Mr Charles has nothing to fear," Marie gently corrected them, "Morag has switched her affections to someone else."

"Oooh!" their eyes went round and they wanted to hear more.

Heavens! Marie wanted to blush again. "I should not gossip."

"Is that why he's sick?" Richard said, "He doesn't have a cold, he has a broken heart."

Goodness, could that be the case? Mr Charles had been with herself, Morag and Mrs Ellwood for the whole day delivering boxes to the tenants, yet only Mr Charles had come down with a cold and not the rest of them. No, surely it must be a coincidence. Mr Charles had been relieved that Morag was so keen on his brother!

Marie was tired enough after spending all day with the boys to want her bed straight after seeing them to theirs, so had little time for a private conversation with Renwick. As tired as she was each night, she still managed a little more knitting, smiling as the second scarf grew nearly as long as the first one. They would both be finished well in time for Twelfth Night.

Once Mr Charles returned to his duties, with profuse thanks to Marie for stepping in, she was quite glad to return to the routine she had become pleasantly used to, joining Renwick in the library after dinner.

"You have had little time to read that book," Renwick

said, observing she had not progressed many pages through the volume in recent days. "Thank you, for taking so much time with the twins."

"It has been a pleasure," Marie replied, "but honestly, quite tiring. I'm not sure how mothers manage, day in and day out!"

"And they are less tiring at this age than when very young," Renwick pointed out.

"Yes." Marie made a little face. "I do not have a lot of liking for small babies," she admitted. "One cannot hold a proper conversation with them."

Renwick seemed to be holding in laughter, but he agreed with her quite solemnly.

"They have been showing me about the castle," Marie said then, "and George mentioned his plans to renovate the North Tower, once he becomes its custodian."

"Did he now!" Renwick did not look displeased by the thought.

Marie wanted to keep the boys' trust, but at the same time was deeply concerned for their welfare. "I thought I should warn you that apparently they have been going up there, and have admitted it's somewhat hazardous at the moment."

He looked at her, his face filled with concern. "Go on."

"They have promised me not to try again until summer, and never to go alone, but…"

"Ah, yes. I thank you for the caution." He looked thoughtful. "I might install a gate, at the foot of the tower, with a key. I'll let them know they may go up whenever they ask, but they will have to ask for the key, which should preclude any dangerous solo adventuring."

"An excellent thought, my lord!" A clever solution, and not difficult to implement before the boys came home again. Marie thought of something else then, which she had been meaning to ask him. "My lord, the boys mentioned to me that they stopped overnight in Hatfield on their way from Eton to Cambridge. You must have known they would be passing through, or close by - why ever did you not have your coachman stop by the book-shop to collect your order?"

Renwick's reaction was oddly defensive. "It never occurred to me to entrust them with such valuable cargo," he said, a slight snap to his voice. "Richard and Renwick Junior are still just children."

"And you're still struggling to call him George," Marie pointed out. "Whatever is the matter with the name? Cannot you simply call him by his middle name, if the name George bothers you so?"

He snapped, "Because Francis is worse!"

It was an outburst, one that quite shocked Marie. She sat staring at Renwick, who had placed his hand over his eyes.

She had touched a nerve, and didn't know what to do with herself. Should she leave him or remain?

"It's not the boy's fault," Renwick said finally. "I know that, and I'm trying, but I hardly know him, hardly know either of them."

"And whose fault is that?" Marie asked dryly. It had been made clear, from her conversations with the boys, that while they had lived their whole lives at Alston with their mother until being sent to Eton aged six - which she thought an appallingly young age, but they had seemed to think quite normal - they had not known their father at all until after their mother passed away four years earlier. He had lived in London, estranged from his wife.

"You're blaming *me*?" He lowered his hand, stared at her with outrage clear on his face. "If you had the slightest idea…"

He might try sharing *the slightest idea*, and then she might be able to understand him better. But the man was a closed book.

Anger, disappointment, hurt all warred in Sebastian's breast. That Miss Baxter could think he had callously cut the boys from his life without good reason! He hadn't thought of the boys collecting his books because … he wouldn't have trusted them. He still didn't know them very well, and that was partly his fault, not not entirely.

He hardly knew what he was saying as the words began to spill out of him, words he had never said aloud to another living soul.

"I don't even know if they are mine."

Far from looking sympathetic, Miss Baxter snorted inelegantly. "My lord, if you cannot see that they are yours, you are blinder than I am without my glasses! Richard is the living image of you, and though George is lighter in colouring, he is very like too!"

She really had no idea what she was talking about. In some ways, it was good that she couldn't tell. Nobody could tell, and nobody would ever know. The likeness to him was convenient in many ways, but galling at the same time.

He was going to have to tell her all of it, the very worst, or she would continue thinking badly of him. That he could not bear.

"They might be my brothers."

She blinked, a little puzzled. "I was not aware you had a brother, my lord. Oh," and now she began to look compassionate, "did he pass away? Was he perhaps betrothed to the countess and you felt obliged..."

She still had it wrong. Every word felt like a knife into his soul as he explained, "I never had a brother, Miss Baxter. They might be *my brothers*," he said again, but this time elaborated to remove any shred of doubt, "my brothers, as in, my father's sons."

"Oh," she fell silent, blinked a few times. "I... see."

She very clearly did not, and from the many expressions crossing her face at this time, she was struggling to work out if he was still the villain in this scenario.

Sebastian sighed and began to explain. "Francesca was fifteen when she came to live here. Her parents had passed, and her father left her wardship to my father, who was an old school friend of her father's. At the time, I thought she was quite the most beautiful girl I had ever seen. She was the granddaughter of a duke, though lacking a title herself, and had a substantial dowry. My father thought it appropriate to betroth us. I was only eighteen, but very amenable to the idea. Of course, I spent the next few years studying at Cambridge, but when I finished my studies and returned home, Francesca and I were married." His mouth twisted bitterly as the painful memories resurfaced. "I was besotted with her. It was only a few months later that she told me I was to be a father; we were all delighted. And then a week after that, I returned home early from a day out hunting, my horse having come up lame ..."

The memories burned acid in his gut and he spluttered, "I found my wife ... and my father..."

He couldn't make himself say it. Thinking back on that awful day stuck in his throat. He wanted to break and smash things. In a moment he might.

Marie stared at him for a long moment, uncomprehending, and then her mouth slowly opened and her eyes went very wide and round. "*No*," she breathed in horror.

"And in case you are thinking that my father was guilty of some villainy in forcing her, that was very clearly not the case," he added. "Francesca was..." he rethought the salacious details he'd been about to reveal. It would be so much easier simply to cut himself open and spill his innards than say the words. They were not fit for Miss Baxter's ears. He softened the blow with a euphemism, "Evidently she was an enthusiastically willing partner."

"Oh, Renwick." Marie's hand covered her mouth, her eyes welling with empathetic tears. "How very dreadful that must have been for you!"

Sebastian nodded tightly. He still couldn't believe he was bearing his soul to Miss Baxter in this way. "I try not to relive that time, as you no doubt understand. I confronted them, demanded to know how long it had been going on for. Neither would answer me, but I eventually came to understand that the *affaire* predated the wedding. I refused to spend another night under Alston's roof while either of them remained here; left that very day. My father provided an allowance for me to live on and I went to London and made myself useful there. Did some work for the War Office. They sent me news when the twins were born, but George's names were a slap in the face. George, you see, was my father's name, and Francis, after Francesca."

"Oh," she said, full understanding finally dawning on her face. "Oh, I *see*."

His entire body prickled as he relived the memories. "I refused to come back, even when my father passed away. That was when the boys were about three. If I had thrown Francesca out it would have been a scandal I had no wish to have made public. The boys would have suffered terribly for it. When she died four years ago, however, I realised that I was the only family they have, so I came home. Looking at George, however..." it was still a struggle to say his name. Marie had been far too observant there. "He has her eyes. They might be mine, but I have no way to know. Either way, he is legally my heir."

"And you are still punishing him for his mother's and your father's sins," Marie said, not unkindly, but the accuracy of the statement hit him to the heart. "Whatever the facts of the twins' parentage, they are innocent children, my lord, and you are not being fair to them."

Suddenly, irrationally angry, Sebastian threw down the book he had not looked at in several minutes and jumped to his feet. "I *know*!" he cried. "Do you think I don't know? Do you think I'm not trying? How dare you come here and make these accusations, you who know nothing of what I've been through? Do not look at me with pity, madam, I do not want or need your pity!"

Eyes blurring and hot, he was almost on the verge of tears. His heart pounded with fear and anger mixed together. He had to get out before he broke down and cried in front of her. Turning on his heel, he fled the library, running out into the hall and past a startled Mr Martin. He dragged open the front door and ran out into the dark, snowy night, his breath coming in great agonised gasps.

CHAPTER 15

Mrs Ellwood Reveals All

Marie sat dumbfounded in her chair, not sure what to do. Renwick had stormed out and she thought she'd heard the front door open and close. She should not be here when he returned; she needed to make herself scarce.

She quickly ran to her room to avoid having to see him again this night. What a fool she'd been to push him for the truth about those darling boys. It wasn't her place to ask such personal questions. The answers had shocked her and from his reaction, he'd possibly shocked himself at revealing them.

It was clear he'd kept the truth bottled up for years; perhaps she was the first person he'd ever told. And the boys didn't even know! Her heart ached for them after Renwick's utterly shocking revelations.

She quickly dressed for bed, trying hard not to put weight on her bad foot. A little while later she heard his voice in the hall speaking to Mr Martin before his heavy tread went up the stairs.

Her ankle was beginning to throb, but it wasn't the pain keeping her awake, it was her guilty conscience. She could not believe she'd pushed him so far. She'd thought he was being cruel to those lovely boys, when all long he'd been protecting them. She lay staring at the ceiling, unable to stop thinking about the agony on his face as he'd revealed the shocking extent of his wife and father's perfidy. And that he'd had to explain things so much before they made sense in her head. But who could ever have imagined that anyone would do something so dreadful? She could not even imagine what he must have felt, seeing his wife and his father... Marie shuddered. She could not begin to guess.

With so many thoughts colliding in her head, sleep was far away, and eventually she sat up and took her knitting into the great hall to try and work using the light of the Yule log fire. It was hard to concentrate and she missed a stitch. The boys would love their presents, but not if they were shoddily made. She stayed for a while, stitching and getting more rows of knitting onto the scarf. Her eyes were dry as she blinked, and her head and heart ached.

Taking herself back to bed, she tried again to sleep, her ankle aching again from dashing about from room to room.

All this time, she'd thought his demeanour was of a man wracked with grief over his beautiful dead wife. She could not have been further from the reality that the memories of his wife and father had eaten away at his soul. That his late wife had named the heir after Sebastian's father and herself was proof enough of this. No wonder he struggled to say the child's name! Every time he looked at the boy would remind him of his wife's disloyalty and betrayal. George's colouring was so much closer to his mother's than Sebastian's or even the old lord for that matter.

Marie moved into her wheeled chair, unable to sleep anyway and needing to raise her ankle on the wonderful design. She had Sebastian to thank for this ingenious invention, and she'd repaid that kindness by goading him until he'd had to relive the most painful episode of his life.

This new knowledge explained so much, but wanting to know more continued to eat away at her.

She did not get a wink of sleep all night.

When the housekeeper arrived with her breakfast tray, Marie took her chance.

"Mrs Elwood, please tell me about the last countess."

The housekeeper pressed her lips together in annoyance and huffed a little as she set the tray down on the table.

"There's little to say," she said, as she fussed about and plumped Marie's pillows as if giving herself a meaningless task to fill the time.

"Please? I have upset his lordship and I need to make amends."

"Upset him?" Mrs Ellwood's hands stilled, and then she set the pillows down. "How?"

"I mentioned the late countess," she left out the rest of it, on the off-chance Mrs Ellwood was not privy to the details. She probably knew much more than she ever let on, because she'd remained at Alston while the terrible events had been taking place. "He stormed off. I know I said the wrong thing, and I want to make amends, but I don't know much about her." It was the closest Marie had come to telling a straight up lie, having left out so much pertinent information.

Mrs Ellwood clasped her hands together in front of her apron and said, "It's not good to speak ill of the dead. Ring the bell if you need anything further."

She made to leave Marie's room, but Marie shuffled herself backwards and blocked the open doorway. The housekeeper could, of course, leave via the music room, but she pressed her lips together again and sighed with resignation.

"What have you heard?"

"Rather a great deal," Marie said, heat warming her cheeks. "A shocking story that explains so much."

"And may I ask who you heard this scandal from? Morag knows better than to spread stories she might have heard whisper of."

"It wasn't Morag." Marie shook her head. She'd made a huge mess of things, and could no longer lie to the woman who'd been so kind to her from the moment she'd arrived. "It was Lord Renwick himself. I ... I confess I challenged him on how he was letting his grief for his late wife affect his treatment of the boys, George especially."

"You *challenged* him?" Mrs Ellwood's brows rose high on her forehead in astonishment.

Marie let out a long sigh of resignation. "I did, and I realise now my utter mistake. I had noticed, over the past few weeks, that he is aloof with George more than Richard, and I pushed him until he told me why."

"Well then," Mrs Ellwood looked around for something else to do and decided to pour tea. As if she needed to keep herself busy at all times. "You know everything then?"

That was the problem, she still really didn't. She wanted to help Renwick and the boys, but she didn't want to make the situation worse by saying the wrong thing and upset them. Well, upset Renwick any more, because she'd upset him a great deal last night. If she'd known more of the details, she would never have pressed Renwick the way she had. She would have left well enough alone. "I know some of it, but by my understanding you've been here since before the wedding. He may have left for London but you were still here… with his father and the countess." She hesitated before adding a final, pointed word. *"Together."*

Mrs Ellwood sighed, and then she sat in the chair at the table and helped herself to Marie's tea, as if to fortify herself.

"What his lordship said is true. I've kept this to myself as it wasn't my tale to tell. There were rumours and suspicions from the very beginning, but I ignored it as gossip. You know how staff entertain themselves sometimes. I imagined many of them must have been bored so they made up wild stories to pass the time in this lonely spot. I didn't want to believe it was true, but…" she sighed as she unburdened herself. "The poor boys, they never knew any of this and they are such sweet things. And they still don't. I helped raise the wee things because I felt it best to keep them out of the way so they wouldn't hear any gossip."

Mary nudged herself closer so they could keep their voices low.

The sweet lady sighed again and said, "That girl. I knew she was no good from the moment she came here, making eyes at his lordship. He should have married her himself, but he was hellbent on Lord Sebastian doing it, more fool him!"

"That would have seemed to be the best solution," Marie agreed, wondering why the old earl hadn't done just that.

"She was a hussy, that one." Warming to her topic, Mrs Ellwood thinned her lips at the sour memories. "They were carrying on long before the wedding - Lord Sebastian shouldn't have married her, but who would dare tell him? We kept it quiet, for his current lordship's sake, but in doing that, they got away with it. After Lord Sebastian left for London when he'd found out what they'd been up to, well, the earl and Francesca figured there was no point hiding it any more. They virtually lived as man and wife in the castle here and it was all I could do to bite my tongue. They would hold hands at the breakfast table and not keep a respectable distance in the library. They shared a bedroom! The way he looked at her, they didn't hide it. Truth be told, I was glad to see the back of the old lord, and then her when she went. I'll probably burn in hell for saying such a thing about my betters, but that's how it is."

And Marie had stumbled right into that emotional

patch of nettles and dragged Renwick in with her. "I think I could use some tea," she said.

"I'll get you another cup," Mrs Ellwood said, getting up.

"No, please, I'm happy to use the same one. Best get this out before we're interrupted."

Mrs Ellwood poured more tea and added some milk and handed the cup and saucer over. Then she finished her tale.

"The old earl died when the boys were only three. I thought the new lord would come home then, but he still wouldn't. He was so hurt, he stayed in London rather than come home to the babes so he didn't have to see his wife. Even though he never really liked the city. I wrote asking him to come home for the boys' sake, but he said he couldn't face her, and who could blame him? He stayed in that stinkin' city for years instead."

Marie took her glasses off and set them on the table, then rubbed the top of her nose as she tried to absorb the terrible truth. *Poor Renwick. Those poor boys.* Thank the good Lord they didn't know.

Mrs Ellwood continued, "When the countess died, well, Lord Renwick came home and did his best, but... the boys were old enough to stay at school and not come home until the summer. Apparently Eton boys mostly don't come home for Christmastide, which sounds pretty cruel to me. Ever since his lordship returned, he makes sure to bring them home to make up for the Christmases they missed. But young George, he has his mother's eyes and ... I'm not surprised his lordship struggles to say the boy's name, because it's his father's name."

A gasp at the doorway had them both spinning around in horror, to discover who had overheard them.

There stood Richard and George, faces ashen with shock.

Marie wanted to cast up her tea immediately. She swallowed and tried to pretend all was well. "Boys, what a lovely surprise!" Her heart raced and her pulse thumped in her ears. *How much had they heard? How long had they been standing there?*

'No, it's not!" George almost shouted, walking into the room.

Richard followed him.

Marie's stomach roiled at the discovery, feeling utterly dreadful and responsible for more pain. The boys should never have heard them. Why hadn't she been more careful? Why hadn't she shut the blasted door?

Mrs Ellwood sighed deeply, "It's not good to listen in to others' conversation, no good ever comes of it."

"I heard enough," George said. His small jaw was clenched with fury, and he had never looked more like Renwick. "Tell me the rest."

Marie swallowed, her mouth dry. "I'm not sure what _"

"Tell me!" George thumped his fist on their table. His aim was poor and the thump so hard, he knocked her glasses off the table and onto the floor.

Marie was sure she'd heard something crack, possibly a bone in George's hand.

"George, you've hurt yourself, we'll get some snow and help it heal."

Richard came over to help his brother and look at his

sore hand. "What did you mean when you said George was named after his father? Our father's name is Sebastian!"

"They said more than that," George said, and Marie realised to her horror that George must have arrived at her door before Richard, and had heard perhaps something about his mother…

Marie was going to be sick. Of all the foolish things, urging Mrs Ellwood to reveal all without making sure they couldn't be overheard was the dumbest, stupidest thing she could ever…

CRUNCH!

The boys froze in position.

"What was that?" Mrs Ellwood said as she shook her head in confusion.

Brain filled with the fog of stress, Marie didn't know what had made the noise.

Richard and George stepped back, and Richard looked to the ground. "Oh dear."

They took another step back, then both of them bolted for the door and ran off, getting as far away from them as possible.

When Mrs Ellwood rose from her chair, she cleared the view for Marie.

One of the boys had stepped on her glasses, which now lay smashed on the floor.

Marie buried her face in her hands. "This has gone so badly!"

"Miss Baxter, we have bigger problems than your glasses." The housekeeper ran to the doorway to see if anyone else was nearby. Then she dashed back. "I think the coast is clear." Then she started packing the uneaten breakfast onto the tray. Her hands shook so much the teacup rattled on the saucer. "The staff who knew, well, they knew, but we all promised to say naught. And now the boys know anyway and I'll get the blame. This is bad. This is very bad."

"I will make sure to keep your name out of it," she said. Marie herself was in a panic, but the housekeeper was fluttering about like a trapped pigeon.

"They'll cast me out with no reference!" Mrs Ellwood cried, giving in to her emotions.

"No they won't," Marie assured her. "I will take the blame. This is my fault. I'm not merely saying that. This really is my fault. I've ruined everything."

Her own last words drummed a tattoo in her head.

I've ruined everything.

I've ruined *everything*.

CHAPTER 16
The Sword of Damocles

Mrs Ellwood fled the room, the crockery shaking noisily on the tray as she did so. Marie buried her face in her hands, her world collapsing around her as she began to panic. She was such a fool to want to know more, and now her curiosity had hurt those darling, innocent boys. Lord Renwick had told her enough to let her know the true reason for his untrusting nature and his poor parenting of the boys. But she'd gone and destroyed her good rapport with Mrs Ellwood, and possibly cost the dear woman her livelihood.

And she'd damaged George and Richard beyond repair!

Badly done, Marie. Badly done! she castigated herself. Why could she not have left well enough alone? Mrs Ellwood had filled in a few extra details, confirming Renwick's version of events, but she had not doubted Renwick was telling the truth. She had not doubted him in any case. What man would admit to devastation like that if it weren't true? She should have been satisfied with that!

The utter betrayal on those young boys' faces burned like acid in her throat.

She had to leave. She could not stay for one moment longer, throwing this family's hospitality and kindness back in their faces.

She was wrecking everything.

"What's the matter?" It was Renwick at the doorway.

Marie dragged in a breath but the words would not come.

Hiding her face so she would not have to look at him, she heard his footsteps growing closer.

"I'm such a fool," she said into her hands, her words coming out in a sobbing rush.

"Don't blame yourself," he said. "How did it happen?"

He was sounding remarkably calm and, dare she hope, sanguine about the entire event. This was completely the opposite of what she expected. She had expected him to lift her bodily and throw her down the front steps.

She brushed her hand over her face and looked over to him. He was waiting for her answer, and she had none.

He pointed to the floor, to her broken glasses, "Did someone break your glasses?"

Fresh tears burst forth at his assumption. He thought she'd become distraught over her glasses, rather than the real reason.

"I'm so silly," she said, making up an excuse.

Anything to spare the boys from any more anguish. "I didn't see them and … I rolled over them."

She had to lie, and it sat badly with her. She had to, because admitting the truth would only cause more heartbreak for all concerned. It could also drag Mrs Ellwood into the story, and that would not do. What a horrible mess she'd made of things!

"Right, hmm." He pulled a handkerchief from his pocket, then bent down to pick up the broken pieces and tuck them away. He appeared to be lost in thought, as if there was something he wanted to talk about. Then he made the most charming smile and wished her a good morning before he walked out.

Marie was terribly confused, which only added to her despondency. She needed to find the boys and explain things, but knowing the mess she'd just made, she could very well make it worse.

She had to keep busy, otherwise she'd go mad. But of course, she couldn't read anything because she'd broken her glasses.

She'd done too much walking in the past few days and her ankle was hurting again. Damn and blast it, she needed to find the boys and talk to them. She needed to find out exactly how much they'd heard.

She got to her feet and tried to reach the doorway. The moment she put her weight on her bad ankle, pain lanced her leg. She swore in French to help with the invisible knives stabbing her.

Hobbling, she reached back for the wheeled chair and rested there.

Knitting. The knitting would help. Even without her

CATHERINE BILSON & EBONY OATEN

glasses, she could hold the scarf out at arm's length and get a good idea of progress, and the rest she could do with her eyes closed.

With her good leg, she pushed her wheeled chair over to the window for better light. That's when she saw Lord Renwick cantering off on Caesar. At this distance, she could see him clearly and he seemed to be smiling to himself, which only added to her swirling confusion.

She spent the next several hours furiously knitting, as penance for being a harbinger of such terrible news to the boys.

Nuncheon came but the boys did not. Marie desperately wanted to talk to them and apologise but that was impossible if they didn't show up. Mr Charles arrived and made the excuse that they both appeared to have developed colds. He then started apologising because he assumed they must have caught their colds from him.

If by colds he meant emotional pain, then perhaps he was correct, but they'd caught that from her, not their tutor.

"Their faces are red and their noses are very stuffy," he said as Mrs Ellwood came in.

"I'll check on them at once," the housekeeper said, catching Marie's gaze. "They need good food to keep their strength up."

"The poor things," Marie said, truly meaning it, but for completely different reasons than a head cold. She'd done this to them, and her appetite vanished faster than one could say 'guilty conscience'. Perhaps Mrs Ellwood would be able to bring them some comfort? She truly hoped so.

She pushed herself back to her room after nuncheon and picked up her knitting, furiously adding rows. The light from the window darkened as a heavy storm blew in, turning the skies foul to match her mood.

If only she'd been content with Renwick's version of events, she would not be feeling like this.

Well, she'd feel awful, but only for the earl, not for the pain she'd inflicted on George and Richard.

What a nasty thing the countess had done by naming her first born after her lover and herself, a permanent reminder of infidelity on her part and no doubt a constant thorn in Renwick's side.

A headache formed as Marie tried to focus on the needles. Holding them out at a distance wasn't helping any more. If she didn't put the scarf down, she'd make a total mess of it.

She heard rather than saw a horse arriving. She manoeuvred onto her knees to look out the window to see it was Lord Renwick, charging back home on Caesar.

He was grinning, looking incredibly pleased with himself. As if riding in a snowstorm was a pleasurable thing.

A short while later, Mrs Ellwood appeared and said, "His lordship has asked me to bring you to the library."

The housekeeper still looked nervous and worried.

Marie herself felt the same. "I've said nothing, and I'll say nothing," she whispered. "How are the boys?"

"Won't talk at all." Mrs Ellwood made a face. "I'll keep them fed, but that might be the best I can do right now." Grasping the back of Marie's chair, she steered her out of the room.

In the library, Mrs Ellwood made a quick bob and dashed out of the room as if her feet were on fire.

"I went to Carlisle," Renwick said, a smile fixed in place.

"Oh?" Marie said, wondering what errand could have taken him so far. "That's a long way, in the storm no less."

"The storm only came on late, and Caesar knows the way home. He's a strong horse and knows the hills. I bought you some new glasses," he said.

Speechless with gratitude and confusion, she stared at him. "You did?" How incredibly generous of him!

"Well, yes, but..." he started and stopped a little, "I didn't know what sort, so I bought several pairs and I hope one of them might help a little."

A great sob of appreciation burst out of her, and she buried her face in her hands again. Would she never stop crying? Guilt was dragging her into an abyss of shame and Renwick was being so incredibly gallant.

"Have I done the wrong thing?" he asked. "Only, I saw how desolate you were because you can't read without them. I wanted to see you happy again."

Could he be any more wonderful? Did he have any idea how badly she'd betrayed him within a day of him baring his soul to her?

"Try them on," he urged, holding out a pair.

She did, but her tears fogged them immediately. He held out a handkerchief and she dabbed at her face and tried again. Oh dear, these glasses made the room swim about. She put them down.

The next pair were good, and she could see more detail in his face. She picked up a nearby book and could make out the text if she held it out. These might work if the others were no good.

The third pair were perfect, perhaps even a little better than the broken pair had been, and she wanted to cry again at the incredible gesture. His face shone happily in front of her, in handsome detail. Seeing his kind face only made her feel more guilty. Should she confess now and get it over with? But it would break his spirit and ruin this most perfect moment.

"These are perfect," she managed to choke out, somehow, and his beam of happiness made fresh tears flow down her cheeks.

"Really, Miss Baxter," he chided gently, "I should not have ridden all that way if I had known my gift would turn you into a watering-pot!"

He had completely the wrong idea, but if he was happy, he should be allowed to enjoy it. A confession now would make him miserable too. She could only shake her head and dab at her eyes with his handkerchief.

He shook his head kindly and said that perhaps she was sickening with a cold too, she had much better rest this evening rather than sit with him.

Oh yes, those famous 'colds' doing the rounds of Alston Castle. Terribly contagious they were, she bleakly told herself.

"After all, you must be healthy by Twelfth Night, and it is nearly upon us," he said.

Now he was confusing her into the bargain. "Twelfth Night, why?"

"Ah, I forget you are not from these parts," he said with a beaming smile. "We have a great tradition of

Twelfth Night where there must be exactly twelve guests at dinner, no more and no less, and I have planned for you to be one of the twelve."

She managed a weak smile, wondering how in the world she could settle her emotional turmoil by then. "You honour me," she murmured.

"It is my pleasure to have you here. Come, Miss Baxter, let me push you back to your room and call Mrs Ellwood, you do not seem quite yourself. Did you overdo it walking up and down stairs? Is that why you're back in the chair?"

"Yes, alas, we had too much fun playing games upstairs. George and Richard were so caring, helping me down the stairs. I must have overexerted myself."

He made a slight frown and said, "Do you need ice? There is plenty just outside the door."

"I might at that," she said.

"I'll get you back to your room and call Mrs Ellwood," which he promptly did.

Mrs Ellwood arrived with Morag, who was promptly sent out to fetch a pail of snow. Mrs Ellwood fussed and clucked like a mother hen, and made great theatre of sending his lordship on his way as they had things well in hand.

The moment the earl left, Mrs Ellwood said, "Is all a'right?"

"I said nothing," Marie whispered in return.

The housekeeper replied with a quiet, "Thank you."

When Morag came back, they set to icing her ankle and the cold helped a great deal.

Mrs Ellwood produced the bottle of laudanum again and raised her eyebrow in question.

"It's so much better already. I shall abstain."

Morag was singing softly to herself, oblivious to the anxiety of her companions. Marie was almost jealous.

When they cleared off the ice, her ankle did feel much better. Mrs Ellwood and Morag helped her dress for bed and she was grateful to be left alone again.

Now she could properly wallow in her self-inflicted misery.

Over the next few days, her ankle improved some more so she approached the twins' rooms to speak with them, but neither of them would talk to her. They barely even talked to Mr Charles, who murmured in some concern that they were talking only to each other in a strange made-up tongue he called 'twin language'.

"They haven't used that since their mother passed," Mrs Ellwood muttered darkly, with a sidelong glance at Marie.

"Will they talk to you yet?" Marie asked the house-keeper when Mr Charles had left.

"No." Mrs Ellwood sank into a chair, deep concern on her face. "I don't know what to do, Miss Baxter! At least they've started eating again, which is a good sign, they had me right frightened when they wouldn't eat for the first day or so! But they've not said a word to Mr Charles, nor to Lord Renwick."

"I think," Marie said slowly, hoping desperately that

she was correct, "that they are working through it by themselves. They have each other, and it's said twins do have a strange bond. Perhaps each other is all they need."

"Lord have mercy, Miss Baxter, I do hope so." The housekeeper dabbed at the corner of her eye with her apron. "Those boys are everything to me. And I don't want to lose my place, wherever would I go, at my age?"

"You would come to me," Marie said firmly. "I shall give you my address, and if ever you have need, you shall write to me and I will pay your fare to Hertford-shire, and my sisters and I will give you a reference, and find you an excellent position with a lovely family."

Mrs Ellwood managed a smile. "Well, that's right kind of you, miss."

"It is the least I can do!" Marie insisted, knowing very well that the housekeeper would not be in such a perilous position if Marie had not pressed her for more details in the first place. "But I already told you, I will take the blame. His lordship cannot fire me, after all, since I am not in his employ. And it really is all my fault."

"I still shouldn't have said anything. But it was almost a relief to talk about it, mind, after all these years." Mrs Ellwood shook her head. "Too big a secret to keep forever, Mr Martin and me have always thought. The boys would have to know one day. Perhaps it's better now, while they're young and resilient."

Resilient or not, Marie rather thought they might never have had to know, but she did not disagree, recog-nising that Mrs Ellwood was carrying just as much guilt as Marie herself over the matter.

"Well." Mrs Ellwood clapped her hands together,

dismissing the subject. "Morag and I picked out another gown for you to wear tonight for the Twelfth Night dinner. Shall I help you into it?"

"Is it pink?"

"No, and I'll be talking to his lordship about getting every trace of that blasted colour out of this house, believe me!" Mrs Ellwood nodded emphatically. "Take all those gowns down to Carlisle and sell them, I will. Not a skerrick of pink left about the place!"

Her determined expression made Marie laugh a little, and then Mrs Elwood brought out a dress so lovely it made Marie gasp. It was a soft silvery grey, with darker grey stitching all over the skirts, and beautiful white Brussels lace at the cuffs.

"Oh, my goodness." Marie touched the lace reverently. "How beautiful!" She would wear this dress and enjoy every moment. It might be the last time she ever had the chance to wear such finery.

"Let's try it on you, miss."

The dress fit very well, much as the others had, requiring only a little tuck here and there from Mrs Ellwood's clever needle to make it perfect on Marie. She swished the skirts about her legs, hearing the rustle of the expensive silk and satin. "Thank you so much, Mrs Ellwood." Impulsively, she gave the housekeeper a hug. "You have been so very kind to me from the moment I arrived. It has been lovely to find such a good friend here."

"Ah!" Mrs Ellwood hugged her right back, her cheeks flushing. "It's been a pleasure to have you here, Miss Baxter. You've put more smiles on his lordship's face these last weeks than I've seen since he was a boy, I'll tell you true."

Marie couldn't quite believe that to be the case, but she hugged the words to herself anyway. Carefully, she made her way with only a slight limp to the great room. The Yule log was down to the last few inches now but it was still burning, a good omen for the coming year.

As she entered the room she was pleased to see the Charles family again; the elder Mr and Mrs Charles with their tall older son were there talking with Renwick. Two older ladies were seated on a chaise, and Renwick came forward to greet Marie and took her over to introduce the ladies as the Misses Tully, two sisters who lived in Alston.

"They were rather dear friends of my mother," Renwick said, smiling down at the two ladies.

"Indeed we were!" Miss Agnes Tully, the elder of the two, beamed at Marie. "And Renwick has been telling us about your bookshop, my dear! Do sit down and tell us all about it."

Charmed, and pleasantly reminded of dear Miss Yates from Hatfield, Marie accepted the offered seat between the sisters and engaged happily in conversation about books. It had the delightful effect of making her feel only marginally less guilty about the damage she'd done to George and Richard.

The younger Mr Charles appeared and was greeted with delight again by his parents and brother; Morag slipped into the room to serve drinks and stared blatantly at the elder Charles brother, Andrew, who stared with a grin right back. Watching the pair of them promised to be quite entertaining, Marie thought, and the Misses Tully were not slow to notice the young couple either.

The last four guests to make up the twelve for dinner were shortly announced, the Stamford family, who Miss Elsie Tully confided were the nearest resident gentry family. A handsome couple in their middle years, Sir Malcolm and Lady Stamford, a young man of perhaps eighteen, and a very pretty young lady of around twenty years. One glance at Miss Stamford's blonde ringlets, blue eyes and pink gown and Marie winced; she was uncomfortably reminiscent of the last countess, Marie thought.

Renwick, however, did not seem to notice the resemblance, as he bowed politely over Miss Stamford's hand.

At dinner, Marie found herself seated between the young Master Stamford, who appeared entirely speechless and applied himself only to his food, and Mr Andrew Charles, who spent the evening staring at Morag whenever the maid was in the room. The only thing that saved Marie from boredom was Miss Agnes Tully seated directly across the table, who did not adhere to convention by talking only to the people on either side of her, but addressed her conversation to the table at large.

At the head of the table, Miss Stamford and Lady Stamford sat on either side of Lord Renwick, and Marie could not keep from stealing glances in that direction, especially as Miss Stamford's loud titters of laughter rang out regularly. Renwick appeared to be enjoying the young lady's company. She was certainly enjoying his attentions, from the smiles wreathed across her pretty face.

What are you doing, Renwick? You're making the same mistake again!

At once, Marie chided herself. It was unlikely in the extreme that Miss Stamford shared any traits beyond blonde prettiness and a fondness for pink with the previous countess, and it was uncharitable of Marie to assume that she might.

But it did seem that Renwick tended to admire feminine beauty of a very specific type, one which Marie herself was far from embodying. She felt like a dull brown sparrow beside Miss Stamford, not to mention that the younger girl seemed to enjoy being the centre of attention.

And then, of course, Miss Stamford was the one to find the bean in her cake and be declared queen for the evening. Marie began to feel quite invisible. Not least because the pretty blonde had barely even deigned to acknowledge Marie at their introduction, and had not so much as glanced in her direction since. She hadn't looked in any direction except at Renwick, and he seemed perfectly happy to give her his full attention in return.

The elder Stamfords were obviously delighted at the situation, exchanging pleased glances and conspiratorial grins. It could not be more obvious that they hoped their daughter might become the next countess.

At the conclusion of the meal, instead of the sexes separating, Renwick invited everyone into the music room, where the twins were to come down to give a small reprise of their carol concert for the company. Marie took her seat at the pianoforte with a little trepidation - they had not practised in days, not since the twins overheard her conversation with Mrs Ellwood - but she need not have worried. The twins performed their parts perfectly, and both even gave her a small smile at the end.

Miss Stamford attempted to make a great fuss of the boys, but they were clearly uncomfortable with this attention from a stranger they had never met, and retreated hastily behind the pianoforte.

"Who is that lady?" George whispered anxiously to Marie.

Thank goodness George was talking to her again, even if it was like this.

"A neighbour, Miss Stamford."

"She looks like..." Richard looked to his feet and then back up, peeping sideways at Marie. "You know."

Richard was talking as well, it was a Twelfth Night miracle. "Is that a bad thing?" Marie asked gently, determined not to prejudice the boys against Miss Stamford. If she could be kind to them, and reminded them of their mother, perhaps Renwick marrying Miss Stamford would be a good thing?

"Yes," George said.

Oh dear. In a whisper Marie asked, "I beg your pardon?" She blinked and glanced about. Nobody stood close enough to overhear. "Why would that be a bad thing?"

George and Richard looked at each other and George said in a low voice, "Mama didn't care about us! She only cared about being beautiful and admired. We hardly knew her! It was always our governesses who looked after us, and then she sent us away to school when we were six, to be rid of us!"

Marie honestly did not know what to say. She looked

at the two young boys in front of her, both almost as tall as she despite their youth, and felt desperately sorry for them. A mother who did not care for them, a father who wasn't sure if he was even their father - for all their privilege and high birth, they were tragic figures.

"Come with me?" she asked quietly.

They nodded and she felt the thaw between them as if it was a physical thing. Taking their hands, she led them into the adjacent room, her bedroom-parlour. "I have some Twelfth Night gifts for you."

"But how?" Richard's eyes went quite round as she retrieved the two parcels, wrapped in brown paper she had begged from Mrs Ellwood. "You haven't been able to go to any shops!"

"I made them." She offered the parcels, and the two boys looked at each other before eagerly beginning to unwrap them.

Inside each parcel was the scarf Marie had laboured long hours over.

"These are wonderful," George said softly, looking at his scarf - blue to match his eyes - and then he dropped it on the chaise and ran to throw his arms around Marie and hug her tightly. "Thank you so much."

"You are most welcome." She hugged him back, glad that the tension between them seemed to have broken. They were friends again, and all was well with the world. Richard wrapped his rust-coloured scarf around his neck and came to join in the embrace too, grinning from ear to ear.

"We don't have anything for you," Richard said.

"You have given me wonderful gifts; your company,

sharing your home with me, and your lovely songs for our concert. I couldn't want anything more." Marie ruffled his dark hair. She hesitated. "About what you heard the other day," she began.

Instantly, both boys disengaged and backed away.

"We didn't hear anything," Richard said.

"Not a single thing," George agreed.

"But..."

Their faces turned still and remote, and they looked just like Renwick when something had annoyed him. Something told Marie she would not get another word out of them on the topic.

"Very well," she said. "I wish you both a happy Twelfth Night... and now off to bed with you."

They were all smiles again, and hugged her again before dashing off, leaving Marie wondering if they fully intended to keep the secret forever. If so, Mrs Ellwood would be safe, thank goodness... and she might retain Renwick's good opinion, at least enough that he would continue to order from the bookshop after she went home. Which was all she might expect, Marie told herself sternly as she re-entered the music room and saw Miss Stamford laughing up at Renwick, her hand on his arm.

The rest of the evening Marie spent quite miserably watching Miss Stamford monopolise Renwick's attention, alleviated only by the entertainment of seeing Mr Andrew Charles go quite boldly up to Renwick and ask his permission to court the maid Morag Campbell - while Morag was in the room!

Renwick looked highly amused and said that of course he might, at which point Morag loudly announced there'd be no need for a courtship, they'd send to the vicar to call the banns right away.

Marie had definitely been around Morag for long enough to understand most of what she was saying and giggled into her hand. Miss Stamford looked dumbfounded and confused.

"Unless ye'd care tae visit me kin o'er the border and ha' an anvil wedding, in which case there'd be no need tae wait for the banns at all?" Morag beamed at Andrew.

The Stamfords all looked scandalised and confused, but the Tully ladies seemed to pick up a fair amount more and appeared delighted to see such a whirlwind romance playing out in front of their very eyes. Mr John Charles in particular looked happy for his elder brother, silently raising his glass in congratulations.

Renwick met Marie's eyes in a moment of shared amusement, and she smiled back at him, but soon his attention was drawn back to Miss Stamford, who was declaring that as queen for the evening nothing else would please her but that they play cards, and Renwick was to be her partner.

It wasn't until everyone had made their farewells and departed, and Marie was undressing and climbing into bed, that she realised what the emotion was that had been troubling her ever since pretty, blonde Miss Stamford had walked in and made a bee-line for Renwick.

"I'm jealous," Marie whispered to herself, horrified. "Oh no. Oh no, no no..." because she had read enough novels to understand that jealousy over a man meant that one's emotions were very much involved.

I can't be in love with him. I absolutely, definitely can not!

"Methinks the lady doth protest too much," she mumbled miserably to herself.

He'll never marry the likes of me. So he kissed me twice, what of it? He's probably kissed a hundred ladies. He'll marry someone pretty and wealthy and probably from a titled family, not a bookshop owner's daughter!

Tears began to slip down Marie's cheeks, and she pulled the covers over her head.

At least her ankle didn't hurt any more, unlike her heart.

CHAPTER 17
Farewell to Alston

Marie's episode of self-loathing did not last long. Not because she gave herself a stern talking to or delivered any confessions to ease her soul, but because a letter arrived carrying far more devastating news that put her introspection into perspective.

Somebody had tried to burn down the bookshop! She read the letter again, feeling more alarmed and frightened the second time around.

"I must get home," she told Lord Renwick as she showed him the letter. They were in the library and he was sitting comfortably. Marie tried to sit but couldn't keep still. She stood up, putting the weight on her good leg, and clasped her hands. Then she tucked her skirts and sat again, the fabric itching her skin.

The urge to flee was also exacerbated by her own poor behaviour, but mostly she was deeply worried about her sisters. The distance between Cumbria and Hertfordshire had never felt so wide.

She stood up again and a twinge shot up her ankle, so she sat down again.

"I can see you're anxious," he said, as he read the letter which she handed to him.

Panic shot through her that the letter might contain a reference to him being the Earl of Demanding; she hadn't read it properly, had been too distressed to check before she handed it over. Time ticked slowly as she watched his face for signs of offence.

Thank heavens none came.

He looked up and appeared concerned more for her than the contents of the letter. "The snow is so deep it would be impossible to head off on your own. And as much as you try to hide it, your ankle is still not completely healed."

"I'm well enough to travel," she said, fidgeting and pushing her glasses up her nose.

"I daresay you are," he said, looking her up and down, "But climbing in and out of carriages and walking up stairs, even at the best inns, will undo all my good work."

She chuckled politely. "All *your* good work. I see."

"I know this news is upsetting." His face filled with concern for her, and it set warm flurries behind her ribs. "But the post coach will be far too rough. I've already decided to take the boys back to Eton myself. We can all travel in my carriage."

"That would be comfortable, I thank you," she managed. He had said something a little while ago about them all travelling together. Now he'd confirmed it, and was determined she should be with them and not leave this minute.

"Then it's decided. I plan to see my man of business in London while I'm there. We can go through Hatfield, and I do have an ulterior motive."

Those warm flurries heated through her, and her mouth turned dry.

He smiled and said, "I'd like to browse Baxter's Fine Books for myself, I've heard so many good things about it."

He was being so lovely about it, which only reminded Marie of how guilty she was for betraying him to George and Richard.

"It will be far more comfortable to travel in your coach, and I thank you for it."

"Write a letter back to Miss Louise and I'll get that off in the mail, it should arrive a few days before we do, so you can at least reassure her you are on the way."

She did just that, after reading the letter again.

Now that his lordship had reassured her of a comfortable journey, she read the letter with a slightly different frame of mind. It wasn't as alarming as she first thought, although it was deeply concerning.

All is well here in Hatfield, although someone did try to set fire to the shop. Mr Jackson thinks a returned soldier might be the cause of it, and he's going to investigate. We have one kitten left who is a proper terror and takes after Crafty in every way, save for some white on him. He will soon clear Alston and I dare say all of Cumbria of mice faster than the Pied Piper. We've taken to calling him Pie.

Marie racked her brain for a while trying to figure out who this Mr Jackson might be. She wondered if Louise might have meant Mr Johnson, who worked at the printers. But why he would investigate anything was beyond her. All the same, she quickly wrote a reply to let Louise and Bernadette know she would be returning soon in Lord Renwick's carriage and if any more books arrived in the interim they should set them aside for him to purchase before they placed the next advertisement in *The Times*.

At nuncheon, the boys were excited about Marie travelling with them in the coach, and they slipped into English instead of French to express their joy. They also slipped into some other chatter that Marie couldn't understand. That was probably the secret language Mr Charles had mentioned.

"I shall be coming too," Lord Renwick said.

"Oh Pa! That's wonderful!" they said. They left their seats and embraced him in a crushing hug.

"Oof!" Renwick said, then laughed. "Calm down, boys, Miss Baxter will still require you to speak French along the way."

Marie laughed behind her hand at that.

"C'est bien dommage," George said. *That's a real pity.*

There appeared to be some kind of unspoken understanding between her and the boys. She'd tried to talk with them again of the terrible news they'd overheard, but they hadn't wanted to. Mr Charles would be with them in the carriage as well, and she doubted they'd openly raise the issue while he was there.

Marie replied with, "Vous l'avez très bien dit." *You put it very well.*

Another pang caught her by surprise at the thought she might not see the boys again once she returned to Hatfield. She could almost feel a headache coming on in anticipation. She would miss George and Richard as if they were her own family.

She would miss everyone.

The day of departure came far too soon for Marie's liking. She should be overjoyed to be going home at last, but as she slowly folded her belongings into her portmanteau, setting aside the borrowed dresses to return, she was hard put to hold back tears.

"Let me do that for you, miss," Mrs Ellwood said behind her.

"Oh, I can pack for myself," Marie said.

She wanted to cry into that glorious dove-coloured gown she'd worn on Twelfth Night, but couldn't bear to damage it.

"It's no trouble, miss. Now why are these gowns over there? You're not thinking of leaving them behind, are you?" Mrs Ellwood put her hands on her hips and frowned at Marie.

"They were only borrowed…"

"I'll have you know that his lordship has instructed

me to dispose of her ladyship's entire wardrobe as I see fit, and I see fit that these are yours now. They are so much warmer and more suitable to travel in the winter than that thin thing you arrived in!" Mrs Ellwood gave a magnificent snort.

With such an emphatic rebuttal to her argument, Marie was perforce obliged to give in, and allowed Mrs Ellwood to help her into the rust-coloured gown, which had become her favourite, and put the rabbit-fur lined cloak about her shoulders.

"There," Mrs Ellwood said, briskly folding the other three gowns and placing them into the portmanteau. "You look lovely, Miss Baxter."

To Marie's astonishment, the housekeeper's lips trembled a little and her eyes grew bright with tears.

"We're going to miss you," Mrs Ellwood croaked.

Marie's eyes grew hot. "Oh, Mrs Ellwood!" Choked up herself, Marie threw her arms about the housekeeper and hugged her tightly. "I shall miss you too, so much. I will write regularly, and you must promise me," she glanced quickly towards the open door and lowered her voice, "should Renwick ever cast any blame on you for what the boys overheard, you must let me know at once and I will do everything I can for you."

"I will, Miss Baxter," Mrs Ellwood promised, hugging her back.

"Are you ready?" Mr Martin came to the door, coughed lightly as he saw the two women embracing. "Ah, pardon me."

"I'm ready, Mr Martin." Marie let go of Mrs Ellwood

and smiled at the butler, nodding as he came forward to pick up her bag. "I wanted to thank you, too. You have been so very kind, making my stay at Alston Castle a memory I will always treasure."

Mr Martin looked a little overcome, and stuttered something about being honoured by her regard, blushing quite profusely. As she preceded him out into the hall, Marie could have sworn she heard him say "His lordship's a bloody idiot, if you ask me," to Mrs Ellwood, but surely not; the very formal, if not downright snooty, Mr Martin would never say such a thing!

Renwick, the twins and Mr Charles were waiting for her in the hall, the carriage drawn up to the foot of the steps outside, and in just a few moments Marie found herself on the forward-facing seat with Richard on one side of her, George on the other, and Renwick and Mr Charles facing them.

"Oh look, everyone has come out to wave you off, look," Marie said to Richard and George as all the staff of Alston Castle came filing out to stand on the steps as the coachman shook up the reins and the horses leaned into the traces.

"They've never done that before," George said in surprise.

"Love you though they do, I'm fairly sure it's not you they've come to wave off, son," Renwick said, his lips curling up in amusement. "And no, it's not me either. This is a tribute to Miss Baxter."

Marie stared at him, open-mouthed, then back at the almost twenty-strong throng on the steps, waving and smiling. "Goodbye, Miss Baxter! Good luck, Miss Baxter!"

she heard them shouting distantly as the coach began to move off.

"You'd better wave," Renwick said, and she did, almost numbly, twisting around to stare out of the back window until they passed through the ruined archway and the crowd was out of sight.

"But why…" she began.

"You made more of an impression than you realise," Renwick said gently.

She truly did not know what to say, but fortunately the boys filled the gap as they began to chatter, pointing out this or that feature of the landscape they passed.

Marie was surprised that the coach turned south instead of north immediately, not turning towards Alston or Carlisle and the way she had come. George was quick to explain that while Carlisle was the closest large town, going that way when one really wanted to travel to the south actually added some twenty miles to the journey.

"A very accurate explanation," Lord Renwick praised, "now please repeat that to Miss Baxter in French."

Marie hid a smile as George gave a great exaggerated sigh, but he did a creditable job of expressing himself in French and she thanked him for the explanation.

The winter days were so short they could not make very great distances in daylight, but they changed horses twice a day and pressed on. Lord Renwick had sent ahead and pre-arranged the horses and accommodations in the best inns and hotels every night, requiring every comfort available, and though the journey south took longer than the one going north in the post-coach had, Marie enjoyed it a lot more. Though perhaps that was due to the company, she thought, smiling as Richard fell asleep against one shoulder, shortly followed by George on the other.

"What is it that you are knitting?" Lord Renwick asked after a comfortable silence had reigned for a while, Mr Charles snoozing with his head resting against the padded side of the coach.

"Oh," Marie looked down at her hands, which had been working the needles unconsciously for quite some time. "It is my own design, my lord." Setting one needle down at the end of a row, she untied her bonnet ribbon and lifted it up on one side to reveal the circular knitted pad over her ear. "I call them ear mufflers. They keep one's ears warm in winter, and have the added benefit of muting sound, just a little. Much though I am fond of your sons, constant chatter can be wearying. I find these help."

Sebastian stared in delight at the clever invention. "What an excellent notion, Miss Baxter! You should sell the pattern for knitting those. I am sure some ladies' magazine would be very pleased to have it."

"I had never thought of that! Perhaps I will." She smiled at him, then returned her attention to her knitting, the soft click of the needles barely audible over the rattle of the carriage wheels and the thunder of the horses' hooves outside.

Dark was falling as they pulled into Lincoln that evening in good time, and stopped in front of the Castle

Hotel, where Renwick always stayed when passing through the city. Tomorrow was a Sunday, and he did not travel on Sundays unless the matter was exceedingly urgent, so they would pass two nights here and travel onwards on Monday.

It had rained that afternoon and there was a puddle between where the carriage had stopped and the steps up to the hotel door, so he did not hesitate to lift Miss Baxter out of the carriage even as she made to descend, and carry her up the steps.

"There was a puddle," he apologised, as she made a funny little squeak. "I did not want you to slip and perhaps re-injure your ankle; I would not for anything return you to your home with a fresh injury!"

She did not demur, and he set her carefully on her feet again once they were inside. An obsequious hotel manager at once approached them.

"Lord Renwick? Of course, we are expecting you. And indeed, we have a maid to assist your cousin Miss Baxter…"

She had allowed him the polite fiction of claiming a familial relationship for the journey, even though she had also laughed and said she did not think her reputation to be in danger. He had still written ahead to every inn and hotel they planned to stay at to ensure they not only provided a maid, but the best and most secure room they could provide for Miss Baxter. Twice he had inspected her rooms only to require them to be switched with his own, the establishment being quite sure a peer of the realm would require the best room for himself.

They dined in a private dining room, of course, not

only to spare Miss Baxter from the stares of the common folk but also his sons - and himself. He had never cared for crowds and the noise that came with them. What use was wealth and privilege if he couldn't use it to spare himself situations which he didn't care for? Escorting Miss Baxter safely to her door afterwards, however, he invited her to the one situation in which he would willingly subject himself to a crowd.

"Would you care to attend church with us tomorrow? Lincoln Cathedral is only a short walk from here and well worth a visit."

"I would be delighted!" Her enthusiasm seemed quite genuine.

They enjoyed a lovely day of rest, attending a service at the stunning cathedral, and then walking about the city to explore a little. They admired the mediaeval Bishop's Palace in the shadow of the great cathedral, walked up to the city battlements, and even looked over some lately excavated Roman ruins.

"This is fascinating," Marie said, her face alight as she inspected an information notice which had been posted beside a part of the ruins. "Thank you so much for this, Renwick. I saw nothing of Lincoln on my way north."

"A great shame." He wished they could stay longer, spend more time exploring the towns they would pass through, especially Cambridge where they would leave Mr Charles, but he had to get the twins to Eton in time for the start of the school term.

He tried not to think about the other reason he wanted to dally and dawdle; that every mile they travelled south was another mile closer to parting from Miss Baxter.

The following morning in the carriage, she handed him something as they set off again.

"What is this?" he frowned down at the dark blue woollen bundle.

"Ear mufflers." She gestured towards her own. "I made a pair for you. Try them on."

Sebastian couldn't quite explain the emotions that came over him at that moment, as he lifted the woollen bundle up and saw the thick round pads of wool, the band that would fit over the top his head and under his chin.

He was an earl. People had been currying favour with him since he was a small boy, but he didn't think anyone had ever given him such a personal, handmade gift, for no other reason than they thought he might find it of use.

"Thank you," he said, his heart full, and he took off his hat and put on the ear mufflers, delighted to find that they fit his head perfectly. And they really did work a little to muffle sound, he quickly discovered, as George and Richard loudly admired Miss Baxter's handiwork.

"I never had the chance to give you a Twelfth Night gift," Marie said, and he froze in sudden horror.

"I did not give you one either!"

"But of course you did!" she laughed, and lifted her finger to tap on her new glasses. "And very useful they are too. I think they might be very slightly stronger than my old ones; I am definitely finding it a little easier to read fine print."

Mr Charles was hiding a smile and looking out of the window. What was the fellow smirking about, anyway? Sebastian was the one who had received a gift from Miss

Baxter, made by her own two hands. His own smile was wide enough to crack his face. He put his hat back on and settled back in his seat to enjoy the rest of the day looking at her face, the noise of the world a little softer around him.

CHAPTER 18

Homecoming

They arrived in Cambridge to deliver Mr Charles, who was in a happy disposition. He was full of thanks and praise for a comfortable journey that was also deeply entertaining. He chose not to elaborate on that, and Senastian chose not to inquire. Then he farewelled the boys and wished them all the best for the term.

He was a good man, Sebastian mused. It was dreadful to think the only way to provide him with a living was if one of his other vicars passed away. Answering the call to God was something of a brutal business, when all was said and done.

Then the tutor turned to Miss Baxter and said, "I do hope we cross paths again in the future." The cheeky fellow then looked at Sebastian with a knowing glance.

You'll keep!

With four of them in the carriage now, Richard swapped sides to sit with him, and they all had a little more room for their feet and legs.

Sebastian now sat directly opposite Miss Baxter, and

he had to force his gaze out the windows to stop from drinking the image of her in. He was making a portrait to store in his memory, but it would not do to stare. How odd that they used to share such long comfortable silences together in the library and yet now he couldn't bear being this close and not knowing what to say.

Oh dear. He tore his gaze from her face yet again and looked out of the window, determined to make a comment about the weather and the landscape, all the while finally recognising that strange feeling in his ribs and belly.

He was in love.

And he didn't have a clue about how to fit inside his own skin any more.

This was excruciatingly uncomfortable and yet so understandable.

He, Sebastian Panton, Earl of Renwick was completely besotted and hopelessly in love with Miss Marie Baxter, of Baxter's Fine Books, Hatfield.

When it happened wasn't quite evident, but it had happened. Somewhere between the first kiss and the second? When he'd caught the bedraggled waif on his doorstep?

He was done for.

So why could he not stop smiling?

He knew a way to make himself stop smiling, and that was to realise the distance to Hatfield grew closer and closer. The minutes seeming to speed by ever faster, until he had to farewell Miss Baxter.

When they reached Hatfield, their rooms were ready at the Red Lion. The grooms and porters dealt with their luggage, while the four of them walked straight into the bookshop that had brought them together.

George and Richard charged in and and yelled with delight, "Look at all these books!"

The sight of so many books warmed his heart, but what was even lovelier was seeing Marie embrace her sisters.

Their housekeeper, Mrs Poole, introduced herself while the sisters were caught in their embrace. She took his hat and gloves and put them aside for him.

The three sisters had tears in their eyes as they laughed and chatted over each other.

Eventually they pulled apart and Marie made introductions. Louise was the taller, sturdier one and Bernadette was a charming, younger copy of Marie, without glasses. There was a young girl named Ruth, a shop assistant, and a boy who Marie introduced as her cousin Brutus, who looked to be very close in age to George and Richard. The three boys took to each other immediately, Brutus leading George and Richard off to explore the shop.

He was tempted to follow the children to see what they got up to, but he really wasn't invested in eavesdropping on children right now, not when the Baxters had promised they'd set aside so many marvellous books. "And where would I find the other books you asked your sisters to set aside for me, Miss Baxter?" he asked Marie.

They were in a locked cupboard beneath the counter, and Marie soon had them out for him. He nearly salivated at the sight of the books they had waiting for him, except it would damage them to drool. There were first editions here and atlases of the known world and hand-illustrated manuscripts from a French monastery which were literally unique. His heart warmed at the sight of them; he needed them like a dragon needed to hoard treasure. He could have sat there all afternoon looking at them, but he didn't have the time. Instead he contented himself with a quick examination to check that each book was indeed what he thought, before going on to the next. Marie stood beside him, making a list of the books in an account ledger and keeping a running total of his expenditure. Her two sisters had moved a short distance away, but he was aware that they were watching him.

He was sure he heard one of Marie's sisters make a comment that included the word "demanding" and then something else about, "but he's nice!"

He tried not to listen, but couldn't help it. He was fairly sure they were talking about him. Marie seemed to be trying to ignore her sisters, and he was glad to have her attention for the small time remaining to them.

He soon had his leather-bound treasures in a pile, but he could not bring himself to leave the shop just yet, or Marie's company. He simply had to browse the shelves and see what else might be in here.

He stacked up some more books he wanted to purchase. There was plenty of room in the carriage for more books with only three of them continuing on to Eton now.

George and Richard had found some books they wanted too, and it was quite a pile when Sebastian reluctantly stopped and asked Marie to total everything up.

"I'll package them up for you to collect them in the

morning before you leave," Marie promised, and he nodded, glad of the excuse to see her again.

Reaching for his hat, he was startled to find it oddly heavy, and then a young black-and-white cat popped up out of it with a miaow!

Miss Louise introduced the cat as the Pied Piper, or Pie for short, the kitten they had been keeping for him. A sturdy little fellow, the boys took to him at once, and Sebastian could not resist their hopeful faces.

"Would you keep him for me, for a week or two? I shall come back this way once I've finished my business in London," he said to Marie, trying not to feel too elated over the opportunity to see her one more time. He'd been feeling miserable at the thought of not seeing her again, but of course he could call back this way on the journey north.

"I certainly will! He is yours. I am sure he'll have a wonderful life hunting down all the mice in Alston Castle for you."

"Mrs Ellwood will like him, I think." They shared a smile, and he could have gazed into her eyes forever.

The bell jangled, and he looked around to see a large fellow step into the shop, a smile coming to his face as Miss Louise greeted him. Sebastian's mouth dropped open in surprise; he recognised the man, though it wasn't someone he'd ever have expected to see here. It was Jackson, who he'd known during his days in London, working with the War Office. He couldn't imagine what an army investigator was doing in a small town like Hatfield. And another thing, he wasn't sure if he should publicly acknowledge that they knew each other, on the off chance the man might still be working on something. A polite greeting later, and Sebastian knew at least one thing Jackson was doing; he was courting Miss Louise. The man could hardly take his eyes off the tallest Baxter sister.

Sebastian knew just how he felt, except his fascination was with the sister in glasses, just then cuddling Pie the kitten and chastising him for leaving a messy pile of mouse entrails on the floor.

"I'm hungry, Pa," George said, tugging at his hand, and Richard declared his agreement.

Much though he wanted to linger in Marie's presence, his sons needed to be fed, and put to bed. He bade a reluctant good night to the Baxter sisters and led the twins out of the bookshop.

They stayed the night at The Red Lion and a hazel-eyed lady wearing ear mufflers filled his dreams. He was aching to see her in the morning, but also wanted to get away as soon as possible to avoid having to say goodbye. He really didn't want to. Then he remembered this farewell wouldn't be for long, and that made his breakfast sit better in him.

He would return this way, along the Great North Road from London, take the cat and any more books he might like, and suddenly his day seemed brighter.

Metaphorically, of course, it was raining miserably.

The bookshop was already open when they brought

the carriage around. How convenient of them to be located so close to the inn.

They walked in to say their farewells, the boys pushing ahead to find Brutus and wish him the best. Then they smothered Miss Baxter in hugs and gave variations of, "We will miss you, Miss Baxter!" and "You're terrific!"

Her face crumpled with grief as she hugged them farewell. "I have one more gift for you, to take to Eton," she said, reaching for a piece of paper behind the counter. "I made this for you."

Sebastian swallowed past the lump in his throat as he recognised the subject matter. It was Alston Castle, from the view of the restored side.

"Oh wow!" George said, "Now we'll be able to see home all the time."

Unshed tears sparkled in Miss Baxter's eyes, his own vision blurred too.

"You must have stood out in the snow to draw this," Richard said. "You had this the whole time?"

Miss Baxter smiled and said, "I drew it last night," as she knuckled away tears from her cheek. "I did it from memory, but I cheated a little and put the snowman up on the hill behind the castle."

"That is incredible," Sebastian said, his voice husky.

Her lips trembled at the compliment. Then she reached for two books and handed them to the boys. "And please take these too," she said, "Your French has come along so well, I thought you might like some stories from France." The boys looked at the bound copies and winced a little. They were *Paul et Virginie* by Jacques-

Henri Bernardin de Saint-Pierre and *Les Rêveries du promeneur solitaire* by Jean-Jacques Rousseau.

"It's not homework, but I thought reading these adventures might be a good way to keep your French continuing."

They made a quick face to each other that Sebastian recognised as a secret twin thing, then they threw themselves on Miss Baxter again.

"Oh boys, I shall miss you," she said, sniffling away.

"Can we write to you?" George asked hopefully. "In English?"

"Of course you can, as often as you like," she said.

Sebastian wanted to ask if she would write to him as well, but recognised it would be inappropriate... until he realised he could ask her to tell him about new books being delivered that he might be interested in.

"Of course, my lord. As soon as the next crate comes from my father," she promised when he made the request.

Then Louise handed him a large, well-wrapped parcel, his purchases from the previous day, and a smaller parcel which was the books the boys had chosen.

With a sudden pang, he realised he had no more excuses to stay.

Marie came out to wave them off. The boys waved madly through the coach's windows until she was entirely out of sight, at which point they both began to cry.

Sebastian put an arm around each of his sons and hugged them tight. There really was nothing he could say to comfort them when he felt like crying himself.

Misery had Marie well and truly in its grip. She made her way downstairs the next morning and checked the hessian at the bottom of the staircase. It looked new and un-shredded. No need to replace it. The floors were free of entrails as well. A sigh of gratitude escaped that she didn't have to do that particularly messy job. It had been one of Estelle's tasks that had fallen to her after their eldest sister had married, but Bernadette or Louise must have done it today.

She moved behind the counter to check the ledgers, sure they might need correcting after her long absence. To her surprise, they were up to date and correct. She didn't recognise the writing; it certainly wasn't Louise's hand. Perhaps she'd hired someone to do them in her place?

Mrs Poole and Bernadette had already been down ahead of her and were lighting the last lamp and the fire, secured behind the protective folding shield. When they were finished, Louise checked to make sure they were secure and safe anyway. Then she checked the front of the store to make sure the fire insurance shingle was secure. It was firmly in place.

Despite missing her family and needing to come home, Marie couldn't help thinking there was nothing for her to do here any more.

Thanks to Felix marrying Estelle, they had far more manageable debts and they also had Rosie to help upstairs. Not forgetting Ruth and Brutus, who arrived at that moment with cheery smiles. They kept the shelves neat and clean, Ruth was learning to serve customers and take money, and Brutus loved assisting Louise with glue-making and book repairs.

If Marie's ankle still ached, she'd have a ready excuse for her misery, but even that had healed quickly.

Over the course of the day, Louise and Bernadette told her to get lots of rest after her travels, they had everything under control.

That was the problem; Marie needed to be useful but her sisters didn't seem to need her.

She almost wished she could fall down the stairs and injure herself again, so she could have a right proper tantrum about the unfairness of the world.

It wasn't her ankle that ached at all, but her heart.

She hadn't slept for thinking about Sebastian. And the boys too. But mostly Sebastian. Louise and Bernadette kept giving her gentle looks of sympathy. Instead of making her feel better, she only became angry that they were showering her in pity. She didn't want pity, she needed to feel wanted. Instead, they kept sending her back to her room to rest.

Knitting helped her pass the time, but soon her thoughts strayed to Sebastian and how much he had admired her ear mufflers.

Dear heavens, she was thinking of him as Sebastian and not the Earl of Renwick. That phrase Mrs Ellwood had used, about reaching farther than your sleeves would allow, hit her hard. She surely was reaching too far to think an Earl would consider marriage to a shopkeeper.

Waking with a headache the next morning, Marie forced down some tea and toast and headed downstairs into the shop.

"Oh!" Her heart bashed against her ribs at the sight of Mr Jackson and Louise kissing.

They pulled apart at their discovery.

Shaun cleared his throat and muttered something about getting back to the accounts.

Louise laughed and said, "Far better it be Marie than cousin Joshua."

Shaun said nothing, but his shoulders shook in silent laughter.

Marie huffed and headed upstairs, her vision blurring with tears.

She made it to the table where Mrs Poole offered her a currant bun and fresh tea. She couldn't eat a thing, and her stomach was almost sloshing from the amount of tea she'd had, courtesy of Mrs Poole constantly refilling her cup.

Her unshed tears spilled over and she knuckled them away.

Louise reached the kitchen, slightly puffed. A moment later, her sister's arms were around her in a tight embrace.

Mrs Poole fussed over her and said she needed to eat something. "You've hardly touched your currant bun."

Louise said, "Oh Marie, I'm so sorry you walked in on me and Shaun kissing..."

"Wait, you were kissing Mr Jackson?" Mrs Poole said, startled, but Louise waved her off.

Marie shook her head, gulping back sobs. "It's not that, Lou, it's... oh, I love him, and... and..."

The end of her sentence drowned in a sea of sobs and tears.

"And he's coming back," Louise said. "In a few days, to collect Pie, you'll see him again."

Marie cried some more and pushed the currant bun and the tea away. "I love him but it's impossible. He's an *earl* for goodness' sake!"

Louise hugged her again. Bernadette arrived home and she and Louise tried to catch her up on all the events that had happened in her absence, most of which seemed to revolve around Mr Jackson, who had apparently been helping Louise with the accounts in addition to kissing her. And there was an arsonist causing plenty of trouble in the town, but they told her that was well in hand.

"I do wish you happy," Marie said to Louise, as her vision blurred again with fresh tears, "I'm so sorry I spoiled what was otherwise a sweet moment. I didn't mean to. I will get over my misery soon. I hope."

"Take as long as you need," Louise said, her eyes filled with sympathy.

Marie wiped her face with a handkerchief and said, "So, you and Mr Jackson?"

Louise grinned back at her, trying to rein in her happiness and failing miserably. Her smile was too broad. "Yes, but we're keeping things quiet until he captures the arsonist."

"At the rate I'm crying, we can put the next fire out with my tears," Marie said, trying to make light of it and failing miserably.

CHAPTER 19

The Sword Falls

The carriage ride to Eton should have been filled with happiness and chatter, but the boys were mopey and sombre. Sebastian was finding it hard to hold on to any happiness himself, despite the snowy landscape that usually dusted everything in quiet magic.

He knew the reason for all their misery, of course. Marie. She'd brought music and laughter into their cold castle, and had softened his stony heart. The glimmer of hope was that he'd visit the bookshop once more on his way home. Firstly to fetch the kitten that was almost a grown cat, and get more books if they'd arrived. He'd started counting down the hours until he could see Marie again.

About an hour out from Eton, George and Richard nudged each other back and forth a few times. Then George asked, "Father, is it true about our mother and grandfather?"

His body froze with horror and shock. Questions

CATHERINE BILSON & EBONY OATEN

raced through his mind and tumbled over themselves, but none could get out.

"That they... that grandfather might be our father, really?" Richard added when Sebastian couldn't speak. As if he hadn't understood the question.

Breathing became difficult the longer the boys looked at him. How could they possibly know? Who could have told them? A croaky, "Yes," fell out of his mouth, and he wished with all his might he could have thought of a clever lie to protect them from that awful truth.

The boys' eyes grew round as he confirmed their question.

"I am so sorry," he said, not really knowing why he was apologising. "You are both my darling boys and I will always love you."

Richard's chin wobbled, as he asked in a quivering little voice, "Does that mean you're not really our father?"

Nausea roiling in his stomach, Sebastian wanted to cast up his accounts. "Who told you?"

They both clamped their mouths shut.

"You're not in trouble," he said, "I promise you're not. And neither is the person who told you."

"Nobody told us," George said. "We overheard. We... we don't know who was doing the talking, we didn't see them."

It could be the truth, but they were most likely protecting the staff member who'd spoken too freely. He knew the sound of everyone's voices who lived at Alston, and they would as well.

"Was it a man's voice or a woman's?" he asked. They remained mute and refused even to look at him.

"Nobody's in trouble," he said again, but as he said that, he started to wonder if it had been Marie who'd misspoken. She'd come close to the truth when she'd questioned why he treated George differently to Richard. She had a hard time keeping secrets, blurting out the details of the Christmas Concert, which he wasn't supposed to know about. That was hardly a hanging offence, he'd been eavesdropping as well.

The more he thought of it, the more he concluded it could only be Marie. Everyone else in his employ who knew, had said nothing. Yet now the boys knew, and the only difference was that Marie had been in the castle with them.

Richard said something else, and Sebastian caught the tail end of it as his thumping pulse calmed a little. "They would hold hands at the breakfast table and not keep a respectable distance in the library."

Then George delivered the cutting blow, "And they shared a bedroom."

Pain lanced his soul.

"We didn't mean to overhear," they chorused, tears filling their eyes.

"George, Richard," he said his eldest son's name without hesitation. Normally he'd be happy that he'd been able to do so, but there was no time to congratulate himself. "You're both my darling boys. You'll always be my darling boys, no matter what."

The boys leapt into his arms for an embrace full of tears and confessions.

"We didn't want to say anything," George said. "We knew you'd be upset."

"But we had to know," Richard said.

A child in each arm, he hugged and reassured them that everything would be all right, but he had to be honest, now that they had asked. "The truth is, I really don't know who sired you, and there's no way we can ever know for sure."

"My name makes it obvious," George said. "Mother didn't name me after you, she named me after herself and Grandfather. That's why you made up so many alternatives."

Dear God, the boy had noticed. "I haven't been fair to you, and that stops now, George Francis. It doesn't matter. I promise, it doesn't matter. You are my heir, you are both my sons because I choose you, do you understand me? *I choose you.*"

Both boys were crying and clinging to him, telling him that they loved him and calling him Father. And perhaps for the first time, he realised that it really didn't matter who had sired them, or what sort of a woman their mother had been. Because he *was* their father.

George and Richard were *his*, and woe betide anyone who ever dared to think of hurting them.

They reached Eton and parted with loving embraces and promises to write to each other. It was hard to see them go, but the moment he was alone in the carriage he gave full vent to his steaming anger at Marie. The beautiful woman who'd bewitched him, but could not keep her mouth shut. Whether she was aware of it or not, her loose tongue had harmed his boys.

He could never forgive her for it.

His foul mood lasted all the way to London, where he

steamed and fumed his way through several days of business transactions. For a time he wondered whether he could by-pass Hatfield entirely, but they might have more books. He could never have enough books.

And they had a cat that would solve the rodent situation at Alston.

So, while he was there, he'd deliver a piece of his mind to Miss Marie Baxter!

It had been seven days since Sebastian had left to take the boys to Eton, and Marie could not bring herself to care in the least about the bookshop any more. She sat listlessly behind the counter now, because someone had to mind the shop and really, it was her turn. Her sisters had held the fort for weeks while Marie was gone. Bernadette was off delivering herbs to someone now, Brutus gone with her to carry a heavy basket. Louise had gone for a walk with her Mr Jackson, and Mrs Poole had gone to visit with a friend. The only person in the shop apart from Marie was Ruth, and Ruth was quieter than a mouse, slipping about like a pale little ghost dusting shelves and petting Crafty and Pie.

Marie dully turned a page in the ledger. Ostensibly she was checking the figures, but she hadn't found an error in twenty pages - Mr Jackson was very good at mathematics, it seemed. Her thoughts drifted as she watched Pie stalk across the bookshop floor.

Would Renwick even come back for Pie? She was beginning to think he might not. Hatfield was out of his way, really, to go back to Carlisle, and he'd taken all the books he'd wanted with him.

And even if he does come back to collect Pie, what difference does it make? He's not coming back to collect me.

He might have kissed her - twice! - but he had made it clear that nothing could possibly happen between them. Indeed, he'd paid more attention to the pretty blonde Miss Stamford in a single night than he'd paid to Marie in almost six weeks.

He's not in love with me, and I have to accept that. Oh, but how the truth hurt! Her heart ached with it.

The bell tinkled, and Marie sighed and looked up, preparing to paste on a smile and try to be polite to customers. The smile which dawned on her face was very real, though, because it was Sebastian who strode into the shop.

"You're back!" She jumped to her feet, fighting the impulse to run around the counter and throw herself into his arms. Her smile slipped a little though as she took in his expression; his eyes were dark, his mouth set in a hard line. "Why, Lord Renwick, you look like a thundercloud," she said, trying to keep her tone light even as her stomach sank. "Did your carriage crack an axle on the way here?"

"Can we talk?" Sebastian flicked a glance at Ruth, who had frozen mid-pet of Crafty just beyond the counter. "Privately?"

Marie gulped, fearing what had happened. The boys must have said something. There was no other possible reason why Renwick would be looking at her as though he wanted to wring her neck. "Ruth, would you mind the counter until Louise gets back, please?" she asked, trying to keep her voice steady.

"Yes, Miss Marie," Ruth whispered, slipping past her to take her place on the stool.

"Come upstairs." Though she would rather do almost anything else, it was time to accept the consequences of her own actions. "Everyone else is out."

Renwick followed her up the stairs without speaking, though the heavy thud of his boots was a drumbeat hammering home the death of all Marie's hopes. Perhaps she'd been harbouring a tiny wish that he might come back and tell her how much he missed her, that he couldn't live without her; she recognised now how fanciful that was; how foolish she'd been.

He's going to rage at me - quite deservedly - and then he's going to leave and I'll never see him again.

"Please, take a seat," she said, gesturing to the table. "Can I offer you some tea?"

"No, thank you." He looked at the table, pulled out a chair, but then shook his head and paced over to the window.

Marie sat down. She had the feeling her knees were likely to give way at some point during this interrogation, and she had best be sitting when it happened.

"I couldn't believe it at first," Sebastian said, stopping his pacing and turning to face her. "And I still don't understand why you would do such a thing."

She hesitated, because he still hadn't specified exactly what he was talking about. Mrs Ellwood was still at risk if Marie said the wrong thing. "To what exactly are you referring, my lord?" she asked, trying to appear composed.

"Telling the boys about their mother!" he barked, a flush of fury rising up his cheeks. "I told you about Francesca in confidence; I never believed you would betray me so!"

She couldn't say that she had never told the boys anything. Thinking quickly, she said "I am so sorry, my lord, I know you never meant for them to know. I hope they are all right..."

"Of course they're not all right!" he shouted, and Marie gulped. Sebastian slammed his fists down on the table, leaning over her. "Just tell me why?" he asked, seeming almost despairing. "Why would you do that to them?"

I didn't! she wanted to scream. Instead she bit down hard on her lower lip and stared at him, shaking her head slowly, willing the tears burning hot at the back of her eyes not to fall.

Staring into tear-filled hazel eyes, waiting for Marie to explain herself, Sebastian had a sudden moment of clarity. It was the picture on the wall that brought him around. A picture of Alston Castle that she had probably drawn from memory, like the one she'd given to George and Richard. What if he was wrong? What if she had not told the boys about their mother? She adored them, she'd made them scarves and drawn them a similar image of

their home that they could look at when they were homesick at Eton.

Marie betraying the boys was so out of character for
her as to be entirely impossible. And suddenly, he
recalled what the boys had really said.

"They would hold hands at the breakfast table and not keep
a respectable distance in the library. They shared a bedroom."

He had never told Marie that. He hadn't even known
that himself; he had never wanted to know any of the
details of what his father and Francesca had been doing.

"You didn't tell them, did you?" he said slowly, and it
wasn't really a question. "I'm so dreadfully sorry I
accused you - I jumped to conclusions."

She shook her head again, something coming into her
expression that looked very much like fear. "No, my lord,
they did hear me. I didn't intend it, but…"

"You didn't realise they could hear you, was that it?
You were talking with someone… with… Mrs Ellwood?"
It was the only logical conclusion.

Marie turned quite pale, and Sebastian realised with a
sudden surge of affection for her that she had been trying
to protect his housekeeper.

Taking the seat he had declined before, Sebastian reached
for her hands, finding them to be cold and trembling. Gently,
he chafed her fingers between his own, trying to warm them.

"It's all right," he said softly. "You don't need to
protect Mrs Ellwood, I promise, she is in no danger at all.
I owe her far too much for that."

"You do?" Marie gulped, obviously trying not to cry.

His heart clenched at the pain he'd subjected her to; he

was a bullying brute to have barked at her in such a way. "Indeed. She and Mr Martin were the only two people who tried to dissuade me from marrying Francesca - of course, they worked for my father and did not dare tell me the whole truth, but they both hinted as strongly as they dared that perhaps I was marrying too young. That I should meet other young ladies, live my life a little before I settled down. After... everything, Mrs Ellwood came to me and told me she deeply regretted not telling me more." He shrugged. "I might not have believed her if she had. It would have sounded utterly preposterous - and at the time I assured her she'd done all she could. I would probably have become angry with Mrs Ellwood instead of Francesca and my father, I would have accused her of being jealous that Francesca would be pushing her out of her position, maybe had her dismissed. If she *had* told me and if I'd then gone to my father, for certain she would have been turned off without a reference."

Marie nodded in understanding. So many awful mistakes made so long ago, yet the ripples were still being felt today. Her breathing had steadied, and the colour was slowly returning to her cheeks.

"I would forgive Mrs Ellwood anything except perhaps murder." Sebastian grinned, trying to inject some lightness into the conversation. "And even then, I'd back her if she convinced me the victim deserved it. She is family to me."

"I shouldn't have pressed her," Marie said, her voice still thin and strained. "But I... I just wanted to under-stand you better. It was so shocking, what you'd told me, I could barely believe it was real, but Mrs Ellwood had dropped some hints that the previous countess wasn't well liked, so I pressed her to tell me more. I had no idea the boys were anywhere near my room and… they overheard us."

He nodded, understanding now exactly what had happened.

"I'm so very sorry, my lord," Marie said, her head drooping. "I would never have hurt George and Richard intentionally, please believe me. I tried to talk to them about it but they wouldn't talk to me, nor to Mrs Ellwood. I've hurt them so badly."

"We had a difficult conversation before we reached Eton," he said honestly, "but they are resilient. Perhaps Francesca did them one favour in sending them to school so young; they had to learn to rely on themselves, and they do at least have each other. I reassured them in the strongest possible terms that no matter what anyone might suspect about their parentage, in the eyes of the law they are my sons."

"And that is what you told them?" Her hazel eyes opened wide.

"It's certainly not all I said," he hastened to add. "I also assured them that they are my sons in my eyes and my heart, and nothing will ever change that. We parted on good terms, I promise you… perhaps in a better understanding of each other than we have ever previously had, and for that I have you to thank."

"Me!"

"Not for letting them find out the truth, because I will always regret not telling them earlier, and finding a way to deliver the news kindly. But you have helped open my eyes. I hadn't been fair to either of them, but especially George, and until you called me out on it, I had not noticed. Or was being willfully blind, I know not which."

"Thank you for understanding," Marie said, using her sleeve to dry her face. "I did rather make a mess of things. You were right to be upset, but Mrs Ellwood was so kind to me, I should never have put her in that situation."

"I'm the one who should be begging your forgiveness." His heart sank at the misery he'd cast her into, all because he hadn't thought the situation through properly. "I apologise most sincerely for barking at you like that. I wasted a perfectly good journey from London to Hatfield fuming all the way. Completely missed the pretty countryside."

"In that case," Marie said with a hiccup. "Sounds like you've already suffered a terrible punishment. I do forgive you. I hope you can forgive me."

"Absolutely." He reached for her hands and clasped both in his. "Goodness, look at us. Don't we make a fine pair of fools?"

"We do," she said.

Mrs Poole arrived back in the kitchen and they slowly broke apart. The woman had the grace to say nothing at all about their tearstained appearances.

Best they get back downstairs to the bookshop, where the dim light would provide more cover for their emotions.

CHAPTER 20
Lord Ferndale Interferes

O n reaching the ground floor of the bookshop, Marie was delighted to see Ruth assisting Lord Ferndale, who'd come in to peruse their latest titles. The girl was such a shy little wisp of a thing, but she came alive when she was helping people discuss books.

Marie stayed close to the counter and out of the way, as Sebastian approached Ruth and Ferndale, looking at the book Ruth was showing the elderly baron.

Sebastian was giving her space and time to recover from her bruised emotions. She loved him for that. She cared so much for him, even though deep down she was well aware an earl marrying a shopkeeper could never happen. He could never be hers, but she'd handed her heart over willingly anyway. Sitting behind the counter, she feasted her gaze on his dear face, trying to keep her composure. Soon, he'd be gone, and she thought it highly unlikely they would ever meet again. Her heart was breaking at the knowledge.

For the next ten or so minutes, the men became deeply

animated about books, especially rare books from the continent.

Ruth let them be and made her way to the counter so she could enter the titles of the books sold - when they eventually got to that part of the transaction. Louise came back into the shop with a stack of new folios from the printer to bind and set them down on the edge of the counter.

The tone of the men's conversation developed a sharpness, as the two began to argue about which of them had the right to buy a book they both wanted.

It was time to break them up, as gently as possible, before this turned to acrimony. She patted her face to make sure the tears were all gone. Her skin felt cool again, so she hoped she was no longer a splotchy mess.

"Lord Ferndale, you live close by and can come into the shop any day you choose to browse the new titles. Please allow the gentleman all the way from Cumbria to buy the book. I shall order you a replacement."

Ferndale wagged his finger and smiled as he mildly corrected Marie. "I keep saying you should call me Grandfather, my dear!"

"Sorry, Grandfather." It was lovely saying that. She smiled fondly at him.

Ferndale then said, "Are you going to introduce us, perchance?"

Marie apologised for her lapse and introduced Baron Ferndale to the Earl of Renwick, then explained to Sebastian, "My eldest sister, Estelle, married Lord Ferndale's grandson, Felix Yates, and…"

"… That's why we're now family," Lord Ferndale said

jovially, "and I am delighted to have four new grand-daughters."

Marie adored that Lord Ferndale and Miss Yates had welcomed all four sisters into the fold, as if it was the most natural thing in the world to do.

"The Baxter women are truly lovely, and so very clever. Each in their own way," Lord Ferndale said, ladling on the praise. "That's why I encouraged the match between Estelle and my grandson in the first place. An excellent connection on all counts. Have you received any letters from them, Marie? They must be enjoying themselves far too much to write, for I have received only one missive."

Marie burned with embarrassment. What she did not appreciate was Lord Ferdale's obvious matchmaking attempts, following his marvellous success with Estelle and Felix. The elderly baron was looking from her to Renwick with a most alarming twinkle in his eye.

"Ah, er, I don't know," she stammered. "One might have come while I was away. I'll ask Louise." She looked about for reinforcements, but Louise had disappeared again. She had to break these two up or she might perish in agonised embarrassment. Lord Ferndale might have been able to convince his own grandson to see Estelle as a suitable match, but Renwick was an earl and under no obligation to appease anyone, much less an eccentric old man he'd just met in a bookshop.

"If you'll come with me, my lord," she said to Renwick, indicating they should walk to the counter with his book, "I'll make sure Louise wraps this with as much care as your last order." She was babbling now, but she had to get him away from their self-appointed family match-maker.

Louise reappeared, and nodded as Marie handed her the book. "A good choice, Lord Renwick. I'll just get some oilcloth to wrap it."

"I thank you," he said, following Louise around to the side of the counter, before freezing in his tracks and looking down. Wondering what had happened, Marie was opening her mouth to ask the question when she saw the expression on his face turn to disgust.

" 'Pon rep! I appear to have stepped in something."

"Oh no. Pie!" Marie cried out in horror. "You little wretch!"

Ruth left the back of the counter to assist Lord Ferndale in his perusals, while Louise and Marie cleaned up the entrails.

"Oh yes, I was taking the cat home too," Renwick said. "I suppose I'll have to keep the windows closed in the carriage so he doesn't scarper off on the way."

Louise said, "We bought a basket for him to travel, so he'll be safe and sound."

"Excellent." He sat on the stool when Marie brought it around from the counter and lifted his boot, so Marie could use a rag to clean the last remnants of entrails off the sole.

Her face was burning with embarrassment. "I'm so sorry about this, my lord…"

"I've stepped in worse, Miss Baxter." His smile was kind, his eyes bright with genuine amusement.

There is the sweet, kind man I grew to know and love in Cumbria. Her heart ached as she put the rag in the ashpan.

Louise had gone back upstairs to fetch the basket for Pie, and Ruth and Lord Ferndale were somewhere deep within the shelves, their voices drifting distantly. Marie knew her conversation with Renwick would not be overheard.

"My lord, as you suggested, I'd be happy to send you a list of new books we receive ahead of placing our regular advertisement in The Times."

Was that too fast? Any time he needed, she'd happily pack a trunk of books and travel to Alston with them.

"That would be most convenient, I do appreciate it. And, of course, you needn't travel all that way, you can post them to me."

He was smiling as he said it, but a chill settled in Marie's heart. He was dismissing her.

Louise came back out with the basket, lined with old cotton rags, with the half-grown cat safely contained within. "There's some bowls here, and a little cut up chicken he might eat on the journey," she said, handing Renwick a cloth bag. "You'll need to provide a box of earth, of course, and his dinner…"

"I'm sure we can find a fish head or two at the inns we'll stop at, eh, Pie?" Renwick accepted the bag and basket, and his most recent purchase closely wrapped in oilcloth to protect the book. "Thank you, Miss Louise." He made her a polite little bow. "Miss Baxter…" He tilted his head towards the door, and Marie followed him out, heartsick. She watched as he placed the cat and his package inside the coach, drawn up waiting outside, before turning back to her.

"It has been an honour and a privilege to get to know

you, Marie Baxter," he said, his tone soft, and he picked up her hand and bowed over it, brushing the lightest kiss over the backs of her knuckles. "Thank you for... well, for everything."

She was trying very hard to hold back tears. "Everything?" she said in a stiff little voice quite unlike her own.

"Indeed, I have so many things to thank you for! For travelling all the way to Cumbria in the dead of winter to satisfy my quite unreasonable demands for personal delivery, for your grace after being injured in the performance of that task, for your charming and entertaining company this Christmastide, for improving my sons' French beyond recognition... and most of all, for opening my eyes to the damage I was doing to my own relationship with them. Thanks do not seem like enough for all you have done for us."

She didn't know what to say. So she bobbed a silly little curtsey and mumbled "It was all a very great pleasure, my lord, and no thanks are needed."

He looked at her for a long moment, as though trying to fix her face in his memory, and then he said very softly "Goodbye, dear Marie," and turned away and climbed into his coach.

Somehow, Marie managed to stand and wave until the coach was out of sight, before stumbling blindly back inside the bookshop and collapsing in tears of utter misery.

CHAPTER 21

Alone at Alston

Sebastian had never really considered before how very long the journey to Alston was, save to be grateful for the distance it had afforded him in previous years before his wife and father had passed on. Always before when making the journey it had seemed comfortable enough; when Sebastian was absorbed in his books he did not particularly notice the passing of time.

This time, however, his extreme agitation of mind would not allow him to settle, even to read the stack of new books resting on the seat opposite him. Not even the antics of the sweet little cat Pie could keep his attention for more than a few minutes.

Pie was charming, though. Sebastian allowed him to spend most of the journey out of the basket, and Pie was quite content to sit on the seat beside Sebastian, occasionally crawling onto his lap as the hour grew late and cold.

"You're a good little creature." Sebastian scratched behind Pie's ears on the final afternoon of his journey, chuckling as the cat popped his head up and two triangular black ears blocked part of Sebastian's view of his book. "Though if you interfere with my reading, you and I shall not be such great friends. I dare say you are well trained not to behave disgracefully around books, considering where you have grown up..." he paused, his thoughts once again inevitably drawn back to the bookshop and the beautiful, fascinating woman he had farewelled.

"Have I made a mistake, Pie?" he asked the cat, who gave him no answer beyond a rumbling purr, as Pie made himself comfortable and began to knead against Sebastian's legs. Fortunately his coat and trousers were thick enough that Pie's claws did not penetrate to his skin.

With a sigh, Sebastian gave up trying to read, setting down the book, and gently stroking Pie's sleek fur, trying to find some comfort in the cat's soothing purrs.

At least Sebastian's ears were warm, courtesy of the ear mufflers Marie had given him. He stared out of the window at the grey, winter-bare landscape, and tried to ignore the fact that his eyes were leaking.

Home at Alston the next day, he felt no better. Everything in the castle reminded him of Marie; several times when he was sitting in the library reading after dinner he caught himself turning to ask her a question only to find she was not there.

In the time he'd been gone, the staff had removed all remnants of Christmastide decorations. The cold, dreary months of winter loomed ahead.

Sharpe noticed his mood, because of course he did. "Perhaps this decorative pin in your cravat might bring some cheer?"

"I don't need cheering," Sebastian snapped.

"Of course not, my lord, you're the most cheerful man in Christendom."

"You'll keep," he growled, marching out of his rooms, sans decoration.

In the breakfast room, Mrs Ellwood produced plum jam. "I know it's one of your favourites, m'lord. Thought it might bring a smile."

"Why is everyone trying to cheer me up?"

Mr Martin entered the room and said to Mrs Ellwood, "How goes our lord and master this morning?"

Mrs Ellwood chuckled and said, "No better."

"Now see here!" Sebastian pushed back in his chair, making the legs groan against the floorboards. "Why is everyone commenting on my mood?"

Mr Martin looked at Mrs Ellwood, and she sighed theatrically and accepted the responsibility of delivering bad news. "Because you're been proper miserable ever since you returned home."

Pie ran into the room and leapt onto his lap, then helped himself to the table, where he licked the butter off the knife.

Sebastian lifted him away and sat the rascal on his lap. "I am not," he insisted, but even to his own ears he sounded petulant.

"Yes you are," Mrs Ellwood said. "Quit your moping. It's all your fault."

He may have previously claimed he could forgive Mrs Ellwood any transgressions, but this morning she truly was pushing her limits. "And, what, pray tell, is my fault?"

"I'd say that's obvious," Mrs Ellwood said. "Leaving your heart behind with Miss Baxter!"

"How dare," he stood up, still holding the cat, "you speak to me like that!"

Mr Martin interjected, making a calming gesture with his hands, "Let's all take a deep breath."

Mrs Ellwood's fists landed on her hips. "Too many years ago I held my tongue when I shouldna, an' everyone ended up miserable. I'll not make that mistake agin. Miss Marie is the best thing that ever happened to Alston, and to you. And the boys adore her so. Why you didnae bring her back with you I'll never know!"

Mr Martin hesitated, and then he nodded. "She's right, my lord. We should have told you then... be damned if we won't tell you now that you're making an enormous mistake!"

His pulse thumped so hard in his ears he couldn't hear anything else. When the two of them eventually stopped giving him a piece of their minds - and they were very large pieces indeed - he did his best not to explode.

"I'll take it under advisement. I should like to finish my breakfast now."

They left him with the cat at the table, and he overheard Mr Martin asking Mrs Ellwood if they should best both make themselves scarce for the next few days as they headed back to the kitchens.

Sebastian took a bite of his toast with plum jam, but it tasted bland and stale. It took another gulp of tea to get it down his throat.

Mrs Elwood had ruined his mood, and his appetite.

At least Pie understood him, as he nuzzled into his

hand for more head and cheek scratches. Alas, it was only the cat caressing him. How he wished it was Marie.

He'd said all the right things to Marie when he left Hatfield. About how much he trusted her. He even said she could post his next delivery of books to him! A groan escaped his throat and he leaned over in pain. The clarity of his loss rang as clear as a bell. He loved Marie Baxter, but he hadn't told her.

He'd thought he'd said all the right things, but she'd said farewell.

Then it hit him, the reason Marie hadn't said anything was because she clearly was not in love with him!

How could she be, with the way he'd treated her so poorly upon his return to Hatfield. He'd been a thunder-cloud and had shouted at her upon his return. Accused her of the worst kind of betrayal. Driven her to tears.

When he'd eventually realised his error - and that she was protecting Mrs Ellwood - it had been too late.

No wonder she didn't love him; who could fall in love with someone who terrified her?

She was probably grateful to see him go.

Sebastian woke the next morning with a gripping headache and Pie sleeping on his chest. Giving Pie a cuddle, he whispered to the cat, "At least you love me."

Climbing out of bed, he nearly stepped on the dissected mouse on the carpet. "Good boy, Pie." The cat was already proving an excellent addition to the house-hold; hopefully his habits of leaving unsavoury gifts would improve, or at least become confined to a single location as Marie had assured him Crafty's were. He pointed out the location of the remains to Sharpe and left his bedroom.

Tea did not shift his headache. He needed the serenity of his sanctuary; the library. Absently browsing the shelves, not finding anything to appeal to his mood, he came across a book he hadn't thought of in years, but which became of brief interest now. The copy of Burke's Peerage would have been his late father's copy. He hadn't needed to replace it with a newer edition. Being removed from London society did have its advantages. However, it was recent enough to have the information he wanted.

He looked up Baron Ferndale and was surprised to see the gentleman only had one heir, his grandson Felix Yates. He was the one who'd married Marie's sister, Estelle, at the urging of Lord Ferndale himself, if he recalled correctly.

So, a shopkeeper's daughter was good enough for the heir to a barony!

At some point, he privately hoped not too soon as he'd rather liked the old gentleman, Felix Yates would become the new Baron Ferndale, and Marie's sister Estelle would be a Baroness.

Good for them, he smiled.

Then it hit him. Marie, as the sister of a Baroness, would suddenly be far more eligible in the eyes of society.

He really didn't like that thought at all. Jealousy made his heart constrict, at the idea of some fop from the ton taking Marie to London on his arm. She would hate that, he felt sure of it.

He put the book back on the shelf and only now noticed there was nuncheon on the table. His staff must have been incredibly quiet bringing it in, not wanting to disturb him.

He'd lost all track of time, but his stomach roiled with a pang of hunger. He needed to eat.

Gulping down the cold soup, he felt his spirits soaring as he came to a momentous decision.

It was time to face facts. He'd never cared about Marie's station in life. He barely cared for his own for that matter, which was why he'd lived so long in isolated Alston instead of bustling London.

If he married Marie and they did eventually venture to London when George and Richard were older, she'd be a countess, and her sister a baroness. Doors would open. They would walk right through. Nobody would know or care about her family's background.

They could marry as soon as they liked!

Oh dear. He'd been so unfathomably awful to her, she'd probably turn him down. Would she even agree to marry him?

Was *he* good enough for *her*?

He'd better hurry up and ask.

The library had served its purpose. It had given him time for contemplation and realisation. Contemplation to know for sure he was hopelessly in love with Marie Baxter, and realisation that he could not waste one more minute in the wilds of Cumbria.

Rushing out of the library, he went looking for Mr Martin, and found him in the kitchen.

The windows showed it was dark outside. He'd lost

all track of time. It could be four in the afternoon or eight in the evening.

"Mr Martin, ready my carriage for the morning, if you'd be so kind. I know I've only just returned, but I must get back to Hertfordshire as soon as possible."

Mrs Ellwood poked her head around the scullery door, a smug satisfaction written all over her face. "What did I tell you, Mr Martin? He's come to his senses."

Mr Martin grinned and nodded her way. "If I recall, you said 'eventually' and I thought he'd be faster than that."

"All right, you two. Yes, I've been an idiot. Take care of Pie for me," he said, suddenly wondering where the cat was.

Out of nowhere, Pie tore across the kitchen floor and darted into the pantry. Something squealed, then the cat reappeared, grey furry trophy in its mouth.

He deposited it at the feet of Mrs Ellwood. "Excellent!" She beamed, then she got him a plate of leftover sausage as a reward. "You are such a good boy. Keep this up and I'll spoil you rotten!" When she finished heaping praise on the cat, she turned back to Sebastian and asked, "If I may speak freely?"

Sebastian laughed and said, "I couldn't stop you if I tried."

That brought a round of laughter from all, including muffled noises from a nearby room. The rest of the staff must be eavesdropping. He deserved every bit of it.

"My lord, I'm delighted you've come to your senses," she said, with a warm look of encouragement. Then her voice turned stern. "But if you return to Alston without Miss Baxter, you may as well not come back at all."

He bit his lip and nodded to his housekeeper, and, he now realised, perhaps his truest friend.

"Write to him, tell him how you feel!" Louise urged. "Don't ruin your chance of happiness with this dear man like Estelle nearly did!"

Marie sniffed and sipped her tea. Mrs Poole refilled it.

Bernadette handed her a fresh handkerchief and said, "Writing will help. You didn't tell him how you were feeling. Men seem to be intelligent, but they can be as dense as an oak at times. How was he to know how you felt if you never told him?"

"But," Marie sniffed again, "what if I tell him my deepest secrets and … he … rejects me?"

"If you don't, he'll never know, and neither will you," Louise said impatiently. "If he rejects you, he's an idiot."

Mrs Poole tut-tutted in the background as she refilled the kettle and put it on the stove.

They did not let up for the next ten minutes, by which point Marie relented and promised she'd write.

It took her almost another ten minutes to think of what to say, but after a few false starts the words began to flow.

"Dear Sebastian," for that is how she thought of him now. If he blanched at her use of his Christian name, then he would most likely hate what followed and she'd rather

know how he felt now, instead of spending the rest of her life wondering.

It has come to my attention, and that of my sisters and dear Mrs Poole, that I have become gripped with abject misery since your return to Alston. Forgive my sentimentality, but I have grown so very fond of you since arriving on your doorstep. I had a very different impression of you from our earlier correspondence where I had come to think of you as the Earl of Demanding. (I hope you are smiling as you read that.) But over the weeks at Alston, you grew in my affection. So did your charming sons, George and Richard. (It's possible their sweet dispositions made me realise you were in fact a kind person after all, and you had a generous heart.)

I'm not exactly sure when it happened, but over time, I came to care deeply for you. That care has a name, and it is love.

This sentiment has most likely come as a shock to you. (A good shock, I hope.) I should have told you as soon as I knew, but it took me far too long to know myself, and now I fear I am too late. It is my dearest wish that you carry the same affections towards me and let me know at the soonest opportunity.

If you cannot find it within yourself to return my affections, or you do not feel that the gap between our respective stations in life can be bridged by love, then all that is left for me is to wish you happy. I would still like to reply to any correspondence George and Richard send me, if they remember, as I would like to keep my promise to them.

(I hope you may reconsider any plans to marry Miss Stamford, however, in light of the discomfort such a union might cause your sons; I pray you will think of their happiness as well as your own.)

Bernadette sanded the letter for her when she handed it over. "I shan't read it, it's between you and Renwick, although I have noticed some tear splotches." She folded the mostly dry letter so that Marie could write his address on a clear section on the reverse, then she sealed it.

Marie took her glasses off and rubbed the bridge of her nose. She had to sit on her hands to stop herself grabbing the letter back. "You'd better post it now before I change my mind and put it in the fire."

"I'll be right back," Bernadette said, and she darted out of the room.

Marie made her way to her own room and slumped on her bed, sickness and nerves taking hold, her tears starting to flow again. "What have I done?"

CHAPTER 22

Reunion

I t had only been a little over a week since Bernadette had mailed the letter, and as Marie walked home from church arm-in-arm with her youngest sister, she found herself wondering if Renwick had received it yet, and if so, what his reaction might be when he read it. She felt a little sick at the thought, pressing her hands to her stomach.

"Are you hungry?" Bernadette asked. "I know I am; that sermon seemed to go on forever. Reverend Millings is getting more boring by the week!"

"Keep your voice down," Mrs Poole, walking just behind them, warned.

Bernadette sighed a little impatiently and tossed her head. "I'm only saying what everyone's thinking, Mrs Poole! Even Cousin Joshua looked thoroughly bored by the end of it."

Marie was not listening, staring in disbelief at the coach just then coming into Hatfield from the north and rolling right past the Red Lion towards them. It looked so terribly familiar… but it couldn't possibly be. How could he even have received her letter so soon, never mind then travelled back to Hatfield all the way from Alston?

The coach stopped right in front of the bookshop. Her incredulous eyes traced over the crest on the door. Somehow, it was Renwick, he was really here. In fact, he was stepping out of the coach, a broad smile coming to his face as he saw her standing, staring at him.

Marie didn't think. She just ran to him as though it was the only possible reaction she might have in that moment, and he opened his arms wide to receive her.

"Renwick!" she cried, almost falling into his welcoming embrace.

"Dearest, darling Marie," he said, and kissed her, right there in the street in front of her sisters and Mrs Poole and Mr Jackson and very nearly half of Hatfield, walking home from church as they all were.

"Lord have mercy!" Mrs Poole almost shrieked it. "Inside, both of you; what a disgrace! On a Sunday!"

"You don't even like travelling on a Sunday," Marie said nonsensically as Sebastian laughed and let her go, his warm hand reaching for hers and wrapping around it.

"And lose another day in getting back to you? Certainly not," he replied.

"But how did you get my letter so fast?" She could not fathom it, unless the mail had somehow begun using winged horses.

"What letter?" he frowned, looking down at her. They were inside the bookshop now, standing by the counter, Louise going about busily lighting lamps so it was not too dark to see.

"I wrote you a letter…"

"Did you?" He reached up to gently tuck a stray curl behind her ear. "I'm sure it will get to Alston at some point and I shall be delighted to read it, but I was barely home long enough to read the mail that had arrived in my absence before I realised I had left something critically important here in Hatfield, and I had to turn around to come back and retrieve it."

"Something important?" Bemused, she blinked up at him. "A… book?"

He laughed, shaking his head. "No, my dearest, though I have no doubt with more time I'll find plenty of those here that I want too. No… I cannot live without what I left here, but it took getting home without it to realise. Can you not guess?"

She couldn't, and she stared up at him, blinking slowly.

" 'Tis my heart, Marie Baxter."

She thought she heard Bernadette give a little shriek behind her, but she couldn't look away from Sebastian's dark, dark eyes.

"I," she started, but then she couldn't think of what to say. "I… I thought you were going to marry Miss Stamford!"

That wasn't what she'd meant to say at all, but somehow they were the words that had come out.

Sebastian looked as puzzled as she'd felt a moment before, and it was quite obvious that he was struggling to even think of whom she might be referring to. "Miss… Stamford?" he said slowly. "Oh!" The light dawned. "Her! Goodness me, no. She might have attempted to catch my eye, and certainly her parents were keen to promote the match, but they were always doomed to failure. I could see no-one but you, my dearest."

It did not seem possible. "Am I in a dream?" Marie whispered. "This is too much, I can't…"

"It's not a dream, beloved." His thumb brushed tenderly along her jaw, and then he stooped to kiss her again, much more slowly and thoroughly this time.

The troubles of the world disappeared in that kiss. A kiss filled with longing, passion and love for just the two of them.

"This is the most romantic thing I've ever seen," Marie heard Louise say somewhere distantly behind her, but Marie could think of nothing but Sebastian, the heat of his mouth on hers, the tender way his hand caressed her cheek. Her knees sagged a little, and his other arm swooped around her waist to hold her securely close against him.

"I love you, Marie. Come away with me, and be my bride," Sebastian whispered, peppering gentle kisses across her face.

She might very well faint, and she *never* fainted!

She wanted nothing more than to say yes, but as he lifted his head and looked down at her, she saw the bell behind his head, recognised the familiar setting of the bookshop.

"Oh, but…" she began to say.

Louise shrieked from behind her, "ARE YOU MAD?"

"What…?" Marie turned to look at her sisters.

"Don't even think about saying you have responsibilities here! You're going to be a countess, you lunatic, say yes at once!"

Bernadette was nodding vigorously. "We'll hire more help if we need it, Marie!"

"And we have Shaun to help with the accounts," Louise said. "So there is absolutely no reason at all to refuse this lovely, lovely *earl*."

Sebastian grinned at Marie's sisters and then said to Marie, "It's still completely your choice, but your sisters do make excellent points in my favour. Plus, I love you with all my heart. Also, not that it matters, but Mrs Ellwood may not allow me to go back to Alston if I don't bring you with me."

Marie had no tears, only happiness. "You love me?"

"Completely. Besottedly," Sebastian confirmed.

Despite their audience, Marie leaned in for another kiss. It filled her with sunshine and light. When she eventually pulled away, she looked into his beautiful face and said, "I love you with all my heart, too. I would be so happy to be your bride."

Behind them, Louise and Bernadette cheered.

The door to the bookshop opened and the bell above tinkled someone's arrival. It was Sunday, so they wouldn't have any customers.

"Oh, no," Louise sighed, then said with a very loud voice. "It's Cousin Joshua, come to ruin a lovely moment."

Marie groaned aloud. Sebastian raised an eyebrow and turned, unruffled, to find Cousin Joshua glaring at him, puce with fury.

"Unhand my cousin!" he barked at Renwick.

Renwick quickly looked him up and down and said in his most languid, aristocratic drawl, "I don't believe we have been introduced."

Joshua puffed himself up and stared at Marie to make introductions.

Louise said, "He's been like this for *months*."

Stepping out of Renwick's embrace, but still holding his left hand, Marie made introductions, emphasising Sebastian's title a little more than strictly required.

The men warily shook hands.

Joshua seemed to miss the significance of his title, or perhaps disregarded it, and turned on Marie with righteous fury. "Young lady, you've disgraced yourself and the Baxter name with your behaviour, out in the street, where all of Hatfield could see. On a Sunday no less!"

Renwick spoke up, his voice calm and steady. "My good man, there is no disgrace, we are to wed. By all means call the banns and we shall marry in Hatfield in three weeks."

"You forget yourself," Joshua said to Marie, a nasty smirk coming to his face. "As your legal guardian, I do not give my permission. There will be no wedding."

Bernadette spoke up, which was unusual for her. "For goodness sake, cousin. He's an earl! Stop being so petty."

"I don't care if he is an earl, I do not give permission and that is the end of it." Joshua was only too obviously enjoying himself as he spoiled the moment. He'd tried with Estelle when he'd at first refused to walk her down the aisle, but had endured that rather than surrender the job to Baron Ferndale.

Marie looked to Sebastian, feeling her happiness slipping away. "My father is not yet returned from France. When he does, he will grant permission immediately, of that I'm sure."

"Your father could very well be dead," Joshua interfered meanly.

Sebastian tilted his head in thought. "Mr Baxter, you are a singularly unpleasant man…"

"I am the head of the Baxter family, and the magistrate of Hatfield. You do not have my permission to marry my cousin!"

Marie's stomach plummeted. She turned to Louise and Bernadette, whose faces were like thunder. Louise said, "We keep hoping he'll calm down."

"You poor things," Marie commiserated.

"Nothing I can't handle," Louise said. Then she raised her voice so that Joshua could clearly hear her, "Now, where did I put that crowbar?"

Joshua took a half step back, but Marie could see he did not plan to relent. Misery filled her. How long would she have to wait? It could be months yet before Papa returned from France!

Sebastian drew himself up to full height and looked down upon Joshua, before saying in a cold voice, "What a petty example you set for the good people of this town. I'd direct you to stick your head in a bucket, but then I'd feel sorry for the bucket." Then he turned to Marie, his expression filled with love. "There is another way. We could travel via Gretna Green and elope on our way home to Alston Castle. It is just over the border, only about fifteen miles from home."

Love warmed her heart. Marie could have floated

with happiness. He'd taken a suddenly awful situation and found a happy and terribly convenient solution. "I will gladly elope with you any day! We can leave as soon as you like."

He gently cupped her face and delivered a kiss in full view of her apoplectic cousin and cheering sisters. "My carriage awaits, my dearest."

The journey to Gretna Green was long, but they didn't mind. They changed horses frequently and even travelled on the next Sunday, because reaching their destination as soon as possible was vitally important. They arrived at Gretna tired and a little travel sore, but elated they could wed. Marie wore the rust-coloured dress with the fur lined cloak, the one Sebastian admired so much on her, and Sebastian found the blacksmith at his forge and handed over a jingling purse of coin for the man to pronounce their vows over his anvil.

From there, it was a blissful afternoon covering the last leg of the journey back south over the border to Carlisle and finally the steep incline home to Alston.

"My wish came true," Marie said suddenly, as the ruined archway appeared in the distance.

"I beg your pardon?" Sebastian turned to her, his brow furrowing.

"When I lit the candle from the Yule log." She nestled closer against him. "I wished to come back to Alston Castle someday."

"Did you indeed!" He laughed.

"But not as its mistress. I did not dare to dream."

"I loved you even then." He cupped her cheek in his hand, and leaned in for a kiss. "I should never for a moment have let you wonder as to my affections, and I promise, I never will again."

As they neared the main castle door, Marie saw the staff hurry out the front to greet them.

"Sit back for a moment, my lovely bride, this will be fun," Sebastian said, a grin coming to his face.

When the carriage came to a stop, Sebastian stepped out of the carriage and left Marie inside.

Peeking through a gap in the drapes, she saw Mrs Ellwood's hopeful face and Mr Martin, along with what appeared to be everyone else from the estate. There was Morag, holding the hand of her strapping farmer, Mr Andrew Charles.

"It's lovely to see you all," Sebastian said. "But please don't stay out, it's far too cold!"

Mrs Ellwood stepped forward and said, "Have you returned with Miss Baxter?"

Marie muffled her giggles behind her hand but remained seated.

"Mrs Ellwood, I am afraid I must inform you that Miss Baxter is not with me."

"What?" The housekeeper exploded, her face turning red. "I told you not to come back without her!"

Rewick laughed cheerfully and said, "But, Mrs Ellwood, I have instead returned with the Countess of Renwick." He opened the carriage door fully and extended his hand.

Marie took it and stepped out of the carriage into the

wintery light. The staff burst into applause, cheering and laughing at Renwick's teasing joke.

Mrs Ellwood rushed forward and wrapped Marie in a motherly embrace. "Welcome home, My Lady! Oh, I am so glad he came to his senses and went to fetch you... this is where you belong, and no mistake!"

As soon as the grooms finished cheering, they took the horses and carriage into the stables.

The staff formed a guard of honour to welcome them home, with another round of applause.

They reached the steps and Sebastian held them back a moment. "Just to be on the safe side," he said.

Marie almost fainted when he picked her up and carried her safely up the steps and across the threshold into the castle to begin their new life together, as the Earl and Countess of Renwick.

We hope you've had a wonderful time enjoying Marie's romance with Sebastian. Turn the page to read chapter 1 of book 3 in *The Bookshop Belles, Louise's Christmas Champion.*

Louise's Christmas Champion

CHAPTER 1 - LOUISE IN CHARGE

Hertfordshire, 1814
Louise In Charge

Louise Baxter, second-to-youngest but indisputably the tallest—and certainly the most capable, at least in her own opinion—of the four Baxter sisters, stood at the edge of the muddy roadway. She waved a brisk farewell as the post-coach carrying her sister Marie rattled away, its wheels kicking up dirty clumps of earth that speckled her boots and hem. The coach was bound for the north, and with each lurch and sway, it carried Marie further along the first leg of her long journey to Cumbria. Louise kept her posture erect, her shoulders squared, and her chin tilted high, determined to appear resolute until the coach disappeared entirely from sight. She owed her sister that much, at least.

Only when the coach vanished around a bend in the road did Louise allow her shoulders to slump. A sigh, long and heavy, escaped her lips as though it had been bottled up there for hours.

"What a lot of work this is going to be," she muttered, turning towards her youngest sister, Bernadette, who stood at her side. The two of them were ankle-deep in the muck of the roadway, the cold damp seeping through their sturdy boots.

"She had to go," Bernadette pointed out practically. Her tone was light, even if her expression was not. Together, they trudged back toward Baxter's Fine Books, the family business that had consumed nearly every moment of their lives since they were old enough to dust shelves and arrange displays. Before stepping inside, they paused at the bootscraper outside the Red Lion Inn next door, scraping away the worst of the mud with practiced efficiency.

"The Earl of Demanding ordered nearly a hundred and fifty pounds' worth of books," Bernadette continued, shaking her skirts free of mud droplets. "But, we had to deliver them personally."

"He thought he was writing to our father!" Louise's voice took on a sharp, frustrated edge, her words clipped as though she were biting them off before they could escape entirely. "I hope he still pays up when it's Marie who turns up on his doorstep!"

"Oh, don't be such a worrywart," Bernadette chided. "He's getting his books, isn't he? It's not as though we've shortchanged him. Marie will charm him, no doubt, and she'll be back in time for Christmas—with her pockets jingling full of coin."

Louise gave an exasperated snort. "And in the meantime, we're left to do all the work!" Her boots thudded against the floorboards as they stepped inside the shop and closed the door, shutting the cold and damp outside.

It wasn't just Marie's absence that weighed on her.

They were already one sister down, with their eldest, Estelle, having married Mr Yates and gone off to Ireland to visit his mother. Estelle wouldn't return until spring at the earliest.

Still, as Louise glanced around the bookshop, her irritation softened into something warmer. The shop felt like home, as it always had. It smelled of musty paper and old leather, a scent she thought might linger in her memory forever, underpinned with the sharp, tangy notes of fresh glue. The light filtering in through the windows was scant, most of the panes long since covered over with bookshelves crammed to bursting. Instead, the shop's many corners and nooks were illuminated by carefully shielded oil lamps hanging from beams and mounted in strategic locations. Their golden glow brought the shelves and stacks to life, casting shadows that danced across the walls.

Ruth Millings, their young assistant, was busily sweeping the floor when Louise and Bernadette entered. Her father, the fiery Reverend Silas Millings—known privately among the Baxter sisters as "Old Brimstone"— had made it abundantly clear that Ruth was to behave with the utmost propriety. Ruth had only been permitted to take the job on the condition that her wages went directly into the church's collection plate each Sunday.

"I didn't go behind the counter yet," Ruth said tentatively as Louise and Bernadette peeled off their coats. Her voice was soft, almost apologetic, and her hands tightened nervously around the broom handle.

"That's all right," Louise replied with a reassuring smile. "I'll take care of it."

She fetched the small dustpan, scraper, and rags they kept specifically for this task and stepped behind the counter. There, waiting as always, was the morning's 'gift' from Crafty, the bookshop's resident cat.

Crafty, whose full name was Wollstonecraft when she was in serious trouble, had been a vital member of the shop's operations for years. She was a skilled huntress, keeping the mice that threatened to nibble at the book paper firmly in check. However, her habit of leaving partially eviscerated 'presents' for her mistresses behind the counter was less than endearing. Recently, her son Pie —a young cat with his mother's talent for hunting but none of her discretion—had joined in the habit, doubling the number of unpleasant surprises Louise had to clean up each day.

"Ugh, Crafty," Louise muttered, wrinkling her nose as she scraped up the offending mess and took it outside to bury in the midden. "And Pie, too! Between the two of you, I'm not even sure the mice are worth it."

Once the floor behind the counter was clean, Louise washed her hands, dried them briskly on her apron, and returned to her post. This had once been Estelle's regular domain, then Marie's. Now, with both of them gone, Louise and Bernadette took turns managing the counter.

The bell above the door jingled, and Louise glanced up, expecting a customer. Instead, it was Rosie, the young maid Mr. Yates had hired for them before taking Estelle away to Ireland. Rosie helped Mrs. Poole, the house-keeper, with the cooking, cleaning, and laundry, which freed the sisters from the household chores they had previously split amongst themselves.

"Good morning, Rosie," Louise said warmly. "Mrs. Poole will be glad to see you when you go on upstairs."

Rosie bobbed a quick curtsey, her cheeks pink, before scurrying off toward the staircase. Louise's gaze lingered on her for a moment, and she felt a pang of envy. How nice it would be to escape upstairs herself, to the quiet sanctum of her bookbinding workshop! There were several projects waiting for her attention—books with cracked spines and fragile pages that needed careful rebinding. It was work she enjoyed, work that required focus and precision, and she longed to lose herself in it.

But someone had to keep an eye on the customers, and Bernadette was busy this morning, out visiting women who needed her herbal expertise. So Louise stayed put behind the counter, ready to greet the steady trickle of patrons who would inevitably wander in.

A steady flow of customers came into the shop, and then young Brutus Baxter arrived. The middle son of their cousins, he was a nice boy afflicted with a terrible name courtesy of his awful parents. He spent time in the book-shop to escape his home, where he was neglected by his parents and bullied by his dreadful older brother.

"Any books to bind today, Cousin Louise?" Brutus asked eagerly. He was showing an interest in book-bind-ing, and Louise was happy to teach him the craft.

"Indeed." Louise thought about it. There were quite a few tasks they might be able to do at the counter, espe-cially with Brutus to be an extra pair of hands. "Mind the counter for a moment. I'll go and fetch down some things."

Mrs Poole came down the stairs, bubbling over with excitement. "You'll not believe what I've just heard from Rosie, Louise!"

"I probably would not, no," Louise agreed dryly. The maid barely ever said a word in Louise's hearing but seemed to be full of Hatfield gossip for Mrs Poole.

"There's been a fire!"

"A blocked chimney or something?" Louise asked, without much interest. Fires weren't exactly uncommon in the winter; everyone needed fires for heat!

"No, deliberately lit!"

Now that *was* newsworthy. Louise gave Mrs Poole her full attention. "Where? Did they catch the culprit?"

"You know that little cottage on the St Albans road, the one just out of town, with the roof falling in?"

Louise did not, in fact, know the cottage. Bernadette was the one who went tramping all over the place visiting people with her herbs; Louise preferred to stay closer to home. But she nodded, because otherwise Mrs Poole would spend all day trying to make her think she did know it.

"Well, nobody lives there now of course, it's not fit, but some of the returned soldiers were sleeping rough there." Mrs Poole made a bit of a face.

They were very grateful to the brave soldiers who had defeated Napoleon and thwarted the looming threat of the French, of course, but there did seem to be somehow more of them hanging around Hatfield than had ever left to go off to war. Certainly more of them than were jobs for men during the winter. Louise didn't quite understand why they didn't go back to wherever it was they'd originally come from, or to towns who'd lost a lot of their men in the fighting.

"Was it one of the soldiers who set the fire?" she asked, though she wasn't sure who'd be silly enough to set fire to a building they were trying to live in.

"No! They woke up in the night to someone throwing a lamp in at them! It smashed and lit fire to the straw they were sleeping on, so they had to get out in a hurry. Lucky nobody was burned!" Mrs Poole nodded wisely.

"It seems like perhaps the culprit is someone who didn't want the soldiers here," Louise suggested. "That seems the most obvious motive."

"Listen to you, talking about culprits and motives! Have you been reading novels about murderers again?"

Louise pretended she hadn't heard the question. She did have rather a penchant for novels, the more thrilling the better, and she had a particular weakness for a novel with a good murder to solve. "I hope the returned soldiers find somewhere better to sleep," she said.

Unable to excite her to further speculation over the fire, Mrs Poole left to find someone better to gossip with, and Louise returned to work.

"What are we doing, Cousin Louise?" Brutus asked excitedly as she put down her supplies on the counter.

"Yet another set of Shakespeare folios, I'm afraid," she said. "If I never see another set, it will be too soon. Every aspiring gentleman seems to think it an essential addition to his library."

"The colour's nice," Brutus said, running gentle fingers over the green-dyed calfskin.

"Yes, and being calfskin, it's not cheap, so we need to do a good job with it, with as little waste as possible. Let's get measuring and cutting…"

"Measure twice and cut once," Brutus said in a sing-song fashion, making Louise smile.

"An excellent motto, I'm glad you've been listening to my instructions!"

They busied themselves with the work, Ruth handling the customers who came in unless they wanted something out of the ordinary or required recommendations.

Bernadette returned in the early afternoon with a basket full of food items folk had given her in trade for her herbs, so they sat down and feasted on fresh crusty bread with butter and honey.

"Would you mind very much if I went back out this afternoon instead of working the counter?" Bernadette asked hopefully, eyeing the neat piles of cut green calfskin on the desk. "I still have some people I'd like to see…"

Louise nodded. "Go on, so long as you're back by closing to help me add up the accounts. You know they make my head hurt. Brutus and I are going to start sewing the sections to the bands this afternoon."

Brutus looked quite excited that she was going to let him help with this specific task, which could be quite tricky and required accuracy. Louise smiled fondly at him as Bernadette scooped her basket up and took it back upstairs to refill.

Soon after Bernadette left again, Benjamin Baxter barged in with the air of someone who believed the world owed him deference, immediately setting his sights on Brutus.

Louise had been in the middle of clamping one of the folios behind the counter when she overheard Benjamin's jeering tone. She looked up to see Brutus shrinking back, his face pale, while Ruth stood frozen nearby, her expression caught somewhere between embarrassment and dread. With a few sharp words, Benjamin had managed to turn the air in the shop sour, his insults aimed at his brother before pivoting to Ruth with a sly tone.

Louise wasn't even entirely sure what some of the words Benjamin said next even meant—though the suggestive tone made their nature clear enough—but she knew they were entirely inappropriate. Without a second thought, she seized the broom leaning against the counter and marched toward him.

"Out," she barked, holding the broom like a soldier might hold a bayonet. "This is a bookshop, Benjamin, not a tavern—and certainly not a place for such foul language."

Benjamin's retort was cut short as Louise raised the broom an inch higher, her expression leaving no room for argument. "Would you like me to tell your father what you said to Ruth? Or should I let Reverend Millings hear it first?" she asked, her voice cold and clipped. She gave the broom a small, purposeful jab forward. "Out."

Benjamin's bravado crumbled in the face of her sternness. With a muttered curse, he backed toward the door.

"You'll regret this," he said, but his attempt at menace fell flat as Louise advanced another step.

"I sincerely doubt that," she replied.

As the door swung shut behind him, Louise gave it an

extra push for good measure. "And stay out!" she called after him, before turning back to Ruth and Brutus. She sighed, setting the broom aside. "Dreadful behaviour," she muttered, shaking her head.

Ruth, still standing near the shelves, wiped away a silent tear.

"Are you all right?" Louise asked, her voice softening.

The girl nodded quickly, though her hands twisted nervously in her apron. "Yes, thank you, Miss Baxter. You were jolly brave, standing up to him like that!"

"Spiffing," Brutus chimed in, his wide-eyed admiration making Louise chuckle despite herself.

"Most bullies will back down if you stand up to them," Louise said, her tone firm but encouraging. She glanced at Ruth, appraising her carefully. The girl was sweet-natured, but far too timid. "And a firmly wielded broom—or a correctly applied knee—can make even the more stubborn ones reconsider."

Several days later, the weather had turned utterly foul, heavy rain intermixed with sleet. It was so wet that the fire in the small stove in the centre of the shop - safely set far away from any bookshelves - went out in the middle of the afternoon.

"I'll clean the grate," Brutus volunteered, "and we can lay a new fire with fresh wood."

"I don't suppose we have much choice." Louise shivered, picking up her winter coat and shrugging into it.

Bernadette was upstairs in the kitchen mixing herbal teas, no doubt enjoying the warmth from the kitchen stove. "We need the shop to be warm, or nobody will browse books long enough to buy anything!"

Brutus set to with a will, scooping out half-burned, damp sticks of wood and ash into the ash pan before taking them out and dumping them in the midden in the back yard. He laid the fire quite expertly and soon had it going again.

"A good job, Brutus," Louise praised. "Best keep an eye on it, though. Use as much extra wood as you need to keep it hot enough so it won't go out again, but don't forget to keep the fireguard in front of it."

"Can I sit here by it and read a book?" Brutus asked hopefully.

"Of course you can. Choose any book you want." She ruffled his hair fondly on her way back to the front counter. Brutus' father, Joshua, was too pinch-penny even to buy a subscription to the circulating library they maintained; he certainly wasn't about to spend money on books for his disregarded middle son. Louise was happy for Brutus to read all the books he pleased in the bookshop; his help was well worth it.

"Wash your hands first," she warned, seeing his ashy fingers. The boy gave her a grin before rushing off to take care of that business.

Settling down again at the counter, Louise picked up the day's correspondence and began working through it. A few orders in response to their last advertisement in The Times, a note from the printer to please collect the next batch of Shakespeares to bind... Louise groaned.

More Shakespeare! The green calfskin batch were still drying in the book presses! Well, she'd send Brutus over in the morning.

The doorbell jangled, and she glanced up with a frown as a damp, chilly draught blasted across her, ruffling the papers on the desk. It was only Mrs Poole coming in, though, and Louise nodded to her and returned her attention to the correspondence.

It was a quiet afternoon, not too many folk straying far from their homes on such a miserable day. The post-coach roared past in a great clatter of hooves and rattle of wheels before turning into the inn-yard, the driver shouting for fresh horses.

It must be almost four, then. Louise sighed, reaching for the sales ledger. Time to add up the day's takings. Although the afternoon had been quiet, they had made a lot of small sales that morning, she noticed, and laboriously began to add them up, hoping her sister would come down and check her workings.

The church clock struck four, and Louise was about to call out to Ruth to lock the door and turn the little sign to say CLOSED, when the shop door opened again. Words of welcome died in her throat as she saw a tall man almost wholly blocking the door with his sheer size.

From the corner of her eye she spotted a black shape darting for the open door, and cried out "Crafty, no!"

The huge man in the doorway lifted a massive boot, neatly fended off the would-be escapee, and shut the door behind him, before coming to stand in front of the counter. Louise stared up at him, quite mesmerised. There were few men in the district who could even meet her eye-to-eye, but this man was a near-giant; he would be a full head taller than she if not even more.

"Where should I put this?" he rumbled, and it was then that Louise noticed he had a crate balanced on one broad shoulder.

About The Authors

Catherine Bilson and Ebony Oaten are long-time collaborators, creating bestselling multi-author Regency romance anthologies over many years.

At the 2024 Romance Writers of Australia conference in Adelaide, they were busy running the Indie Book Store when they came up with the idea for this series. A bookshop would feature strongly - they were living their fantasy of selling books to readers anyway.

Why not set an historical series in a bookshop itself? With sisters who each find love in a bustling town. Instantly they brainstormed complications and issues - what if their father raced off to France after Napoleon was exiled away on Elba, to gather rare books? The characters weren't to know Napoleon would escape only a few months later and wreak havoc on France!

Also, at this conference, Catherine won the RUBY - the Romantic Book of the Year award - for her novella *The Bride Said No*. This novella had started life in one of their collaborative anthologies, of course.

Ebony had also won the Ruby several years earlier, for one of her sweet romance novels, *The Girl and The Ghost*.

With their powers of romance combined, surely they could come up with something wonderful.

You can follow the authors by heading to their respective websites and joining their newsletters.

Catherine is here:

www.catherinebilson.com

Ebony is here:

www.ebonyoaten.com

ABOUT CATHERINE:

"I grew up in a 14th century manor house in North Wales and spent most of my youth making up stories about the people who might once have lived in it. I ran off and married a handsome Australian a few years later and now live with him and our two sons in the permanent sunshine of Queensland.

I write original Regency romance, Austen-inspired variations, and Pioneer American romance. I also write contemporary romance and romantic suspense under the pen name Caitlyn Lynch."

ABOUT EBONY:

Ebony is from Melbourne, Australia and used to be a journalist at several suburban newspapers across the city. Then she turned her hand to writing romance and hasn't looked back. She married a Welsh 'boyo' and they are raising their son in Melbourne, where it can be stinking hot one day, pouring with rain the next.

The Bookshop Belles

NOVELS:

Estelle's Ardent Admirer

Marie's Merry Gentleman

Louise's Christmas Champion

Bernadette's Dashing Doctor

EXCLUSIVE BONUS NOVELLA FOR SUBSCRIBERS:

Matthew's Willing Widow

www.ingramcontent.com/pod-product-compliance
Lightning Source LLC
Chambersburg PA
CBHW030611170726
48283CB00002B/561

* 9 7 8 1 9 2 3 1 9 5 0 9 7 *